KING OF
THE OUTLAWS

P9-CBE-175

The name of El Tigre was one that even brave men dared only to whisper. Few had ever been face to face with him, but those who had remembered all their lives the Indian with the long hair, the face twisted by a hideous scar, the burning eyes.

For three years El Tigre had been plundering Texas. From his hidden lair deep in Mexico, he struck across the border with lightning raids—and as quickly vanished again.

Since they couldn't get him on his swift raids, they decided to forget law, to send one of their own men to Mexico to bring back El Tigre—or die in the attempt.

It was a million to one chance. And they picked Joe Warder for the job. Because he was tough—and experienced—and the only lawman on the border who would take the job.

SOUTH OF RIO GRANDE was originally published by Dodd, Mead and Company, Inc.

Books by Max Brand

Ambush at Torture Canyon
The Bandit of the Black Hills
Blood on the Trail
The Border Kid
Destry Rides Again
The False Rider
Fightin' Fool
Fighting Four
Flaming Irons
Ghost Rider (Original title: Clung)
The Gun Tamer
Harrigan
Larramee's Ranch
The Longhorn Feud
On the Trail of Four
Ride the Wild Trail
Rippon Rides Double
Rustlers of Beacon Creek
Seven Trails
Singing Guns
South of Rio Grande
Steve Train's Ordeal
The Stingaree
The Stolen Stallion
The Streak
The Tenderfoot
Thunder Moon
Tragedy Trail
Trouble Kid
The Untamed
Valley of the Vanishing Men
Valley Thieves
Vengeance Trail

Published by POCKET BOOKS

SOUTH OF RIO GRANDE

•

Max Brand

PUBLISHED BY POCKET BOOKS NEW YORK

SOUTH OF RIO GRANDE

Dodd, Mead edition published 1936
POCKET BOOK edition published November, 1946
5th printing...................November, 1973

This POCKET BOOK edition includes every word contained
in the original, higher-priced edition. It is printed from
brand-new plates made from completely reset, clear, easy-to-
read type. POCKET BOOK editions are published by POCKET
BOOKS, a division of Simon & Schuster, Inc., 630 Fifth
Avenue, New York, N.Y. 10020. Trademarks registered
in the United States and other countries.

L

Standard Book Number: 671-75790-3.
This POCKET BOOK edition is published by arrangement with Dodd,
Mead and Company, Inc. Copyright, 1930, by Street & Smith Publica-
tions, Inc. Copyright renewed, ©, 1968, by Jane F. Easton, Judith Faust
and Frederick Faust. This book, or portions thereof, may not be repro-
duced by any means without the permission of Brandt & Brandt, 101
Park Ave., New York, N.Y. 10017.
Front cover illustration by Jack Thurston.
Printed in the U.S.A.

Contents

SOUTH OF
RIO GRANDE

1 . . . Hard Hit

IT WAS during my last conference with the chief before I started across the border on the El Tigre business that I first saw the kid.

The chief had hit me hard. So hard that I had to look out the window, and looking out there into the street, I saw the kid in the middle of trouble.

But I have to get back to the chief, because he's the proper starting point. He had his coat off, and his sleeves rolled over his hairy forearms to the elbow. There was perspiration in the wrinkles of his fat forehead. Even in midwinter he perspired across the forehead when his temper was up, and I've only seen him twice when his temper wasn't high. Twice in five years he has said: "Joe Warder, you've done a good job!" The rest of the time it has always been perspiration, and cursing, and trouble, and blue-brown tobacco smoke, with the chief barking through the mist. His cigar sagged in the middle under the grip of his wet fingers.

"I haven't any authority on the Mexican side of the border." I told him. "My badge and my commission wouldn't be worth a penny."

"Of course they wouldn't," said he.

"Then why should I go?"

"Because I tell you to!" said the marshal.

He punched his fist through the cigar smoke as though knocking out a hole in order to see me better; but I glared back at him.

"What would your own higher-ups in Washington think?" I asked.

"They wouldn't think. They'd simply fire me!" said the marshal.

That softened me a little.

He went on, hotter and hotter: "You've been sitting here in the saddle rolling cigarettes and dropping matches all over the landscape, with your horse asleep, and you

1

asleep, and for three years El Tigre has been coming across whenever he feels like it. Haven't you any pride? Can't you keep your eyes open?"

I swallowed that. You had to swallow a lot when the chief was hot.

"Now, *you're* going to cross the border," said he; "and you're going to find him; and you're going to bring him back with you!"

I jerked up my head and confessed: "I'm scared to go. I've been there before. They know me and they're laying for me. I'd never get deep enough to land El Tigre."

The marshal leaned back in his chair with a grunt, and he sneered at me: "Whatcha want anyway, Warder? A house, and a wife, and kids, and a quiet life?"

"Well, why not?" said I.

He raised his voice to a roar that was thick, and harsh, like the bellow of a walrus in a zoo.

"Go look at yourself in a mirror!"

I lifted my hand to my broken nose; I didn't need a mirror.

"How old are you?" he boomed.

I was forty-two. But I knew he wasn't asking the question because he expected an answer. He was showing me to myself.

"You got the kind of a past to attract a nice wife, too," said he. "A jail bird, a crooked gambler, a gunman, a yegg!"

It was too much, even for him.

I laid my left hand on the desk and leaned into the smoke.

"I won't take that much from you," said I. "You and the service can be—"

He drowned me out with his roar, pretending that he didn't hear. "Who else can go, except you? I'm too fat to ride Mexican deserts. Rayns hasn't the nerve. Clifford's a fool of a kid. Jackson don't know the country. Barker talks too much. Who does that leave? It leaves you! You're all I've got. You're not much, but you're the best that I can offer."

It was almost a compliment, but I was angry, and my heart was hot in me. Everything that he said was true. I was forty-two; thirty years of gun smoke and dust had blown into my eyes; and a face that never was very pretty

2

had been entirely spoiled when "Shorty" McMahon dropped the butt of his Colt into the midst of it.

Still, all women don't marry a man because of his looks, thank Heaven!—and perhaps I still had a chance at an ordinary life. I didn't want much. Any sort of a shack, a wife, a kid; I was willing to work with both hands to keep things together.

"I wouldn't go even if—" I began.

But the chief was talking over me. "I hesitated a lot before putting the job up to even you. When I thought of the distance you'd have to ride, the guns and the knives that you'd have to face, the fight on your hands before you got to him—why, I was about to throw up my hands and say that even Warder wouldn't tackle the job. And then, all at once, I remembered that you'd never said 'No.' "

He got up and came to me through his cigar smoke.

"If you do this job, I'm going to make you famous, Joe! I'm going to step you into the newspapers. I'm going to make you better known on the right side than 'Billy the Kid' ever was on the wrong side. I'm going to put you in the position where the kids will follow you like a circus parade, and the girls will turn pale when they hear you're coming by. I'm going to make you, Joe!"

Well, I knew that he meant it. and I knew that he could do it; but I also knew that mine was one chance in a million.

He took the thought out of my mouth before I could speak.

"You're like the man who owes a million. He has to put everything down on one number. If he wins, he's fixed. If he loses, he's dead. If you cross that border again, you'll win or you'll die."

He didn't say any more, but he dropped his thick, hairy hand on my shoulder and waited in silence, while I turned my head and looked out at the street. I vaguely saw the white road, with the heat waves shimmering up from it, the thick dust rutted by big, four-inch tires, and dimpled where the buggy wheels had whipped through. And vaguely, too, I read the blacksmith sign, and the notice over Palmer's saloon: "Wines and Beer."

When had there been any wine in Palmer's place, except the white wine that's made from corn?

These things were drifting through a part of my mind,

3

but the rest of it was stretching south, far south across the glare of the deserts, and over the naked mountains, until I looked down from the farther side of the white, clear image of San Clemente, where, rumor said, El Tigre lived. He had shown his genius by picking out quarters at such a distance from the border which he crossed for plunder. Neither did he dwell in the midst of his band, but when he wished to strike, he sent out the word, gathered the chosen ones of a thousand candidates, and swept up north, hundreds of miles, splashed through the Rio Grande, then whirled back south again.

Other bandit chiefs had tried the same system, but they lived too close to the northern land of opportunity, so their methods could be studied; they lived with their followers about them, which opened the way for treason, jealousy, betrayals, and all the work of the stool pigeon. El Tigre, however, kept his lair at a distance, struck from afar, suddenly retired, and lived at the end of such a long trail that it had been impossible either to check his raids or to spy upon him.

It was of El Tigre that I really thought as I looked out at the street. I could win everything that the chief promised if I succeeded with the Mexican bandit. But my chance was one in a hundred. One in a thousand, perhaps. However, as the marshal had stated, I was not one to pick and choose. At my time of life, with my past, with my face, I had to accept some desperate hazard, and perhaps this was it.

That was the melancholy point to which I had come in my reflection when I saw the doors of Palmer's saloon knocked wide open and the kid came spinning through them.

He landed in the deep dust of the street, which exploded into a cloud around him; over the blowing top of that fog I saw a lantern-jawed cow-puncher emerge from the saloon with his fists still clenched, and many grinning faces behind him.

It angered me. I've always hated to see a big man hit a little one; besides, the kid was a tenderfoot. He looked as soft as a girl.

"There's a fight down there at Palmer's," I told the chief. "I'll go down."

4

"Let 'em fight," he answered. "I'm waiting for an answer."

I forgot my own troubles for a moment, however.

The kid was down, but not out. He came through the dust he had raised and jumped at the cow-puncher's throat. Of course I knew what would happen. As the youngster went in, I saw the man of the range make a move for his gun, but he changed his mind when he saw the still empty hands of the tenderfoot. Out went a long arm in blue, sun-faded flannel; I heard the crack of an iron-hard fist getting home solidly, and the boy tumbled head over heels.

I started for the door.

"What's what, Joe?" shouted the marshal.

"Dang it, I'll take the job!" I snapped at him; and whirling away from his big, hairy hands, I slid through the door and hit the street in two jumps from the head of the stairs.

It wasn't finished. There was a circle of twenty gloating men, and in the middle of the circle I saw the cowboy head and shoulders above the rest, laughing and grunting as he hit the kid away from him. The poor tenderfoot was pretty battered but still game to the core. He was punch-blind, running into those cutting fists as if against a stone wall, so I brushed him back and took the big man by a twist of his collar and the wrist of his gun hand. I jammed him back against the wall, while he told me that if I didn't happen to be a deputy marshal— Well, I suggested that I chuck my badge away, and my guns with it, if he wanted to have this little fracas out to a finish; but he blinked and gulped and then slunk off down the street with a good deal less reputation than his shoulders should have carried.

The bystanders looked sick, by this time. They saw they had been cheering on a yellow bully, and some of them tried to brush the kid off and talk kind to him; but he twisted out of their hands and got away.

I followed him into an alley and found him leaning against a board fence with his head in his arms. He wasn't five minutes more than twenty, even timed by a fast watch. I don't suppose he was more than five feet eight in bare feet, and, besides, he was very slenderly made.

I thought at first that he was crying, but he wasn't. The

5

thing that made him shudder and shake was the groan that bubbled in his throat.

"It's all right, kid!" said I. "You did fine. You showed you're game. The whole town's with you!"

He whirled about at me and showed me his bruised face twisted in knots.

"All right?" he shouted at me. "I've been beaten like a cur. And I'm a MacMore! I'd like to die! I'd like to die!"

He lurched for the mouth of the alley to find the other fellow again and butt into those same hard fists, I suppose. But I slung him over one arm and kept him back. I didn't talk, however. I was suddenly remembering that on the spur of the moment I'd given my word to the chief that I'd ride south to San Clemente and look for El Tigre. That was enough to stop my breath.

2 ... Across to Mexico

AFTER I had stopped the kid, I tried to comfort him, but that was like trying to pet a hostile bull terrier. He was as edgy as a bolt of lightning and still shook in his boots, not with fear but with a great appetite for eating up about half the world that had seen him beaten and shamed. I tried to tell him that there was no disgrace in being overcome by a bigger and older man, but he could not see it that way. He was a MacMore! He thanked me for helping him, but he nearly bit his tongue off getting out the words.

Of course I understood.

And I went back to the chief deciding that, if I had my own way, I would have a special State fund for such cases as this; to put them on the train and ship them back East, where a man can be as small and as soft as you please so long as he knows how to walk and talk. The kid was all right; he meant no harm; but he was simply loaded with excess energy that couldn't take care of itself, and, of course, that meant trouble of the worst kind that far west of the Mississippi. I figured that he would be calloused

6

with knockdowns before he got through with this West of ours. That would either break his spirit so that a China-man could slap his face, or else it would leave him as sour as a green persimmon as long as he lived.

When I got back to the chief, I forgot the kid and re-membered my own sorrows. They were plenty! He was perfectly matter-of-fact about it, now, and took it for granted that the consent he'd torn out of me was a sacred promise which I wouldn't go back on. I could see his policy clearly enough, but I couldn't see a way to retract. I started to protest a few times, but he cut into the middle every time. I never seemed able to say what was on my mind and before I knew what had happened, he was say-ing good-by and wishing me luck.

He should have been a diplomat, not a Federal marshal.

It was a ragged, mean, low-down, crooked, dirty border town. When I stepped out onto the street again I looked up and down its one street and wondered that the thin sides of its wooden shacks could hold in the murders, the stranglings, the knife fights, the gun plays, the robberies, treacheries, and thousand kinds of crime which they had known. But still the old town looked good to me when I thought what lay ahead of me on the far side of the border; just as a chill rain in Texas can seem warm and balmy when you think of a good Alaska freeze. However, I was in for it, and from that minute I decided that I must not think too far ahead; otherwise, I'd be apt to stall be-fore I got going.

I went ahead making up my pack. I traveled light, of course. I didn't put in a frying pan, a coffeepot, a hatchet, flour, beans, or even bacon. I didn't even pack two can-teens. One would do for me and the horse, no matter how far we had to go. As for provisions, I had the lightest weight and the most nourishing substance that ever was devised on the face of the earth; I had what used to carry the Indian raiders over the trail when they rode toward the Mexican Moon, where I was riding now. Parched corn, in other words. You can't beat it. You need good teeth for it, but mine will bite through a bone; you need a good appe-tite, also, but fifty miles a day under a hundred and fifty degrees of sun will give anybody plenty of appetite. The other half of my provisions consisted of salt.

Of course, what really counted was the rations for my

7

Winchester, which I hoped to turn into a good many pounds of meat, even if it had to be the dry, stringy meat that runs on the desert. I carried plenty of rifle food, you can be sure, and enough for the Colt that hung under my left armpit, as well. I promised myself that, when I finally went down, some of the other side would have to digest a few of the leaden noses of those slugs.

The rest of the day I spent on my horse outfit, getting new saddle blankets, and wondering whether it would be the gray or the roan that I took, but all the time I knew it would be the roan. He wasn't as tough as the gray, he couldn't last as long without food or water, and his sprinting powers didn't offset the gray's ability to rock along at a steady lope for hours together. The gray was the horse for the desert, of course, but right from the first I knew that I would take the roan. He might not have the ability, but he had the heart and the brain; he was, you might say, my old bunkie. He knew what I said, and I knew him. He would watch me at night, run for me till he died, and fight for me like a bulldog with teeth and hoofs, if the pinch came.

So I took the roan, with new saddle blankets under the old saddle, and a new center-fire cinch, and an extra light bridle with a plain snaffle bit. That bridle looked like nothing at all, compared to the jingling, heavy, sweaty, cumbersome headstalls of a Mexican bridle, but it was enough for Larry. For that matter, a bridle was a luxury on him; he knew the cant of my body or the pinch of my knees, and could take orders by them, or by voice. I mean to say, Larry was a cutting horse and his everyday brains were better than the Sunday wits of most human beings.

At sunset I had supper.

"Makee tlip?" says the Chink waiter, watching me get outside two pounds of steak with eggs on top and onions on the side.

I was making a trip, all right, and when I walked out onto the veranda of the hotel after I finished eating, I didn't dare to stop to roll a cigarette, because I knew that once I paused it would be pulling teeth to get started again. I sauntered on to where the roan was waiting for me, with lead in my boots, a chill in my heart, and cold snakes working up and down my spine.

He saw me coming and whickered at me.

"Bless you, Larry," said I, rubbing his nose, "and

8

Heaven forgive me for the trail that I'm going to ride you on now!"

He saw there was something wrong, and went off up the road with his head turned a little, the better to study the cant of me in the saddle.

Every little thing connected with that evening is burned into my mind deeper than fire burns a design in leather. I remember the hot twist of whirlwind that choked me and Larry with dust when I came to the Widow Saunders' house, and how Petrov, the Russian, was standing at his front gate with his heavy arms resting on the top of the pickets, apparently not feeling their sharpness. He was nodding, not at me, but at the goodness of this world which furnished him with the shack at his back, work to do, money for that work, doctors who had cured his sick boy and his sicker wife, a vegetable patch in the rear yard, and two apple trees which were trying to grow in front. Everybody liked Petrov, and everybody laughed at him; but I did not laugh at him now. I envied him. It made me envious to think of his security every morning and day and night of the life that lay before him.

Just before I came to the bridge, out of the Larkin house, Bud Larkin shouted: "Hey, Joe!"

It was nearly pitch dark; the lights were beginning to break into spangles as they shone through the black, and the stars were tumbling down into view. I reined Larry over to the fence.

"How'd you know it was me?" I asked Bud.

"I seen your slant in the saddle," he answered. "I wanted to tell you. I seen Guthrie last week when I was up to town. I seen Guthrie!"

He came closer to me, and his husky voice barely reached to me, though I could hear him pant very distinctly.

"Guthrie's out. He's finished his term. He's got the best job planned that you ever listened to, old-timer. He could get anybody. But he only wants you and me. We're in. Come inside and I'll tell you about it!"

"I'm through with that line," I told him.

"Come on!" said Bud. "You've been putting up a great front, but I know where your heart is, old son—it's with the easy money."

"I've had the easy money, and I've worn stripes for it,"

9

I told him. "You can't talk to me. Besides, I'd be no good. I've lost my nerve for that line. So long!"

I went on, but it wasn't easy to go on. I wished that I hadn't spoken so quickly. I wished that he'd sing out after me and give me an excuse to turn back, because anything seemed better than the job I was riding on, even being on the wrong side of the law again! But Bud didn't call after me. He merely cursed, and I heard his voice still snarling after the dark had blotted him out completely.

Now, I suppose I could have met with a thousand better people to speak to, but somehow nothing so perfectly represented for me the end of life as that meeting with Bud Larkin. The good we've done is its own reward, I suppose; but the taste of the old days, the evil days, the crooked days, were sweet in my mouth. Those were the times when money came in a flood and went in a flood; when my spoon-handled spurs were gold, and golden bells hung on them; when colored silks were plaited in the mane of my horse, and the flash of the Mexican gold-and-silver work made all eyes trail after me. When I slid east to New Orleans in those jolly times, the old town hummed like a guitar for a few days, and the bookmakers rubbed their hands together. I could read a wine list like a Frenchman, and head waiters seemed to know me by my step.

Now, here was Bud Larkin calling me back to those days. He and Guthrie were two of the best; they flew high and they flew fast. A handful of soap and a flash of "soup" might open the door to a fortune for all three of us—a last coup for me that would enable me to settle down peacefully to the end of my days. These things were calling after me, but Bud Larkin did not shout, and the good roan gelding was stepping away toward the new life which meant much toil, and little pay, and no bonus except, at the end of the trail, a spoonful of glory to flavor a ton of desert dust.

We reached the fork of the road, and there, looking back, I saw the lights of the town trembling behind me, then I pulled Larry with an unnecessary jerk onto the left turn.

He stopped short. When I spoke to him, he merely flattened his ears and I had to touch him with the spur to make him jog forward again. That pause of his troubled me more than you could guess. Reason might say that he balked a bit simply because he didn't want to leave the comfortable stall and feed box so far behind him; but reason couldn't soothe the qualm that pinched me, because I felt that a ghost had drawn on the reins and warned me to go no farther.

He slowed up again when we came to the bridge, and as I forced him across it, I thought that the echoing fall of his hoofs was spelling out deeply: "Dead! Dead! Dead!"

These fancies took such a hold on me that at last I put Larry to a brisk gallop that carried me down the slope toward the river.

On the bank above it, the gelding paused an instant while I watched the starlit water swaying around the bend; then Larry stuck down his nose and descended to the stream. I didn't dare to check him, or to look behind over my shoulder, or to let my very thought fly back; but, instead, I thrust Larry into the shallows, and we plodded and stumbled and swam across to old Mexico.

3 ... Gentleman in a Hurry

I KNEW that a lot of people—old hands, a good many of them—believe in starting the day with the first pink of the dawn, and working straight through to the dusk, horse and man; but it seems to me that from the time the sun is eleven o'clock high in the morning to its four-o'clock point in the afternoon, the desert is not meant for human labor or equine labor either. Besides, I had worked Larry overtime in getting south from the Rio Grande as fast as possible. All up and down its vicinity were too many eyes that knew me, and too many hands against me; therefore, I wanted to make the first stage a long one, and I jogged Larry steadily all through the night. Sometimes, when I felt very sleepy, or found the gelding going dead beneath me, I swung down to the ground and ran ahead, with Larry patiently trotting behind me. This freshened him and kept me from growing saddle weary.

It's a simple and a pleasant thing to do, and I think it adds at least ten miles to any forced march.

But when eleven o'clock of the next morning arrived, I was mighty tired, Larry was fagged out, and the blue glint of water that I found in a hollow among willows looked like authentic heaven to me.

We camped there under ideal conditions, except for the mosquitoes. That low-lying, marshy ground was fairly peppered with them. They were the long-beaked kind. It was plain that they'd been fasting for a month, and they tackled the two of us with a vengeance. However, there was grass here for Larry, firewood for me, and water for us both. In a half hour I had unsaddled, eaten half-raw jack rabbit singed over a low fire, made a small bed of the springing willow boughs, and was asleep on them.

I wakened with Larry snuffing at my face.

There was one weakness in the fine character and training of Larry. When he waked me while we were camped out in this manner, I never could tell whether he was warning me that some strange animal or man approached, or if he simply was lonely and wanted my conversation. He was that sort of a horse.

I sat up now and saw that the sun was slanting from the four-o'clock spot in the sky. It was time to think of moving on, no matter how far we had marched since leaving home. So I stood up and turned to Larry for guidance. In case he had seen danger approaching, what was its present direction?

He showed me at once, turning about and facing to the north. A moment later, I made out through a gap in the thin foliage of the willows a single rider on a slender bay horse coming down to the water hole. I got out my glass and turned it on him when he dismounted to drink. When he stood up again, I could make him out clearly enough. It was the youngster who inadvertently had made me give the chief my promise to tackle this lost cause; it was young MacMore.

To see him here, headed south through this country, was as much of a shock as, say, seeing an infant walking through a snowstorm. I was about to go down to speak to him when I remembered where I was and where I was bound.

It's well enough to consider the other fellow, but it's

12

better to have a bit of an eye to one's own hide. Every human being who knew I was south of the river doubled my danger.

That did not prevent me from having a guilty feeling when I watched him water his horse and then turn off on the trail once more. Of course, he was wrong in doing that. If he had been riding through the whole heat of the day—and I judged as much from the dust and sweat which covered the horse—it was high time for him to make camp for that evening. But it was exactly what one would expect a tenderfoot to do.

I waited until he was out of sight over the rise toward the south, then I ate the last of the rabbit, rubbed down Larry, saddled, and remarked with a sinking heart that this single march had appreciably lessened the girth of my gelding. However, he would be thinner still before ever I had a sight of the white walls of San Clemente.

I slapped the last mosquitoes from my face and neck, waved off the lingering cloud of those pests, and left the marsh for the higher ground.

It was still very hot. There was no stir of air, but the atmosphere was so intensely dry that it blotted up the moisture as soon as it sprang out on my face. That which generated beneath the band of my hat ran only a short distance down before it shriveled away to a streak of thin salt. However, the sun was dropping fast, now, and before long it was bound to lose its power. In the meantime, there is nothing like an early sweat to loosen the muscles of a horse when it begins a long march. Larry was well rested. He snorted the dust from his nostrils and stepped on with his short ears pricked.

We came into broken country, the rough land tumbling down from the mountains to the right, and as the sun dropped into the fork of two hills and poured a shallow valley full of golden light, Larry tossed his head and stopped short.

I knew well enough what that sign meant, and would have turned aside to get shelter among the rocks, but it was too late. The sand which covered the trail had dulled the noise of approaching hoofs, but now a rider swung around a sharp corner and loomed just before me.

I saw sudden apprehension in his face when he discovered me. He actually dodged his horse to the side and at

13

the same time slid his right hand into a saddle holster, but by that time I had him covered. None of his own actions concerned me so much as the horse under him—it was the same bay on which the young tenderfoot had previously been mounted!

The Mexican pulled up with a rattle of rapid Spanish which declared that he was no enemy of the gringos, but a dear friend to them, and above all that he always had respected, loved, revered, and in every way esteemed the celebrated general, hero, man-crusher, and so forth, José Warder.

That meant me!

I was so disgusted at being recognized that I almost sent a bullet through the narrow forehead of that yellow rat on the first impulse. I mastered that temptation, but let him cool with his hands in the air, while I fanned him and got a pair of guns and a cruel-looking long knife away from him.

After that, I asked him about the horse.

He blinked, and winced distinctly in the region of the stomach, as though just there he expected a .45 caliber bullet to plow through his vitals.

Then he told me that I might, perhaps, imagine that he had stolen the horse. As a matter of fact, that was not the case, but he simply had made an exchange with another man on the trail. Did I know that man, and was I his friend?

I admitted that I knew him; I even went so far as to say that I was his friend, and the Mexican watched me hard, blinking rapidly, as some people do when they are thinking. He had given up his own mustang and fifty dollars to boot, he swore, and the reason was that he was in such a great hurry to go north. If I would now return his weapons to him and permit him to continue on his way, he would be greatly pleased and would, as always, remember my name with his next glass of tequila.

He talked smoothly enough to be telling the truth; but he grew hot; a ragged scar on the side of his chin stood out more clearly.

Finally I said: "You're a liar. Maybe you're a murderer too. You and I will go back up this trail together."

He fell into a perfect agony of apprehension. As a matter of fact, he said that he was riding on an affair of life and death. His wife lay critically ill. His children, too, were in a dangerous condition. If he did not hurry on, neither Heaven nor man would ever forgive him for arriving too late!

By this time, I was beginning to feel more than a little worried. I told myself that the lying scoundrel really had killed poor young MacMore, and I swore inwardly that if I found the body, I would drop the greaser on the spot. So I made him turn his horse, and in spite of his groans and appeals, I forced him to ride back along the trail.

He grew silent, after a while. His head bowed a little, and I saw him covertly moisten his lips two or three times. It was plain that he was frightened to death and was trying to get at some words, but he couldn't find any to suit the occasion. By that time, I would have ventured a Canadian quarter on the chances of poor MacMore!

It was clearly my fault. I should have stopped him and talked to him, found out something about his business, perhaps; but, at least, I should have come in touch with him and no doubt either would have persuaded him to camp at once in the willows or else I would have accompanied him for a little distance along the trail. In either case, he would not have fallen into the hands of the Mexican who was now beside me.

There are Mexicans and Mexicans. Many Americans put them all down as a bad lot, but I've been south of the Rio Grande too often to make that mistake. In the ripe old days, most of the frontiersmen felt that the only good Indians were the dead ones; the same sort have the same feeling now about Mexicans. But now that the truth about the Indians has been investigated, a new school of thought has risen, and intelligent men will tell you that the Indians are as fine a race as ever stepped. The same thing is true about the Mexicans. They simply go more to extremes, I'd say, than their whiter cousins north of the Rio Grande. When they're bad, they're poison; when they're good, they furnish you with a finer type of gentlemen than any I've ever sat with from Texas to Montana. But when I took one look at the man beside me, I guessed that he was poison. He wasn't ugly. But his ratty, quick eyes made my blood cold.

I said nothing to him for a few minutes, until he suggested that if we were going to overtake my friend we'd

15

better hurry on. By that I guessed we might be near interesting information that instant. I reined in Larry and whistled to him the call I'd taught him to answer with a neigh. At once he responded, not overloudly, because I was on his back, but with a whinny which had hardly died down before an answer was in the air from the rocks at our left.

I looked aside at the Mexican with a grin, but he was not in the smiling humor. He looked a sort of olive-gray and bit his lips.

"Ah," says he, "what can that be? Be careful, señor!"

I waved him ahead of me, and in a few mintues I came in sight of the nag he had "exchanged" for the bay. It was a poor cartoon of a beast, all bones, and skin stretched loosely over them. There was a hideous saddle sore on its projecting backbone, and a great ugly red patch where the spurs had been constantly driven home. Still, the mustang had kept enough life to leave off its cropping at the grass and send a whinny of answer to Larry's call. Suddenly I wanted to see that brute of a greaser saddled and treated like the horse.

But where was MacMore?

4 . . . MacMore Rides

AROUND the corner of the hill I found him.

I've said that Mexicans are poison when they're bad. Now see what this scoundrel had done to MacMore out of pure malice of the heart!

Young MacMore was lashed hand and foot to a projecting stump of rock that stood up like a fragment of a tree. Everything of value about him had been stripped away—the boots off his feet, the coat from his back, his very trousers. Half naked, he had been bound against the rock so hard that the projecting points of it pressed deep into the flesh of his back. A noose had been used to strain his head back in an agonizing position, and into his mouth was stuffed a rag, wedged in so hard that he was now purple in the face, his neck distended, and the look in his eyes

16

was that of a dying beast—full of terror and hopelessness, that is.

When I came into sight of this, the greaser turned a bit in his saddle with a desperate expression—his lips twitched far back—as though he were on the verge of throwing himself at me with his bare hands.

I nudged him in the stomach with the muzzle of my Colt and made him dismount. With his own hands he had to set MacMore free, and then I tied my brown friend's hands together behind his back and gave my attention to helping the boy get his wind again. He lay for a moment gasping. When he could get up, he lurched straight at the Mexican with doubled-up fists.

There was a sight which I would have liked to show to a few of the parlor theorists who talk about the wild men of the open spaces without even having seen them. This Mexican of mine was low stuff, as I've already said, and he had squirmed freely enough when he first felt the shoe pinch, but now that he was helplessly caught, he changed. They are fatalists, nine tenths of them, and they accept blandly what can't be avoided. This chap stood up to the rush of MacMore without stirring an eyelid, and looked him straight in the face. He would have looked down the barrel of a gun in exactly the same manner.

I did not interfere. It's out of times like that that a man can see deepest into his fellows. But when MacMore was on the verge of wrangling the greaser, he stopped himself so short that he staggered on tiptoe.

"Set his hands free," he shouted at me.

I grinned. It was what I had hoped. The kid was white, and that color went clear to the heart.

"He'd strangle you!" I told him.

MacMore hesitated an instant and then let his hands fall to his sides. "It's true," he admitted. "I'm not man enough to fight a rabbit. I'm no good at all!"

He told me what had happened. It had started with a mere greeting on the trail, and then as the Mexican talked on and saw that the white man was as green a tenderfoot as can be found, he presently had a gun under MacMore's nose. In five minutes he had the youngster stripped and tied.

"I would have been dead in another two minutes!" MacMore said. "Murder wasn't enough for him; he want-

17

ed to torture me to death! I've heard what fiends these Mexicans are; I'd believe it after this! What harm had I done to him?"

He had been through about as much as a man can endure. He was white, and there were lines sunk in across his forehead and beside his mouth. When he clenched his fists, his whole body trembled. Of course, slow strangulation is about as close to death by fire as anything you can imagine in the way of horrors, and I was not surprised that MacMore still had a wild look in his eyes.

But there was my prisoner, with as dull, expressionless a glance as ever, staring through MacMore and beyond him toward the horizon, where he saw, I had no doubt, the gods of his race. For he was Indian—seven eighths at least —and he knew that he already had one foot on the border of the happy hunting grounds. Still, not a stir of the face to express his emotion. Invincible brute, you may say—hero, I'd rather put it. Life was as sweet to him as to you or to me, but I knew from one glance at him that he would go through fire before he would utter as much as a groan.

I asked him what had made him do this, but he shrugged and answered me quietly: "Señor Warder, I am tired of talking."

Not impertinently, but as if he meant what he said.

"MacMore," I said to the boy, "this fellow has nearly murdered you; but I'd like to have the disposing of him. D'you mind?"

" 'To the victor belongs the spoils,' " said MacMore. He added with a fine flash: "It won't be anything more than a whipping, I hope!"

I liked that, but it almost made me laugh. That Mexican would rather have endured ten deaths than one thorough shaming.

I cut the cord that tied his hands and gave him back his guns and the knife.

"There's only one thing that I want out of you," I said, as MacMore stopped in his dressing to stare. "Promise me not to load a saddle onto the bare back of this horse of yours."

Not very much to ask of a man as the price of his life, you'd say; but this Mexican gaped at me as much as to ask if I really expected him to walk; then he looked down at the narrow toes of his boots. There is only one worse pedestrian than a Texas cowpuncher, and that is a Mexican vaquero. I showed him how he could arrange the saddle blanket so that the weight of the saddle would be raised from the backbone of his mustang; he bit his lip and watched and nodded.

I asked him for his name. It was Pedro Oñate, at my service.

So I said: "Promise me in the name of San Pedro that you won't ride this horse for three days."

He made a wry face, but at last he consented, groaning as he did so, and naming the saint as though he were tasting fire. We had no thanks for letting him off so lightly, but as we rode off down the southern trail he remained behind us, staring alternately at the pony and at the leagues of rocks around him. I knew what was passing in his mind.

"The callous brute!" says the kid to me. "He might have thanked you for leaving him his miserable life. He'll be on the back of that horse before we're half an hour away!'

"MacMore," I told him, "that would be the worst bet you ever made. There aren't enough guns in the world to force him back into the saddle before the three days are up."

"Is he as honest as all that?"

"He doesn't want St. Peter laying for him at the end of his trail. That's his honesty."

The kid thought of this for a while and then broke out: "I haven't thanked you, for that matter!"

"You don't need to," said I. "If you've got your life back, you're not going to keep it long."

He blinked at me. "I don't follow that," said he.

"Son," said I, "suppose you saw a blind kitten dropped into the middle of the Mississippi, what would you give it as chances of reaching the shore?"

"Am I a blind kitten?" asks the kid.

"No," I answered, "and this isn't the Mississippi, either."

He considered this for a while, and seemed to get at my drift; he blushed.

"Look here," said he, "I know I'm not much good down here. But I've had my share of bad luck and ought to get through from now on."

"Trouble isn't bad luck in Mexico," I told him. "It's just nature. When the ground grows stuff like that—"

We'd come through the hills into a flat stretch of sand with the naked Spanish bayonet standing up like skeletons all around us. But the trail was marked like chalk straight before us, and the white of that chalk was made up of bones. Bones of horses, of dogs, of cattle that had dropped on the long trail. I don't mean to say that they were always underfoot, but any long section of the trail was blurred white by them.

Well, that picture should have made my idea clear enough, but I went on and put it into words.

"Even the plants down here wear teeth," I explained to him. "And everything on four feet has either speed to get away, or extra strong jaws to grab and hold. Look at the rabbits. They're so dried up that they're hardly more than a puff of fur strung together with tough sinew. They can run like the wind and they're tough and wise as witches, but still the foxes and the wolves catch 'em. Look at the wolves. Just a roll of loose skin pulled over a frame of bones; but they can run all day and fight all night. The men are the same way. You've seen the manner of that Pedro Oñate. He was as calm as you please when he thought that he was going to die the next second, and the reason is that the only thing people are thoroughly accustomed to in this neck of the woods is death, because they can always see it in the air."

The sun was down, but the broad red flare of the afterglow stretched around the horizon, and in that light the buzzards came down low, circling their effortless wings. I jerked my thumb up at them, and the boy kept his face raised toward them after I'd finished speaking.

It was pretty plain that I'd made my point to him. The flush had left his face by this time, and he was pale as the bones along the trail. At last he said: "I understand what you mean. But the fact is that I have to keep on."

"Keep on," said I. "Keep on, but keep north. Turn your horse around and start north, and keep him at it until you've got the Rio Grande behind you again. Otherwise, young fellow, you're going to be turned into one more chalk mark on this trail!"

He listened to me with a shudder. Perhaps I had dwelt on the thing a little too long, but I hated to see that youngster taking chances in a game where the cards were marked against him.

Well, then, I made surety doubly sure, and struck while the iron was hot enough to take the impression of the hammer.

"Down here where even the grass is thorns, MacMore, you don't know how to use a knife, except at the table; and I'll put my money that you couldn't hit the face of that black rock over there!"

He looked at me with a sigh. "I never used a gun in my life," he admitted.

"Then for Heaven's sake go home!" said I.

He shook his head but didn't say a word. When I saw that I had wasted all my words on the young dolt, when I saw that he was, in fact, a real man under that soft girl's skin of his, it made me sick. We'd come to the mouth of a draw that led to the right, and I determined to make that my trail. Why should I bother myself with such an incubus as this on my way south, when taking care of my own hide would be job enough?

"My way goes here," said I. "So long!" Then I added: "Where are you bound?"

"San Clemente," said he.

5 . . . Trail Companions

THAT wasn't so very odd, seeing that San Clemente was the biggest marker on that trail going south; but this was the third coincidence that tied me to that kid. In the first place, I'd run into him in God's country just at the wrong moment, the moment that had started me south; in the second place, I'd blundered into him on the way down; now, in the third place, I discovered that he was bound for the very town that I wanted to reach.

It took my breath, though it doesn't sound so strange in the telling, not till you realize how much lies inside of the horizon in that big country.

21

"San Clemente! San Clemente!" I shouted at him. "What the deuce do you mean by going there?"

I had actually started Larry off on the right-hand trail, but now I pulled back to the kid and glowered at him.

He sat a little straighter in the saddle. "You're not my father confessor," said he, and looked me slam in the eye.

"You young loon," I roared at him, "that's El Tigre's town! He has thin-skinned tenderfeet like you served up in his camp instead of lamb chops. He eats 'em two at a time, head first. San Clemente! You'd better start for home!"

He heard me with a shrug of his shoulders.

"Nevertheless," said he, "to San Clemente I certainly am going."

"What business have you got there?" I sneered at him. "Are you going to find another gold mine for yourself?"

"I'm hunting for my brother," said he.

It was another facer for me.

I knew San Clemente—having paid for that knowledge and with the receipt of payment in full still written on my body—and I knew the sort of Americans and other foreigners who hung out there. As choice a lot of thugs as ever were listed! San Clemente, in short, was *"muy diablo"* for foreigners. The reasons were strong. They had gathered in the choicest of mining properties in the old days when ten dollars properly placed in Mexico City were worth ten thousand honestly invested in the country; and having got the mines they had exploited them, kicked out the legal owners by force of hired ruffians and bullies of all sorts; and now that newer times had allowed the peons to lift their heads and call their souls their own, these foreign wolves howled loudly for help and sent frantic appeals for "justice" to their home governments in Washington and London.

They wanted a corps of U.S. marines marched into the country at once to protect their "rightful interests." Whereas their rights were as clearly defined as the rights of a gang of pirates to a stolen ship. Such were the masters of the mines, and they had gathered about them exactly the sort of followers you would imagine—outcasts, thugs, brigands, yeggs, throat cutters, purse stealers, drunks, and drug fiends—any sort of a man was a good man to them as long as he would use a knife or a gun, it didn't matter whether he struck from behind or from in front. No matter what was true about the rest of Mexico, the Mexicans themselves, whether they were high-bred Castilians or broad-faced peons, had learned to hate the foreigners, and the foreigners had done most of the teaching. Not without flare-backs, of course, in the land of teeth underfoot and claws overhead.

I say that I knew San Clemente, and when MacMore said that his brother was there, it's hardly too much to say that a picture of that brother jumped at once into my mind. Not the sort of picture that would do to hang on the wall! In short, I saw in my mind's eye a drunkard, a scoundrel, a gunman, a murderous ne'er-do-well, whether brave or cowardly.

"Who is your brother?" I barked at the boy.

"He is Patrick MacMore," said he.

"And how long has he been in San Clemente?"

"Eight years," said he.

I blinked. I revised my picture of the brother in certain details. If he had lived in San Clemente for eight years, he certainly was a rare hero or a rare cur. The average time limit was, I should say, not more than two or three years. And usually twelve months was enough to make the hardiest fellow yearn for a ticket home!

"Eight years!" I repeated. "What's his business?"

"Mining," said he.

"Ah, he owns a mine?"

"He has a little diggings of his own."

"Has he? A little diggings—that he works by himself? Is that what I gather from you?"

"Exactly that. Why do you stare?"

Well, it was possible, of course. Anything is possible in Mexico. But not one man in a million would have the courage to live alone in the San Clemente hills and rub out his ore with a coffee grinder. Such little claims were the particular meat of the organized ruffianism of the big owners. They bought in such claims with the price of one rifle bullet, and then operated the place on a larger scale. It was possible that a white man could live alone for eight years in those mountains, but it was as highly improbable as anything I can put my tongue to.

"I was only thinking of the lonely life," said I.

"Yes," said the boy with a good deal of feeling. "It's

haunted me, too. That's one reason that I've decided to go south to him. Eight years!"

"He's had luck, I suppose? Just enough to keep him grinding?"

"Is it luck," said the boy, "for a man to have to spend eight years slaving for his family?"

"Ah?" says I. "Married, eh?"

"I mean for our mother, and my sister, and for me. I'm ashamed of it. But I can talk to you—out here. Why, he put me through college! He's done everything for all of us. He's sent us tons of money! But he keeps slaving so hard that he won't come home. Won't! That's why I'm here."

"To fetch him?" I guessed.

He laughed a little.

"Nobody could 'fetch' Patrick MacMore," said he. "I should say not! I'd try to persuade him—or to take his place at the mine while he made the trip out home."

"Does he know you're coming?" said I, grinning a little at the thought of this poor tenderfoot taking any real man's place in this part of the world.

"I suggested it to him a long time ago. He wrote back peremptorily ordering me to stay home."

"You came anyway?"

"Yes, I'll surprise him."

I couldn't help wondering how big a surprise that might be.

"But he ordered you to keep away?"

"Well, I'm a MacMore, as well as he," said the boy.

"You're a fool!" I said, half under my breath, but only half.

"What's that?" he snapped.

"I said, 'I'm changing my mind.' As a matter of fact, I'm heading straight down for the same town you want, and I'd as soon take the left-hand trail with you. That is, if you want me along."

"Want you?" said the boy, with a ring in his voice. "Why, man, it's more than I dare to hope!"

I pointed out to him that in some ways I was the worst companion he could possibly have, because trouble was apt to come my way. I could even say that I was reasonably sure to attract it, in fact. He made light of that. A companion was what he wanted.

At any rate, I found myself riding into the dusk of that

day on the hardest job I ever had undertaken, with the extra burden of the greenest tenderfoot that ever had been dropped on the hands of any long-suffering man. But it was my duty. To let that lad ride into San Clemente was like letting a helpless child slip into a den of tigers. My mind caught and hung on that word. A den of tigers indeed, with the great El Tigre himself as their king.

We rode on into the dark of the twilight, and watched the night coming thickly about us, then clearing strangely as nights always do when the brightness of the day is forgotten and the stars alone are in the mind and in the eye.

The boy's horse began to stumble. It was weary, not with his weight, but with the awkwardness of his riding; poor Dennis MacMore in the saddle was shifting from one side to the other but always finding that raw skin was present. I knew that his back was broken, his head reeling, his stomach cleaving against his backbone, but he did not complain. He was the true stuff that men should be made of, and I admired his spunk with all my heart. The right material out of which to make a Westerner, and I felt that I would not be the worst hand in the world at shaping him; but my time was short, mighty short, and liable to be made still shorter if Pedro Oñate buzzed abroad the fact that Joe Warder was south of the Rio Grande.

I did not suggest a halt. I pushed on until we found a fairly comfortable camping spot. That is to say, we found water, and enough brush to make a fire, by walking half a mile to collect it. The water tasted like a full solution of alkali, but it was wet, and that is all one can ask of water in the desert.

I watched the boy without letting him see that I was on the lookout after him. He did well. He was so worn out that his knees sagged and his hands hung helplessly, but he did not give up or sit down, forcing himself to do as I did, whether in collecting wood, starting the fire, unsaddling, hobbling the horse, and so forth.

That boy could learn. I promised myself that in ten days I would make him comfortably at home on the trail.

In the evening, I had dropped a brace of the same leathery, long-legged jacks that had given me my last meal, and this was what we cooked. The boy skinned and cleaned his share, then sat opposite me, toasting his meat on the end of splinters, as I was doing. His head sagged with sleep;

his face was lined and hollow with exhaustion. But whenever I scowled at him, he grinned back.

In fact, it was good to have him along.

If he could control himself in the day, he could not after he was once asleep. And that night I did not have much rest, listening to the youngster fight through the day again in his dreams. Besides, the hard rocks bit through his blankets and bruised his flesh against his bones, I knew, and that was why he twisted and turned.

At last, I slept myself, and had my own share of dreams in which a striped tiger turned into a man, and the man back into a tiger again, crouching beside me with its great paw on my throat.

I wakened at last, choked with fear, and was mightily glad to see that day had commenced.

6 . . . Headed South

WE RODE south day after day, with never a cloud to hide us from the hand of the sun, but still no enemy stood up to block the way. However, I was not deceived, really, but knew that trouble would overtake me before the end. As surely as thunder brings the rain in Panama, just so surely I knew that I could not avoid meeting the danger here; my only hope was to delay the meeting as long as possible and, when it came, dodge to safety. Of course, I could have felt ten times safer if I had been alone. The boy was not only no added strength to me, he was a definite and significant handicap in every way. I would rather have taken along a herd of a hundred cows, I think, with nobody but myself to ride point and rear in that job.

He was helpless and hopeless.

I had told myself that he was going to make an apt pupil because he had two of the best qualities in the world —he was intelligent and he was willing. But all my teaching was wasted.

I showed him everything I knew about rifles and revolvers, and he fired off pounds of ammunition each day for a long time, but he seemed to grow worse and worse. When he was shooting, there was only one safe place on the whole landscape, and that was directly behind him. He was anxious to shoot well. He fairly panted with a desire to hit the target. But he had less than no talent. Finally, I persuaded him to give up the target practice on the ground that he was wasting too much ammunition, but really because I saw that he never would be able to hit anything smaller than a mountainside. He gave up, then, but consoled himself with the prospect of being taught by his brother later on. The MacMore would teach him. The great Patrick!

I was sick of hearing about that man. "You're his brother," I used to say. "Why not call him Pat? Or Paddy?"

"But he's The MacMore," the boy would answer, and open his eyes at me, so that you might have thought that The MacMore was a saint, or one of the upper level of angels at the least. Dennis had a sense of humor, well enough, but that sense died when he began to speak of his brother. He was never too choked with alkali dust and baked with thirst to start an oration about The MacMore's wit, and wisdom, and strength of hand, and daring, and general all-around greatness. He used to tell me in detail about The MacMore's exploits in the home town, and how the doings of the great man were remembered by a whole generation of boys after his time. The MacMore could run faster, jump farther, hit harder, shoot straighter, ride better, than any other man.

The boy fell into an ecstasy admiring this absent brother of his; but the more he talked on the subject, the more I wondered what was the fly in the ointment. Patrick MacMore was evidently a straight shooter, because during all the years of his absence, he had kept his family well supplied with money. He had talent, too, or he would not have been able to make a good income so young. I admitted all that, but I told myself that there was something in the past of Patrick that his younger brother did not know; otherwise, he would have come out of Mexico for at least one visit home.

I used to say: "Well, Denny, when we find your brother, we'll take him along and watch him bag El Tigre for me, eh?"

And he would answer: "Oh, he'll do that for you, all right! You've been so kind to me, Joe, that Patrick will do anything in the world for you. He'll take care of you, too, and see that you get out of Mexico safely."

Finally I broke out at him: "You young jackass! Do you think that this MacMore is as strong as an army?"

Denny looked at me fairly soberly for a time.

"You don't understand," he said at last. "You will when you see him."

"He's got one eye in the middle of his forehead, I suppose?" said I.

"He has eyes that will give you a chill," said Dennis MacMore, and all at once he began to laugh softly to himself, nodding a little.

I must say that that impressed me—as though, after all, The MacMore was such a wonderful person that words were pretty useless to describe him, and the only thing that served was the ability to remember the man he was.

But whatever The MacMore might be, the younger brother who was with me was interesting enough. There was never a day but what I wanted to wring his neck.

If he used the hatchet, he was sure to turn its edge on a rock, or cut his boots with a wrong stroke, or break the handle by overreaching. I think that there was something wrong with the focus of his eyes, or else he closed them just at the moment of impact. I know that was his habit when he was shooting a rifle or revolver. The meat he cooked was either raw or a cinder; it took him half an hour to saddle his horse; and he never left a camp to which he didn't have to return for something or other.

And every time he turned back, I had to remind him to make a cross to keep off the bad luck of a false start. He couldn't remember anything that was really useful.

His line was books. He knew tons of them—by heart, it seemed. He could quote to you by the hour—tell you whole stories in verse with all the rhymes put in straight, and everything like that. Music was a stronghold with him, too. He knew piles of it; he could whistle like a bird; and he sang mighty well, too. You would say by the sort of girlish look of him that he was a tenor, maybe, but he wasn't. He opened his throat and turned loose a baritone

28

voice that knocked the spots off of anything I ever heard, and I've heard them good.

A fine thing is music and a loud voice—a fine thing for a man in his own home, with his own dogs outside keeping watch; but a mighty bad thing for a pair of fellows on a mantrail who already had a better chance of being hunted than of hunting. I used to dang him and his singing up one side and down the other, and he always would apologize and tell me that he had quite forgotten where he was.

Well, he meant that. I'm sure that he never intended to offend in any way, and that he had the most obliging nature in the world. But what good did his nature do, when he let his voice slip a half dozen times in the day with a roar that set the echoes whooping through the hills and dwelling and ringing in the cañons? On the whole, I never saw a more helpless man on the trail, or a man who learned slower, or a man who had less sense about the real values of things.

By that, I mean to say that while he might have been a fine critic of everything that was written on the pages of books, he couldn't follow the meaning of signs which were written in stones, and grass, and animals, and all such things.

One day we camped and I sent him out to collect wood. He was gone so long that I was afraid he had lost himself again—a thing he could accomplish in a one-acre lot with a column of smoke to guide him home. I went out to look for him. I shouted myself hoarse. And finally I came on him a quarter of a mile away with a stick in his hand, poking at something that writhed and jumped on the ground.

A snake—yes, sir, a full-grown, five-foot brute of a rattler. I didn't yell any warning. For a fifth part of a second I was half of a mind to let the snake get the tenderfoot and teach him one lesson he never would forget, but I didn't hold to that idea long. I pulled out my Colt and put a slug through the vermin.

Young MacMore wasn't grateful. He didn't have any idea, as a matter of fact, that there was anything to be grateful about.

"I was about to succeed," said he.

"Succeed in what?" said I.

"Why, in catching him, of course," said he.

"Catching him?" I yelled.

"Why, of course! That's why I had the forked stick. That's the right way, isn't it?"

"Yes! But not a forked stick only half as long as your arm! What in the name of everything this side of a madhouse did you want with that snake?"

He had to think a while. "He had a mighty pretty skin," then said he.

"Did you want to skin him alive?" said I.

He did not answer, but he looked hurt and terribly depressed on the way back to the camp. Twice he stumbled and lost his load of wood. It was always that way. I had to do all the real work or else go crazy on account of his delays. However, when we got back to the fire finally, he turned on me with one of his quick smiles that lighted up his face like the flash of a lantern.

"That was a great shot!" he said. "Right through the head! I don't suppose that even Patrick can shoot very much better than you do it!"

"A snake does the aiming of a gun," said I.

He blinked at me.

"It points its head at the muzzle," said I, and went on with the cookery, leaving him to puzzle out this great problem for himself.

These things may give you some idea of how we stumbled and struggled south, with the boy getting thinner and browner day by day, never learning an item about camp life or the lessons of the trail, never riding a whit better, though he began to withstand the fatigue more easily. However, his spirits never sank except when I lit into him; and seeing him downhearted I never could keep my grouch very long but would have to tell him that it was all right. And then he brightened up again in the most amazing manner. Five minutes after I called him down for singing and raising a racket in a narrow ravine, he was singing again because he was so pleased that I'd forgiven him!

What can you do with that sort of a lad?

Well, all this time, as I said, we had escaped trouble and dangerous people. But two days north of San Clemente I saw a whirl of dust that was not raised by the wind, and that dust cloud behind us dissolved and opened into a distant picture of four horsemen cutting diagonally in to strike our trail well ahead of us.

There was no good reason why horsemen should not be

riding there; plenty of reasons why they might be in such a hurry. Thirst, for one thing, with a good water hole charted not more than three miles ahead of us. However, I didn't hesitate. I'm not superstitious, and I don't care a hang about most intuitions; but suddenly I knew that those four hard-riding men were after my scalp.

I told the kid in a shout, and in another moment we were kiting down the trail as fast as the ponies could leg it.

7 ... San Clemente's Lights

ALL DOUBTS about the strangers disappeared at once. They took after us like mad and came so fast that I knew it was going to be a tough job.

We did a mile that blew the dust out of our eyes, I can tell you; but when I looked back I saw that we hadn't gained a foot. The four were still there behind us.

However, if Larry could hold them in the first mile, I knew that he would leave them in the second. Their flogging quirts told that they were taking everything out of their mounts to get at us.

But if Larry could hold his own, the same thing was not true of the boy's bay horse. Its head was bobbing like a cork in rough water, and it began to roll a bit uneasily in its gallop. Even young MacMore had sense enough to see that something was wrong, and he looked to me for an explanation.

"Your horse is done, kid!" I shouted to him. "But it's me that they want, and not you. Steer off to the left, there, and get out of the way. I can beat them with Larry, and I'll circle back and pick you up after dark in that patch of baldheaded hills, yonder. Start right now!"

He gave me a nod and a jerk of the hand. It made me a little sore to think that he didn't have a bigger heart and want to stick the thing out with me; but, after all, I had trained him on the trail to do exactly as I ordered without asking questions until the job was completed. However, no one likes soldiers who are too quick in the retreat.

I settled into my work with Larry, as the boy turned off to the left and disappeared behind my shoulder. I did not look after him; there was not a chance that any of the four would take after the youngster. I knew that it was me they wanted.

Well, in about three seconds, I heard a terrible screech behind me that made an Indian war yell sound like the whistle of a lark. Guns started cracking at the same time.

"They're making their last rush at me," I said to myself, and turned about to measure chances and distance.

Well, sir, I saw the strangest sight that ever I had looked at. The kid—the helpless kid—the blunderer—the rottenest shot—the bad rider—was humping it straight back down the trail as fast as his horse would run!

Mind why, I mean! He was charging those four hand-picked bad ones with his revolver stuck out in front of him, firing as fast as he could work the gun!

Why one of the bullets didn't go through the head of his own horse, I can't tell; but whatever I thought as I watched him bumping around in his saddle, I knew that he was a goner, and I unshipped the rifle, feeling sicker than I ever felt in my life. It was perfectly plain. The lad thought that I was trying to save him at the expense of my own danger, and he was playing with a bet as large as his life.

I swore to myself that I would get one of those four to pay for the boy in part; just as I was deciding that, those four wild riders fanned out to either side, wavered, and then jerking their ponies about, they made off as fast as spurs and quirts could extract speed from horseflesh.

As I write this down, I can't help laughing, and I can't help wondering, too. I never saw a braver thing done.

All the time he was screaming like a madman, and the four of them couldn't stand that charge. I hardly blame them, because they couldn't really know what I knew, though they might well have suspected it by his manner of riding. At any rate, their nerve thinned out fast and they raced off, two of them down a shallow draw, and the other pair scudding for a gap in the hills through which we had just come.

The boy had sense enough not to follow. As a matter of fact, he could not, because his gelding was plumb beat.

As I came up, I saw him reeling in the saddle from side to side, exactly as a man does when he has been badly hit

32

by a bullet. But it wasn't a bullet that had hit Denny Mac-More. Instead, he was plain paralyzed with laughter. He laughed until he cried. He laughed until he was in agony. He grabbed his ribs with both his arms and hugged himself with all his might to keep his sides from cracking.

It was a long time before he could speak, and when he did, his voice was almost inaudible with the hoarseness brought on by his yelling during the charge.

I asked him what fiend made him fly in the faces of those four. He only laughed again, with a sort of groan.

"I was tired of having you ashamed of me," said the kid. "That's why I decided to finish the thing off one way or the other. If you were ashamed of me, wouldn't The MacMore be a whole lot more ashamed when he met me, and I his own brother?"

Always The MacMore! He was at the bottom of everything that passed in the mind of that boy! I swore at him, openly, and jerked Larry around on the trail. He might have confessed that he had done the thing partly on my account, and not so much for that eternal Patrick Mac-More!

Well, I was in such a grouch on account of this, that poor young Denny didn't dare to speak for another hour. Then, at last, I clapped him on his shoulder.

"I'm jealous of The MacMore for the first time," I said to him frankly. "I wouldn't mind having a kid like you in the family myself."

Young Denny got hold of my hand and gripped it as hard as he could, which was nothing to write home about.

"You are one of the family, Joe," said he. "Wait till The MacMore hears about some of the things that you've done for me and he'll—"

"Like going ahead when you turn back to make a charge, eh? That oughta please him a lot!"

The boy grinned in his pleasure.

"Aw, he'll understand that, of course. It wasn't anything. I couldn't branch off and leave you in the lurch very well, could I?"

"I'll never ask you again, kid," said I.

I meant it. He had buckled himself to me, by that little job of his that day.

I haven't been able to tell you how the thing looked, or how small he appeared stacked against those four huskies,

33

or how he flopped in the saddle, or the yells that he kept letting out. But I'll tell you what, if it's terrible to see a man go crazy in the wrong direction, it's a grand thing to see him go crazy in the right way. And the kid had the power of going wild in him, but he never would go wrong.

It was all very well to have scared those four hunters off my trail for the moment, and it let us get a good long start into the broken country and the mountains north of San Clemente; but I knew perfectly well that though they had been shaken off, they had not given up the trail. Mexicans are not made that way; they stick to a trail as patiently as hungry wolves in the snow time. Back would come those four, and the second time they wouldn't be in a humor to scare so easily. They had been bluffed once so very badly that none of the four would care to meet the eyes of his fellows until he had got his man.

I didn't push straight on. I pulled off into a hiding place and laid up for five whole days. During that time I did not allow the boy to talk louder than a whisper—which was the only possible way to prevent him from singing. I did not light a fire once, day or night, and I did not venture to use my rifle on the game that was always thick around us.

We lived on water and parched corn, during those days, but we had the pleasure of seeing the horses rest and fatten on the good pasture.

From this place, I suggested to the boy that since he really had not a great deal to fear in San Clemente so long as he could locate his brother at once, it would be wise to ride on in alone and try to locate The MacMore.

He gave me a single withering look in answer to this suggestion—a thing that made me recall my promise of the day of the chase. No, he would stay with me to the end. Right to the moment when he and The MacMore and I clamped the irons on El Tigre, not until that moment would he feel that he had sufficiently repaid me for what I had done for him.

Silly stuff, you'll say. Of course it was, but the sort of stuff that is good to hear, no matter how foolish it may sound!

At the end of the fourth day of parched corn and water, we were pretty pale and flabby, but I knew that the trailers had completely missed us. By this time, the reports must have gone in that I had turned into a puff of smoke, which was another idea that delighted me, because I was sure that I had played their own Indian game of "now you see me and now you don't" and beaten them from the start.

In a way, I was glad to linger over this first small triumph, because it was apt to be the last success that I would taste on the trail of El Tigre.

On the fifth day, I took some small bird snares which I had made in the meantime and caught enough meat to make three meals for us—big meals such as half-starved men can eat. Then I took some very dry wood which would burn with practically no smoke and we roasted the birds slowly over a flame no larger than a man's hand. We spent that fifth day feasting and resting and getting our strength back. On the sixth day we were ready to attack the enemy.

So we pushed on through the San Clemente mountains, and coming out through a long night march, winding back and forth among the ravines, we reached at last to the outer rim of the hills. There we halted on a shoulder that hung steeply over the town. A scrubby patch of manzanita grew there and promised enough of a screen from any curious eyes that might come near us; we could camp here for the day and go down to San Clemente that night.

We sat for a while after unsaddling and ate cold roast meat and drank spring water, so cold that it made our teeth ache, and looked down through the dark of the valley to where the little lights of San Clemente shimmered and twinkled as if they were being tossed up and down on waves. The river growled like a lion somewhere off to our right, and I felt almost as though the vibrations of that sound were making the earth tremble beneath me; but I knew that was merely my own jumping nerves. But young MacMore was singing softly, under his breath. No nervousness about him! He sang with joy in his heart, and suddenly I knew that the young scoundrel loved life never so well as when it was spiced with danger.

I rubbed my hands together. They were clammy and cold.

8 ... The Hornets Hum

WE RODE down to San Clemente through the dusk and watched the night rise up from the valley like water in a great translucent pitcher. The boy was delighted more than ever, and as we came into the town, he turned and called my attention to a strange color that lay on the face of the San Clemente River. It was enough to startle any one—a long crimson streak that appeared to be self-luminous. As I stared, it tarnished and disappeared, and looking up into the west, I could see the cloud fade and go out in the sky. It was as if some one had thrust down a great red torch and then withdrawn hand and light again.

"Looked like the water was on fire," suggested young MacMore.

"It looked like blood," said I. "But blood will boil without fire."

"Ah, Joe," says Denny, "cheer up, man, will you? We're not dead till our hearts stop ticking."

As we came in, keeping close to the side of the river, we found that the houses around us seemed devoid of inhabitants except children who played in the street, or fled around the great rough trunks of the cypresses, or ran down to wrestle and shout by the edge of the river, their voices flatly and loudly echoed by the water.

I was mighty glad that the eyes of the older people were not on us. For, although it might well be that I could walk through all the streets of the town without being recognized, I would a good deal rather have walked through fire. This was the night, but now and then the diffused shaft of light that struck outward from open doors, open windows, touched upon the pair of us, and every time it was like the pointing of a gun, to me.

Young MacMore was simply delighted and at home in the midst of my trouble. He commented on everything; because as a rule he talked gayly, restlessly, like a child who speaks his thoughts rather than a grown man who expects

36

an answer. He spoke of the thickness of the dust of the street; of the acrid smell of it in the air; of the scent of the town itself, so different from the odor of an American village. That is to say, there is in Mexico the fragrance of stewing peppers of a hundred varieties, such as the village wives pick out for the beans, the sauces, the meats which they are to cook that day, and the aroma of the tobacco is a different matter, also, and all things tell the nose a different tale. One might say that life has a different taste in Mexico, because of these things.

A delightful impression young MacMore was getting. He babbled along about it, and spoke of the music of the children's voices, and the hushing of the river between its banks, and the softness of the wind, and the smell of the green fields which walked in upon it; but where were the grown people?

I told him to listen harder, and the next moment, because the wind which had been blowing the sound away now fell down, we were able to hear clearly the sound of the band which played in the Plaza Municipal, so that I could all at once see as with an eye the currents of the people moving around the park, and the bright, keen glances which the men and the women cast at one another, covert, and therefore more penetrating, for a Mexican deals subtly, but with a point.

I told the boy that the people of the town, mostly, would be there. That was all the more to our purpose. What we wanted to do was, first of all, to get to the address to which the MacMore family had been sending letters for Patrick—a forwarding address of one José Guadalupe, who should be able to put the boy on the right track to find his brother. So we made two inquiries and eventually got to the place. It was not the sort I would have expected. Usually, an American is in touch with the higher classes, but this was a narrow street flanked by the low houses of the peons. This particular address took us into a small patio at the entrance to which we stopped a scooting boy and learned from him that José Guadalupe was home, and that he lived at the second door on the right.

It was one of the typical compounds where the peons live in Mexican towns, several houses surrounding the patio, with two more families in every house. From the open door of one of them a guitar was twanging loudly, accompanying a voice which sang huskily some of the native songs; and always, in the distance, there was the snarling and snoring of the band in the Plaza Municipal.

At the second door on the right we found a man squatted on the threshold. Behind him I saw the dimly lighted interior of a room where a woman was sweeping the dirt floor. It was the kitchen, with its raised fireplace in view, and the blackened pots hanging from their hooks. The pungent sweetness of Mexican cookery was still sharp in the air.

"Is José Guadalupe at home?" said the boy in his scholastic Spanish.

The squatted form on the doorway did not answer for a moment, as though translating these words into his native dialect. At last he raised his head.

He was that bulldog type, so familiar south of the Rio Grande. No breeze stirred in this patio, and the side of his face glistened with perspiration where the light touched him.

"I am José Guadalupe," said he.

"I've come to ask about Patrick MacMore," said Dennis.

Guadalupe rolled to his feet with a lurch. He dropped his cigarette to the ground and came out a step suddenly toward us.

"Who are you?" said he.

"I am his brother," said Dennis.

José rubbed his hand across his forehead and came still closer, staring earnestly upward into the face of Dennis; he then looked toward me, but not so fixedly, before he replied.

"This is his uncle, also, I suppose?"

It made me double up a fist to hear him chuckle; Dennis was surprisingly patient.

"I am really his brother," said he. "I've come here from the States to find him or to learn why we haven't heard from him for such a long time. Can you tell me where to find him or his mine?"

Guadalupe turned his back on us.

"Why," said he over his shoulder, "should I know anything about the gringos, even about the king of the whole tribe?"

"Ha?" said Dennis.

He had started in the saddle, and flung down to the ground. Guadalupe waited for him in the shadow beside the door, with the gleam of a knife in his hand.

I was fairly cursing with anger, disgust, but not with disappointment. I had only faintly hoped to be able to get the boy off my hands at once. Now, he was bound to be a long trial!

I slid out a revolver and told Dennis to stand back.

"José," said I to the Mexican, "you had better say a quick prayer to San Guadalupe. I have a gun pointed at your head."

"Ring, Alicia," says the peon, as calm as you please.

Instantly, I saw the flash of the woman as she sprang across the kitchen floor, fast as a leaping cat on the kill. She was bare-footed; her brown legs flashed to the knee as she ran, and I had a glimpse of a brown, pretty face, of white teeth.

She was out of sight at once, and I heard a gong, or a brass pan that served as a gong, struck three times in rapid succession.

"There's some mischief up," said I to the boy. "Let's get out of here while we have a clear retreat."

"You go," said the young loon. "I have to stay here. I mustn't be bluffed out by any one. Besides, if I miss my brother here, where shall I pick up the trail?"

I didn't have time to argue with him. My impulse was to take him by the nape of the neck and jerk him back into the saddle; but now, from the corner of my eye, I saw a shadowy form dart out of a door near the patio entrance, then the gate slammed heavily, and the bolt of a big lock clanked home.

All quickly, neatly, without any trouble—and here was I trapped as securely as any rat, all because this unlucky boy had asked in the wrong place about his brother. For the moment I almost hated Dennis; certainly I hated that omniscient Patrick about whom he loved to talk so much.

But there I was, caught. And that trap had teeth, as well. The guitar stopped jangling across the inclosure; I heard a subdued muffling, and swore to myself that I could distinguish easily and clearly the hollow sound of a rifle stock striking against stones.

At that signal, I felt as though twenty pairs of eyes were

watching us covertly, and twenty hands prepared to strike for our hearts with steel or lead.

Dennis was, as usual, apparently delighted by the presence of danger. He sang out to me as cheerfully as you please: "I can hear the hornets hum, Joe! Shall I jump this scoundrel?"

"That same scoundrel will cut your throat if you come near him," I told the boy. "Guadalupe, the bullet in this gun is already hitched to the middle of your forehead. Personally, I should enjoy splitting your head open like a cantaloupe, and if you budge a foot or a hand, I'll do it. Do you hear me?"

"Amigo," says this cool rascal of a greaser, "I hear you perfectly. Thank your kind fate that I did not have a gun or you would have dropped into the dust before now!"

Nevertheless, he did not back up or try to bolt through the doorway. Into that opening I saw the form of the woman suddenly step. She was no more than a girl—eighteen or nineteen, say—but she had a gun at her shoulder leveled fairly at the first possible enemy.

That happened to be young MacMore.

I had much rather face a weapon in the hands of an expert than in the hands of a novice. Those unpracticed hands of hers were apt to pull the trigger even against her will. I barked: "Guadalupe, if that gun goes off, you're a dead man!"

Guadalupe did not answer. He could see for himself that I meant what I said, and perhaps he guessed from my handling of my weapon that, though I don't pretend to be one of these "Deadeye Dicks," still, I hit reasonable targets at point-blank revolver range.

But Dennis MacMore was speaking before any of us could say another word. He raised his hand—Heaven alone kept her from shooting at that moment of his—and taking off his hat to her he says with a bow: "Cara mia, I am not yet in good range."

Then he stepped straight up to the muzzle of the gun!

⦁ ... Alicia Whispers

I was standing enough to one side to see his smile and the flash of his eyes, so that I suddenly knew this incredible youngster was not giving the slightest attention to the rifle. All that mattered to him was the pretty brown face of the girl behind the sights.

Perhaps I haven't said that young MacMore was as handsome a boy as ever broke hearts; but certainly he had quick effect on the daughter of José Guadalupe. The rifle wavered suddenly; I knew in an instant that she could no more harm this gringo than she could shoot her own brother.

Guadalupe stirred a little beside the door. The point of this had not been lost on him.

"Fortune and women," said he, "both favor fools. Alicia, go back into the house and stay right there till I call for you."

She disappeared, but slowly, and still staring at the boy, and he fixedly after her. He even was rash enough to take a step closer to the door—and to the knife of that savage Guadalupe.

I stopped him with a word and saw him start like a sleepwalker suddenly wakened.

"It may be," said Guadalupe to MacMore, "that you are the brother of the man." He whistled—a long, soft, swelling note. Then he added: "We are all simple people here, friends. We are afraid of the wild caballeros from the north!"

He grinned as he said it, but put up the knife; and, a little later, I heard the bolt of the patio gate grind, and the panels fold back. Apparently, the trap had opened again, but I had seen enough to know that our safety here was as uncertain as life.

The guitar began to strum once more, and the unseen singer recommenced his song. But I felt no more safe than a bird under a cat's paw.

"You are the brother of Patrick MacMore," said Guadalupe dryly. "You have come a long way on your horse to find him. So!"

He said this with infinite irony, adding: "Perhaps he has been unable to write to you, señor?"

Dennis MacMore came closer to the burly Mexican. It was a way he had, of standing close to any one when he wished to speak seriously.

"I have letters from him in my pocket," said he. "Would that be a proof to you?"

"Sometimes," said the Mexican, "children pick up eagle feathers on the mountainside."

It was a fairly neat way of conveying his doubt, but MacMore laughed a little.

"You'd think," said he, "that Patrick never spoke about me, or else that he had to be protected from people."

"Ah?" says Guadalupe.

He shrugged his shoulders, which might mean anything. Then he added: "As for me, I know very little about the Señor. He keeps a mine in the mountains and rarely comes to San Clemente."

He seemed to speak this honestly enough.

"Where is the mine, then?" asked Dennis.

"Where is the key to the safe?" sneered Guadalupe. "Of course, that is a thing that he must tell to every one, but he forgot to tell me. If I ever see him again I shall ask, so that I can be able to tell every one who wishes to know."

Dennis turned to me.

"This is a rude fellow," he remarked. "I wouldn't believe that Patrick could have anything to do with him, except that he was always apt to have friends of all kinds. Perhaps even this kind, down here. What are we going to do?"

"Get out of here as fast as we can," said I.

He turned back to make a last effort. "My friend," said he, "if you cannot direct me, tell me who else would be likely to know where I can find him?"

Guadalupe merely shrugged.

"Well, then, let me at least know what has happened to the letters which my family has been sending for the last year. Has Patrick come here for them?"

"That I don't know," said Guadalupe.

"You don't know whether letters have come?"

"I don't know how long since the last one came."

He added: "I don't remember any letters. I know nothing about you and your business, señor."

This put a stop to further talk. Even Dennis could see that, and he was swearing beneath his breath when he remounted his horse.

"We've had this work for nothing," says he. "What's the mystery behind it all? People must be trying to get hold of Patrick's mine, and he's sworn this man to secrecy." He called back to Guadalupe: "If you see my brother again, tell him that I have been here. I'll come every day again, if I can, to find out what you've heard from him."

Guadalupe merely grunted, yet he walked a little distance toward the patio gate with us. This might have been a concession to good manners, though I had a very shrewd suspicion that he was staying with us as long as possible in order to note down a good description of both of us. In this respect, the chief center of his attention was not young MacMore, but myself, and I would have been glad to have him take his eyes away from me.

He turned back, at last, with a surly good night, and we went on toward the street completely baffled in our first attempt to get on the trail of the elusive Patrick MacMore. If I had suspected that there was something wrong, before, I was reasonably sure of it by this time. Yet it might only be that the older MacMore was studiously covering up the secret of his hidden mine. Stranger things than that had happened in San Clemente, I was well aware.

We were in the passage of the gateway when a slender form slipped out beside us, and a hasty, cautious voice was calling to us:

"Señor! Señor!"

It was Alicia.

Young MacMore was out of the saddle faster than a puncher at a tying contest. He stood so close to her that it looked almost as though she were in his arms, and I could make out the dim flash of her teeth, her eyes, as she looked up at him.

She was saying: "Amigo, amigo, you are in danger. Leave San Clemente; never come back here!"

"My dear," says the boy, as cool as you please, "tonight I've found another reason to stay in San Clemente. I've

43

never found a place that I liked so well. I intend to liv
here."

"You will die here, only," said the girl to him.

The big, snarling voice of Guadalupe roared from in
side the patio: "Alicia! Alicia!"

The guitar player ceased again. I saw the girl winc
back from the boy at the sound of her father's angry cal
but MacMore followed her. I had seen ample demon
stration that he feared no man in the world, and now
could guess that if he was brave against men, he was ;
positive hero with women. I heard his low, mischievous
chuckling laughter as he endeavored to pursue her a fev
steps.

She, however, lingered to warn him again.

"You will not go, Señor? Not for my life?"

"Not for ten lives, Alicia."

"Ah, brave!" says she, with her voice trembling in ;
way that should have shamed him. "Then I'll tell you th
name of a man who may help you to see Señor MacMore
Only, swear that you really are his brother!"

"By your own sweet soul I swear it," said this easy
tongued young deceiver.

"It is Don Ramon. Señor Don Ramon Cantaras—"

"Alicia!" bellowed the father.

"I must go," she gasped.

"In one moment," said the boy. "I have one thing els
to say to you."

"Say it, then, and let me go!"

"It is a thing which must be whispered, Alicia," says he.

It gave me a chill of the blood to see the brazen easines
of the young rascal. He stepped in and took her into hi
arms and kissed her deliberately.

I saw her squirm for freedom, but she made a very fee
ble struggle. Then he let her go. I heard the gasp of he
taken breath and saw her stagger a trifle—then she wa
gone as swift as a bird, not back into the patio, bu
through a small door that opened into what seemed th
heart of the wall at the right hand of the gate.

The door whisked shut behind her and young MacMor
swung up light as a bird into the saddle.

"You've had your throat half cut before, on this sam
night," I told him as we rode out into the street, "and fo
the sake of what you've just done, it will probably be cu

he rest of the way before morning. D'you know that the
Mexicans are the most jealous race in the world?"

"Are they?" says the boy, carelessly. "A good lot, I find
hem to be; and I can't believe anything bad about them,
oe. You're a cynic, Joe. A confounded cynic. You don't
elieve in anything except Larry and your six-gun, if that's
he right word for it."

"It isn't," said I, "except in books and on the tongues of
underfeet."

"Exactly," says he, "but if you believed in something
more than horses and revolvers, you wouldn't discourage
a poor fellow who's trying to learn the world."

"Bah," says I; "they'll dissect you—they'll cut you to
ribbons!"

"Isn't it worth it?" says he.

"What's worth it?"

"Why, such a girl!"

"A peon!" says I, sounding a good deal more disgusted
han I felt.

"A brown Venus," says he. "Not brown, either. But
live. A sunburned olive, I'd call her. Roses in her cheeks,
oo, Joe!"

"And garlic on her breath!"

"Sweet as violets, by Heaven!" says the boy, "or roses,
r lavender, or—"

"Or a cow's breath," says I.

He laughed at that. "You're not angry," says he.

"Not a bit," says I. "I'm a fatalist. But if anybody could
urry on the finish for two men, you're doing it. Look over
our shoulder."

"Well," says he.

"You see that old fellow riding the burro?"

"Yes. I see him."

"Well, he sees you, too; if you can follow my drift."

10 . . . Sent by El Tigre

I HAD spotted this shadow some time before, or at least so I thought. But the boy would not believe that I was speaking the truth.

"This would make it too much like a romance," says he. "As a matter of fact, nobody can know about us in this town."

"Have you forgotten pretty Alicia and her growling father?" said I.

"He could not have spread the alarm so soon," says the boy.

"You'll see that he's the one who has sent that same old man on the burro, however," says I.

"Will you be able to prove it?" cries Dennis.

He didn't wait for me to answer, but spoke up himself at once, half laughing and half sighing.

"Did you ever know a pretty girl without a currish father?"

"I'm thinking about the safety of my hide and not about pretty girls," said I. "Besides, I don't have any luck with the pretty ones."

"Do you go in for brains, Joe?" said he. "Well, for my part I think that brains in a woman are like salt with meat. A little seasoning is all very well, but too much of it simply parches the throat."

I stared at this boy who could not shoot, who could not ride anything much rougher-gaited than a rocking horse, but who rode along as serenely in a town where already we had made one hairbreadth escape, and where we already were being shadowed by a spy. But still he could talk about beauty in women!

I was rather of the idea that he was bluffing me, so I carried on the talk with him along his own lines, while we went toward the house of Cantaras. In the meantime, after we had asked our way, I kept the old man on the burro in the corner of my eye. He managed to follow us in all of our turns and windings.

"A good heart is better than a fine complexion," I suggested to Denny.

"Of course," said he, "but you can't see the heart except in the face."

"You can see kind actions, Denny," said I.

"There's nothing left but kindness for a long nose and yellow skin and a pair of spectacles," says he.

"How often have you been in love, Denny?"

"Twice a year," said he, "since I was twelve years old."

"In the spring, I suppose, when the flowers begin?"

"Yes, and in the winter because they are gone."

"You'll never be able to stick to one woman," I told him. "After all of these calf-love affairs."

"Practice makes perfect," says he. "And that old man on the burro is still practicing on our trail. Shall we catch him?"

"Why?"

"To find out who sent him."

"I'm glad that you're willing to look at men and burros," said I, "after that pretty Alicia."

"Not pretty. That's a word for a child. She's lovely. Dress her in red with a rose in her hair and she'll make half of the pale-faced beauties look like nothing at all."

"Denny," I assured him, "you're going to waste half your life in this love business that you're so fond of. Besides, here is rather the wrong time to be casting eyes."

"There's never a right time if you wait for it," he told me. "You have to shoot what you can, on the wing. If you wait for the birds to settle, you'll never dine."

This metaphor pleased him so much that he laughed softly at it, but I was beginning to be more interested in the old man on the burro than I was in the vagaries of my companion.

The burro had fallen back to some distance, though it still followed us in all the windings of our way. After all, the boy's suggestion had been a good one, for there were several things that the spy might be able to tell us—such as how we had been recognized, and who it was who ordered him to follow us.

When we came to a thick growth of willows that fenced in an alley that ran down toward the river, I turned in here, and the boy behind me. According to my direction, he took the horses back among the shadows of the trees, while I placed myself near the alley's mouth.

Presently I heard the quick, light beats of the burro's trot. Sure enough, its grizzled head turned in at the entrance to the alley of willows. I was half choked by a whirl of acrid dust raised against my face by a thrust of the wind. As I blinked the mist out of my eyes, the little burro was at hand, the long, thin legs of the rider, unsupported by stirrups, reaching almost to the ground.

As if on purpose to make matters easy for me, he reined in the little animal at that moment and looked fixedly before him, then with a quick jerk of the head aside toward me.

He had the mouth of a Colt to measure when he looked my way.

A gesture with that gun was enough to make his hands go up into the air above his head. I could see now that he was one of those people whom age dries a little more and a little more, from year to year, shriveling and preserving them, extracting more and more of the juice of life from them, but still keeping in them life itself.

His loose sleeves fell back, and showed his arms, skeleton thin, with the elbows sticking out crookedly; his chest was hollow, so that the white beard flowed straight down; and from under the brows, his eyes looked out at me through a deep shadow.

He looked like a meagre-faced saint, but when I searched him, I took out an old single-shot revolver that certainly had done duty overtime; and inside the leg of his boot I found a pair of long knives. He did not mind the removal of the gun, but his old clawlike hands jerked and contracted when I took the knives away.

"You're following a winding road to-night, father," I said in Spanish.

"My burro," says he, "knows the way home as well as I do, so I let him follow his will. Sometimes one way, and sometimes another."

"And sometimes turning back on yourself?"

"Perhaps he even does that. I am thinking of other things, and, therefore, I do not mark the road that he goes. You, señor, have taken me for some rich farmer going

48

home with the gold from the sale of his crops. See what I am—a very poor man—and let me go on my way."

I put the point of one of his own knives through his bush of beard and scratched the neck beneath it.

"Come, now, father," said I, "and let me have the true story of why you have been trailing me this night?"

"I? Trailing?" He laughed in despair and in scorn. "Who should I trail? Am I not—"

"No matter what you are. The thing I wish to know is the name of your master. Who sent you on this trail after me?"

"Does the wind have any other master than Heaven?" he asked me. "Why does the dust blow? I have no master, kind señor."

He said it with a rich conviction that filled his throat. However, in that instant I recognized the eloquence of the natural liar, and began to think that I had the old fellow in my hands.

"Look!" said I. "Is this knife yours?"

"Yes, it is mine, and I know that you will not rob an old man of his last treasure."

"Do you think other people would recognize it?"

"It has been seen in my hand during these forty years!"

"Then it would be known?"

"You never could sell it at a pawn-shop. They would recognize the knife and accuse you of killing poor—"

"Killing you? On the contrary, if the searchers after me should come upon you with the knife buried in your throat, the belief would be that the old man had collected so much wisdom that at last he understood the folly of clinging to life. They would say that you had opened the door to the future with your own hand, my friend."

"You gain," said he, "exactly one old burro, too slow to keep up with you, the gun that you have stolen from me, and the rags in which I am dressed. As for the knives they are not worth speaking of, for even a kitchen wife would be ashamed to use such old, dull, soft, blunt things."

"That's the second or third time," said the voice of young MacMore in English, "that he has mentioned the knives. There must be something about them that he values or is afraid that you will learn."

"Look them over, then," said I, and passed them to the boy.

The old man actually gnashed his teeth when he saw this done. But he swallowed his curses perforce and submitted.

I went on: "I'm not interested in killing you, old man. I simply want a little talk out of you. Who sent you to follow us to-night? Will you tell me that?"

"Listen to me, friend," said the old fellow smoothly, "I have been to the great United States, and I know the justice of the people there. They do not kill harmless old men for nothing. I have told you the truth—"

There was a little exclamation from MacMore, at this point, and he came hurrying up to me.

"The butt cap of this knife," said he, "twisted loose between my fingers, and this is what I shook out of the inside of it."

He showed me the little heap in the palm of his hand, a dozen small diamonds. In every Latin there is an instinct for hoarding, and I knew that this represented the savings of the veteran. When he saw MacMore's discovery, he lowered both hands a little and made with them a futile, fleeting gesture toward recapturing his small treasure. But the movement of my gun drove him back, though he groaned, and his little eyes glittered wickedly at MacMore, who had made the discovery.

For my part, I was willing to let him off as painlessly as possible, so I said: "Look here, father. You get back your gun, your knives, and the jewels inside of 'em. But tell us first the answer to a few questions, beginning with this one: 'Who sent you on our trail?'"

There was not much light, only the thin arc of the moon stamped like a strip of silver paper against the blue-black sky of Mexico; but still I was able to see the tremor of the body of the spy, and the glistening of the drops that sprang out on his face. His white beard wagged and his teeth clacked together as he started to speak and then suddenly changed his mind; but I took the jewels from MacMore and made a fountain of them, tossing them into the air and catching them again.

The old man watched with a groan, clasping his hands together like a mother seeing her child dandled by savages. Then he cried out to have the gems given back to him and he would tell us.

I gave them back; he cherished them against his breast, the bloodless old miser. So, breathing hard, he gasped out:

"El Tigre sent me! Heaven help me for speaking, and Heaven help you for hearing it!"

11 . . . At the House of Cantaras

THIS WAS as unpleasant as any news I ever received. My hope had been that by lingering that week among the hills I should be able to get at last into San Clemente unnoticed by the bandit who already had had me chased through the more distant plains, as I have described. Now, however, he actually had his eye upon me in San Clemente itself. And I felt like a field mouse when the shadow of the owl sweeps over it.

More clearly than ever, I saw that I must get the boy off my hands by finishing his business, and for that purpose I must get on to the man named Cantaras, who had been mentioned by Alicia. He was our only present clew to the whereabouts of Patrick MacMore.

I tried to get some information from the old man about Cantaras, but he swore that he had already fulfilled his bargain with us by naming El Tigre, and he demanded his freedom.

I let him go. In fact, he was so trembling and shaken with fear that I was ashamed to keep him with us any longer. One might have thought that the word he had spoken was the name of a cruel and avenging spirit which now would be on the wing to overtake and punish him.

He sent the burro scurrying away like a big dog, and after the little beast was out of sight, we still could hear the heels of the rider thumping cruelly against the hollow sides of the donkey.

This is the time for me to make the register of a very fine and brave offer which young MacMore now made.

He said: "The thing for you to do, Joe, is to get away from me and get about your business. This long-range eye of El Tigre has found you out. I think that the man must be a spirit to have spotted you so soon. At any rate, what has made it possible is the fact that you have me to cart about. I'll go on with my own affairs; we'll say good-by, and I'll go on my way."

"Denny," I answered, "are you pretty sure that your own business is perfectly safe?"

"Entirely sure," says he.

"So safe," I went on, "that when you mention your brother's name and ask where he can be found, gates are closed behind you, a whistle brings armed men around you, and you practically have a knife at your throat! Suppose there had not been two of us when we asked that question about Patrick MacMore?"

He nodded in the moonlight, so seriously that I knew he had thought well over all of the details of the business. He understood that there was something very wrong, though he was entirely willing to try to work out the matter for himself.

"We were careless about that," he declared. "But this next case is sure to be different. If—"

His voice was blotted out by the rapid beating of a horse that galloped at full speed past the mouth of the alley and on down the street. When I heard the boy again, he was saying: "Cantaras will put everything straight; I don't think that the girl would send me to the wrong man."

"I don't think so either," I agreed.

"Then good-by, Joe. We'll find each other again, one of these days. When I get hold of Patrick, the two of us will join your stag hunt. Don't forget that."

I agreed with him that it would be a great day. I felt no particular desire to part from him, but it was plain that I was myself in a good deal of danger, and it was only fair that he should begin to play his own hands.

We said good-by, he jumped up into his saddle almost with the swing of a cow-puncher and rode back into the next street, from which we had turned into the alley, and he was gone.

Now the instant that he was out of my sight, I knew that I had done wrong in letting him go. I started after him at once and was about to call to him when it occurred to me that it might be as well to look on from a distance and see how he got on with his adventure single-handed. If he went along smoothly with the thing, all very well. If he did not, at least it might be possible for me to rescue him.

These were the things which I had in mind when I trailed Denny MacMore down the street. They seemed to me good, sane reasons, at that moment. They still seem logical to me as I write them down, but that goes to prove that logic isn't worth a rap compared with instinct, and my instinct on that night told me that I was doing wrong— told me that I ought to keep at the side of the youngster every instant he was in this land of danger.

At any rate, I saw him lose his way before he had gone two blocks, and immediately afterward, I observed him asking questions of three people one after another.

I began to gape at the sight of this foolishness. He might as well advertise himself in the newspapers as to talk as freely as this!

However, at length he appeared to be put on the right track, and I followed him until he came to the entrance of a good-sized private park. The gate of it was closed and here he spent a few moments arguing with the gate keeper, but at last—I think it was after five minutes or so—the gate opened and he disappeared, the hoofs of his horse clinking musically on rough gravel.

Now that he was inside, I was more minded than ever to keep a closer lookout for him. I wished that I never had left him; but I decided that I would not try to get through that gate where he had just passed. I had showed myself too much in San Clemente!

Instead of that, I took Larry back into a thick patch of woods that filled a block or more near that park which was the apparent residence of Ramon Cantaras, then I went up to the high adobe wall, capped with stone, that surrounded the place.

The moon was giving an amazing amount of light, considering its size. Altogether, I was pretty uncomfortable about scaling the wall and getting into the tangle of trees whose heads I could see above the coping. But if I wanted to help the boy, I had better start at once. I swarmed over the wall, therefore, hung by my fingers from the inside, and so dropped silently into a bed of leaf mold.

It was a crudely made park. That is to say, there were no lawns that I could see, and very few elaborate flower beds, except near the house itself. The rest of the park was covered with a rough, shaggy growth of trees, and even the underbrush had not been properly cleared away in all places.

I was glad of this, but would have been gladder if I had not been wearing riding boots. A hundred times during and before expeditions of this sort, I've sworn to myself that I would furnish myself with riding boots and walking shoes. The riding boot is perfect for its own job, but if you want to know its imperfection, try to stalk silently through woods like those as I did that night in the park of Cantaras! The paths twisted in unplanned fashion, simply following the lie of the land, or turning with awkward suddenness around the trunk of a tree, or even a big fallen log which had been allowed to decay until it was probably not worth the cost of its removal.

When I had stumbled up these paths for a time, I was guided by a ray of light, and this led me straight to the door of the Cantaras house. It was by no means as pretentious as I had expected from the extent of the grounds. It was just an ordinary two-story affair, built around the usual patio. Its appointments seemed extremely rustic, even for San Clemente. For instance, just behind the house I found one of the big wells with a sweep attached at the mouth so that mule power will drag up the heavy buckets or work the pump. This I found later. My business at first was to get as far into that patio as I dared.

It was as naked as the palm of a man's hand, and there was only one shelter for such an advance as mine, and that was the series of cellar casements, each big enough to hold a man who knew how to make himself small.

I got to the entrance of the court in time to hear a door squeak open and then a remarkable man's voice speaking. Remarkable, I mean to say, because it was so deep, so strong, so musical. The voice of young MacMore, sounding wonderfully thin and boyish, made answer. He declared in his fine, academic Spanish that he wished to learn how he could find Patrick MacMore and had been directed to this place.

"Ah," says Cantaras, for he had introduced himself by that name, "who sent you to me on such an errand?"

I wondered what sort of a lie the boy would tell, but he was saved from the need of an answer by Cantaras, who went on smoothly: "But that's not of importance. The main thing is that you are here and that you are a brother of Patrick MacMore. Of course I know him. Better perhaps," he went on with a brief laugh, "than you know him yourself. I am glad to have you here. Come into my house, señor. This is an honor. A *mozo* will take care of your horse at once."

In fact, a couple of servants came out of the shadows and instantly took the horse by the head and led it off.

In spite of the fact that Cantaras was so cordial, I almost wished that young MacMore would limit his visit to a few more questions and refuse to go in. But I had let him cut adrift; it was late; he was tired; and perhaps all of those reasons operated together to make him enter the house of this stranger.

They passed inside and the heavy door swung slowly shut behind them.

I did not start back for the trees at once, but remained where I was, crouched in the embrasure of a cellar window, looking over the strength of the house on the moonlit side of the patio. Like the houses of all well-to-do Mexicans, it was furnished with bars across all of the lower windows, which gave it somewhat the look of a prison, but it was sure to be stocked with comfort inside the walls. Those walls were seven or eight feet through, a good guarantee that the heat of the summer and the cold of the winter would not penetrate them.

In short, it was a strong, solid place, and the sort of a house that a Mexican likes to call home. Rifle fire would never have any effect upon it. A bomb would hardly nick its walls to the core.

I was deciding these things and about to start slipping back for the trees, fairly satisfied, when a man walked straight toward me out of the shadows on the farther side of the patio.

When he was opposite me, he turned for the gate of the court and paused there a moment to light a cigarette. He was armed heavily, with a rifle slung across his back, army style, but it was not his weapons which attracted my attention. It was his face. For this fellow was that same scar-faced Oñate whom I had met earlier on this expedition— the same who had taken the horse from young MacMore!

12 ... Inside

OBLIGINGLY, Mr. Oñate waited there until he had lighted his cigarette and allowed me to spot the gun on his right hip, and the bulge of the other beneath his left armpit. Then he sauntered on, and I breathed more freely, but with a conviction that I had been a fool when I turned him loose back there in the mountains. The good you do to the bad ones comes back to you like poison on the waters. I have tried a hundred times to be kind to yeggs, thugs, deadbeats, card sharps, crooks of all kinds such as littered the border. I think I can say that I have sown good seed from Mexico City to Butte, but I never ran across any returns, except once I was black-jacked by a new "friend," and another time I had a gunbutt used on me when it might have been a bullet. Still I had kept on with Oñate the same stupid game I had played before, when I should have split his skull with a chunk of lead and let the buzzards pass their judgment on his merits.

This was what I thought to myself as I looked after him from the mouth of the patio of Cantaras. Oñate had been headed north the last time I saw him, and that was a long time ago; here he turned up pat in San Clemente in my path a second time, and though I hadn't much reason to think that it was my business that brought him here, instinct in this case shouted loudly and long that he had come here to help in the taking of Joe Warder's scalp.

Certainly that scalp felt loose on my skull, just at that moment.

That instant of thought, while I watched Oñate sift out of view among the trees, was split apart as the bright steel of an ax splits dark-grained wood. Voices, and words, and cries, are light and dark—I mean, there is a palpable darkness in a groan and a palpable brightness in a scream. I've heard an Indian squaw shriek under certain circumstances of a tribal war, and even the memory of the sound leaves a dazzle before my eyes. Now, I felt light jump across my brain, for I heard a loud shout from the interior of Cantaras' house.

It was a shout to stop the traffic anywhere, but it fairly congealed my blood, for I recognized the voice of young MacMore, raised in fear, rage and resistance.

Other voices closed around that call rapidly, muttering, smooth, assured, savage. I tell you that I could see the scene and the treachery. There was a heavy, crashing blow, like the noise of a chair splintered against the wall; a whirl of confusion and uproar, then the heavy boom of a Colt revolver, with a last wild cry of despair to answer it and end the confusion.

Not one murmur, not one breath of sound after this; but the final cry was that of Denny MacMore!

You will wonder that I should have remained where I was during all this uproar that was taking place around my friend, but, as a matter of fact, I had begun to move at the first outcry. I knew that the doors would take a lot of investigation, and all the lower windows were more than safely secured with bars. Well, I climbed up the face of one set of those bars, swung myself violently on a ledge over them, and so gained the window next above.

There I slipped into the dark of a room and remained on my knees for a moment, slowly gasping back my breath. At twenty, or twenty-five, I could have managed that little climb like nothing, but at forty-plus a man can carry a weight, but he cannot run with it.

As I got the dizziness out of my head and controlled my breathing a little, I wondered at the echo of other breathing in that room; but changed my wonder for another emotion when the echo got out of step with me.

Some one else was crouched there in the thick black hand of the darkness, some one who might be taking a bead on me, with the faint moonlight sending a ray or two through the window and onto my head and shoulders.

I slipped to the floor and crawled forward like a prowling tiger, with the revolver ready in my hand. It was the worst bad luck that I had entered a dark chamber where some one was asleep, but I had to do something about it.

I pulled off my boots, when I was a fair distance from the window. That was leaving evidence against me, all right, but I would have left more than that, for a secret exit from that room. I spotted the breathing. It had not left the corner from which I first heard it. And now I started slinking toward the corner from which it came.

I was close, very close, when the voice broke out in a faint groan, stifled by fear and therefore having a horrible bubbling note in it. I never have heard a worse thing than that. You may talk of seeing death, but that was like hearing it.

I pushed my empty hand before me and found a cot, bed clothes, long, coarse hair—an old woman in bed and absolutely frightened to death by my entrance!

It was an ugly affair, for me. I struck a match for one instant. It showed me the door through which I would get access to the interior of the house; it showed me also the woman, old as the wrinkles of her skin had suggested, her hair a grisly gray, her eyes closed, but her mouth still faintly puckered in an expression of horror that was a sickening thing to see.

I pressed my hand over her heart. There was nothing to feel. I wasted another ten priceless seconds in putting my ear to her breast, and then at last I heard the feeble pulse of life, with a flutter and tired pause in it.

However, she lived, and that was enough for me. I did not pause to administer any restoratives, I can tell you. Instead, I went across that room, through the door, and into the corridor beyond as fast as I could slither, and I did not wait to pick up the boots I had taken off.

In the hallway, I started to the right, and turning a corner I almost ran into the arms of three people. Two men and a woman were coming, one of the men carrying a lamp, with the flame jumping in the throat of the chimney at every step, and the light wavering up and down along the hallway.

I turned myself almost inside out starting back the other way. Before I reached the first door—it was on my right— the lamplight gleamed on me, so I wrenched that door open and jerked it shut noiselessly behind me as I entered.

They might have seen me; they were almost sure to have seen me; but what better thing could I do than thank Heaven that I had put one heavy door between me and them and look for another way out of the place?

Already I was thinking that I had played the part of a monstrous fool by venturing into this house so blindly, when I knew well enough beforehand that it was loaded with danger to the ceilings thereof. What chance had I here to help the boy, whereas I might conceivably have worked for him from without!

I stepped to the window. It was quite a large room, and apparently, from what I could see of the dark loom of the furniture about me, a living apartment rather than a bedroom. It seemed that the floor had been sprinkled recently for the sake of coolness—I remember that there was a damp feel to the air and a humid scent in it.

I reached the window—and touched iron bars! I cannot tell why that fact chilled me so much. It was only one point of escape cut off, and yet the discovery struck me with a shock. I gripped those bars with a foolish impulse of terror, and flattened my face against the iron; it was an outside room, and therefore I was able to look across the dark heads of the park trees, faintly touched upon by the moonshine, here and there. It gave me a wild and romantic sense of being girt about by black waves in a lonely castle—a childish impression which disappeared at once.

That silly idea barely had come to me when the door knob turned with an abrupt rattling.

They had seen me enter here, then?

I got behind a tall-backed chair with one long stride, and pulled out both revolvers. I had had my back to the wall before, but never quite as badly as this, since I could remember!

But I thanked Heaven when I saw a man come in bearing a lamp high before him—a lamp with the flame jumping in the chimney at every step he made!

No, they did not know that I had come in here, but by a most ungracious stroke of circumstance I had picked out by chance the very room toward which they were making!

At that, I ducked back into a corner and got behind a sort of low settee which was covered with white goatskins. I depended on the shadows and on the intervening furniture to cover my retreat to that place; but once there, ensconced in the angle between the back of the settee and the corner of the wall behind it, I was fairly comfortable and able to see and to hear everything that happened.

I had enough to use my eyes and ears on at once.

The lamp carrier was a long-legged fellow, with a vast pair of shoulders, and huge arms; most uncommonly ferocious looking. He was dressed in cheap white-cotton clothes, like any peon, and his straw *huarachas* creaked a little as he moved—a proof that they were on the new side.

This monster, after he had put down the lamp, stepped hastily back out of the inner flame of its light. I could see him, after that, in the background, as a sort of gloomy witness of the affair, unpleasantly ready to execute sinister orders.

The second man in the room was Cantaras himself—I heard him addressed by that name by the peon almost immediately after they came in. He was a sleek, smooth man, with a dapper air, and very quick with his gestures. At this moment he was apparently so nervous that he walked constantly up and down the room.

However, I was not so interested in the giant *mozo* or in Cantaras as I was in the woman. For it was that same Alicia who had directed poor MacMore to this house.

No matter what my own danger, I felt pity for her at once, because I could see that she was frightened within the very verge of her life. She sat in a chair against the wall, with the lamplight full against her face, making her skin appear a sickly yellow-white. Her head had fallen over to one side; the eyes were very wild, but fixed; and the hands gripped each other in her lap with frantic strength.

She looked the picture of one who has just passed through a paroxysm of terror, and now rests and patiently waits for a still greater dread to overwhelm her.

As far as that was concerned, every one of the three seemed to be waiting for some one or something in that room; all three had an odd air of awful expectancy, though, of course, neither of the men appeared half as terrified as the poor girl.

Cantaras was the first one to speak.

13 ... The Señor

DRAGGED in as she had been, like a criminal in terror of death, or torture at the least, I had expected that Cantaras would quiz the girl first; but, instead, he talked to the *mozo* as he paced up and down the room. That giant kept his monstrous arms folded across his chest and stared at the girl while he answered the questions of his master.

"Old Manuelo," said Cantaras, "he should have been on the heels of the young man."

"Old Manuelo," said the giant, "was trapped by them like a blind dog running on the scent of a pig."

You can believe that I sharpened my ears at this. It was not hard to infer that Manuelo was the name of the veteran whom we had caught.

Cantaras stopped in his pacing and hissed with surprise.

"There was no better pair of eyes in San Clemente!" he declared. "Otherwise, would I have given him that work to do?"

The giant unfolded one arm to make a gesture of indifference to this question. I could gather that he was only partly under the control of Cantaras, or he would not have dared to be so free.

"Gualtero," says Cantaras, "did you see Manuelo caught?"

"Yes, I followed along behind him all the way, and I was not surprised when he was trapped. Old men get dim eyes, even though Señor Cantaras will not believe it!"

Cantaras snapped his fingers in vexation.

"What did you see? What did you hear, Gualtero?" he demanded. "Mind you, my friend, because the Señor speaks to you now and then, you are a fool to give yourself airs with me!"

The giant smiled, and it was as evil a grin as I ever saw. However, he answered obediently enough: "I saw the gringos catch him in the narrow road through the willows. I

61

slipped up close enough to hear them ask who had sent him on that trail, and the old man answered that El Tigre had sent him."

Cantaras threw up both his arms in a silent gesture of fury. And I saw the girl tilt forward and grip the edges of her chair, as though the mere sound of this name made her forget some of her personal terror.

I was not surprised. From what I knew of that man's exploits, I myself feared him almost like a ghost.

"How did they force him to tell? Torture, Gualtero?"

"They promised faithfully to let him go free."

"Ah? And then he went loose?"

"No. When they had what they wanted, they cut his throat and dragged him into the brush."

Cantaras seemed indifferent enough when he heard this fluid lie. But I could guess what had happened to old Manuelo. If the giant had been close enough to hear the words of Manuelo, he was also close enough to see the glitter of that little handful of diamonds, and I could guess where the jewels were now. I could almost see the huge man leaping on the rider of the burro from behind. It would have been a noiseless death, at least.

Or perhaps this monster in the corner with his vast shoulders and his little head was a sort of walking conscience who strode the by-ways in the service of El Tigre and overwhelmed treacherous servants of the ubiquitous master.

"Manuelo is gone," said Cantaras at last, "and that is the end of those who betray El Tigre!"

He glanced at the girl as he spoke, and she shrank back with a faint moan, entirely recalled to herself.

"And this girl?" Cantaras asked. "Did she come willingly?"

Gualtero turned his head and regarded her fixedly.

"She came—willingly," said he.

"He will come here directly," said Cantaras, still walking up and down, "and he will bring word directly from El Tigre. It is always that way. Why El Tigre should prefer to give his authority into the mouth of a gringo, I cannot tell. But we know that that is what has happened. The Señor has promised to be here at once. He will look at the girl, too, and tell us what to do with her. Tell me, did you speak to her father?"

"I spoke to him," said the giant.

"What does he ask?"

"He is a wise man. He does not consider a daughter a treasure. However, he has a need of her in the house, if it is convenient to let her live."

"He will soon be here," said Cantaras, nodding to himself and speaking almost under his breath. "I hope there will be no blood," he added more loudly. "I hope that. For my part, I am a man of peace."

"Yes," said the giant, "you never have ridden in a raid!"

Cantaras cast a blighting look at the big man, and for some moments after this he continued his walking up and down.

"Warder?" he asked suddenly.

My own name startled me, even when given a Spanish pronunciation.

"He is to die," said the giant with perfect calmness.

It was almost as though my arms had been shackled behind me and I had heard a judge speak, there was such calm surety in the voice of Gualtero.

"He is to die," said Cantaras. "Yes, that I can understand. Though it may not be easy. I have talked to Oñate, who knows all about this man."

It was a compliment for which I could not thank Oñate, the traitor.

"Oñate," said the giant, "is a coward and a fool. Hush!"

He lifted a great hand above his head, with the forefinger extended. Then he said quietly: "The Señor!"

I write that word with a capital because of the peculiar manner in which both Cantaras and the big man spoke it —very definitely, reserving a certain air of respect and reverence, almost, for the special occasion.

I think that Gualtero must have heard a step in the hall, because he glided at once to the door and drew it open. Into the opening stepped a well-built six-footer—who was not a Mexican!

This was the gringo who appeared to be in the confidence of El Tigre.

"Señor MacMore!" said Cantaras. And he hurried forward to take the hand of the newcomer.

This was Patrick MacMore, at last!

I strained forward until I almost lost my balance and

toppled against the settee. This was the man of whom young Denny was never done sounding the praises. This was the breaker of ladies' hearts, the conqueror of fighting men, the man of many devices, the keen wit and the cunning brain!

Well, it's human nature—at least, Western human nature—to take all stories of prodigies with a distinct grain of salt. But when I saw the silent, springing step with which the Señor crossed the floor I knew, that instant, that young Denny had not exaggerated anything he said about the strength of the man. Physical power is an attribute that shines out from some men just as great intelligence shines out from the faces of others.

And when The MacMore, as Denny was so fond of calling him, came into the circle of the lamplight, I saw a very pale, handsome face with not much likeness to that of Denny, but with a lofty forehead and deep-set eyes that stirred me even where I crouched in the shadow at the corner of the room.

He shook the hand of Cantaras briefly, gave the giant a mere nod, and then looked at the girl.

That look brought her out of her chair. She flung herself on the floor in front of him and stretched up her arms.

"It was only because he was your brother, only because of that, Señor!" said she.

And again that little breathlessness in the speaking of the title. As though she were calling him "marquis" or "grand duke," you might say!

"Because the young rascal said that he was my brother of course you had to believe him?" said the Señor.

"Ah, Señor, I was unwise!"

"There is no great harm done," said he. He took her hands and drew her to her feet. "Go home to your father," said he.

Her head tilted back, as I have seen the head of a boxer do when a hard punch landed. She swayed where she stood.

"And tell him?" she gasped.

"Why, tell him that everything is forgotten and forgiven. Hurry, my dear. Because we have other things to talk about, here!"

She ran to the door gladly and swiftly enough; there she

64

whirled and gave the Señor one glance over her shoulder, and was gone.

Said the giant, as the door closed: "If it should be that El Tigre heard of this, and the message had not come from him—"

He paused ominously.

"You have done one murder tonight," said MacMore quietly, "that is enough for you to think about. Just where do you keep the diamonds, Gualtero?"

I thought that the big fellow would run at MacMore; he actually crouched like a beast for the spring, but he could not confront MacMore—not for an instant! Then he straightened and I could hear his husky breathing.

"I keep them for my master," said he. "But as for the traitor who—"

"You lie," said MacMore. "You keep them for yourself!"

He turned his back on Gualtero and faced Cantaras, who was blinking like one brought out of darkness to face a strong light.

"Ramon," said he, "what is the word of the other—of Warder?"

"He has been seen. He will be followed, Señor."

"He has been for hours in San Clemente," said MacMore. "You were warned. You were told the very hour he would arrive. But still he has been left free. He must be a dead man before the morning."

Cantaras started to speak, but apparently the Señor was not a man to be argued with. He remained silent.

"That man is dangerous," said MacMore. "Hunt him with couples. You hear?"

"I hear."

"As for the young fool who calls himself my brother, he is young enough to be pitied. Take three good men, with Gualtero to command them, and let them take the gringo down to the sea and put him on a ship for New Orleans."

He turned quickly about.

"Gualtero, El Tigre may forget even the diamonds!"

14 ... MacMore, Miner

EACH in his own way, I should have picked Gualtero and Cantaras to be about as difficult men to handle as one could find in a year's search, but this MacMore had taken them both in hand without trouble. I admired the way he had put the whip on that big brute, Gualtero, and the casual way he disposed of Cantaras. Those people were afraid of him, and only partly because he represented their mutual master—El Tigre.

It was a hard pull on my imagination to jump from such a man as Patrick MacMore to the still greater figure of El Tigre himself. That long-haired, copper-skinned Indian who was the pet terror of the border, was even a greater man than I ever guessed if he could turn a white man like MacMore into such a subordinate as lieutenant.

MacMore turned Cantaras and Gualtero both out of the room by saying that he wished to write a letter. They went at once, Cantaras as though he were not the master in his own house, and Gualtero stalking out first, keeping his dignity, but not able to control one shudder as he turned his back on MacMore.

That was the final touch in building up the picture of MacMore. Gualtero shivered when he turned his back on the man, and that gave a really grisly suggestion of ferocity and power.

I thought that the remark about letter writing was a joke, but I was entirely wrong, for no sooner was the door closed than MacMore sat down at the table and took writing materials out of his pocket. He wrote with a pencil, and the lines flowed rapidly behind it; I was fascinated by the skill and the speed with which he wrote, which was so great that it seemed as though the pencil were running in an irregular groove. A slight creaking sound began—the table trembling under the vibrations of the man's heavy arm.

Under cover of that sound, small as it was, I dared to

stand up from behind the settee. I slipped around the end of it, gripping my revolver hard.

It was like stalking a tiger with a mere Colt for a weapon. I had to force myself back to the truth that this was only a man, after all, and, therefore, capable of being knocked flat and killed by a .45-caliber slug.

When I was halfway to him, I saw his head jerk up a trifle and he turned rigid; then the pencil continued its same rapid writing! But I knew very well that in that instant he guessed there was another man in the room—or danger of some kind coming up behind him. He was using the interval of writing to try to formulate some plan in self-defense —about the coolest exhibition of nerve that I ever saw!

I stepped into the plans, whatever they were, by saying: "Don't move, MacMore!"

"All right," said he, in the most undisturbed voice. "It's Warder, I suppose?"

If he only knew it, I was so staggered by this instant recognition that he could have done almost anything with a quick effort; but he could hardly understand how much I was upset. I never had set eyes on him before, or he on me; I never had heard his voice, or he mine; but he had been able to name me offhand at the first words that I spoke!

"Yes," said I, "this is Warder."

I stepped slowly around him, with the gun ready, but he did not attempt to stir. When I was fully in front of him, he smiled and nodded at me and my leveled revolver as though we were both old friends.

He was one of those men who grow as you come closer to them. Even when he entered the room at the first moment, I had been able to write him down one man in ten thousand. But here at close hand he was one in ten million. He had looked strong, before; he now looked panther-quick, as well. But chiefly the difference of effect lay in the eyes, for seen close up they were the eyes of a man who never has been checked. No matter what the obstacles, he always had broken through to get what he pleased out of people or out of life. It is hard for me to analyze the exact effect they had on me, unless I say that when I was coming up behind him, it was like stalking a great beast of prey, and now that I was in front the similarity was even greater. It was an effect of perfect ruthlessness.

I did not doubt, now, what young MacMore had told me about the powers of this older brother of his; boy or man, he was bound to conquer. With all the advantage on my side of a drawn gun held on him, I still was about as badly frightened as ever I've been in my life. Being fenced up in the peon patio with enemies all round me was nothing compared with this.

"Sit down, Warder," said he.

I merely smiled, and he nodded.

"You think I might push the table over on you, eh?" says he.

Of course I thought that! At any rate, I felt much better at a little distance from him, with my two feet under me, so to speak, so that I could dodge thunderbolts even if I could not forestall them.

"How did you know me?" I asked him. "How did you know that I was behind you, even?"

"Shall I give away my secrets?" said he.

Then he smiled at me, and there was something wonderfully winning in that smile. It invited confidence as much as the smile of a boy.

"There was a slight tremor in the floor," he told me. "Perhaps, besides that, there was something in the air. I saw you with the nerves in my spine, Warder!"

"You saw me?"

"Ah, you wonder how I knew that it was you?"

"That's it."

"That's perfectly simple. Some one was in this room who wasn't supposed to be here, some one who was not exactly a friend of mine. Who could it be? Why, no one but the friend of young Dennis MacMore, as he calls himself. You know the story—kill one snake and its mate will come back to it the next day."

This may have been perfectly clear reasoning to him, but there were a good many missing links in the chain, from my viewpoint—perhaps from yours, also, as you read it. But the reason I never have set the world on fire is just because I lack that ability to skip the links in between and make big jumps to strange conclusions. Genius is the only name for that.

"You're clever, MacMore," I told him.

"Yes," he agreed surprisingly, "I'm clever. What will you have of me, Warder?"

"Your company back to the border."

"You're going to arrest me?"

"Exactly."

"Here in a foreign country where your badge of office isn't worth a pie plate?"

"I won't arrest you till I have you safely on the farther side of the Rio Grande."

"And what's the cause for the arrest?"

"Plotting against the life and welfare of an American citizen."

"You'll have no witness that I've ever done that."

"On the contrary, I'll have an eye-witness."

"Come, come, Warder. Who will that be?"

"Myself."

"Hello! Have you ever laid eyes on me before this night?"

"I'm the man you plotted against, and I heard you in this room."

He made a little gesture that almost got him shot.

"I was a fool to forget that, of course," said he. "I'll keep my hands still, hereafter, too," he added. "I saw your trigger finger move just then."

"You were a sixteenth of an inch from eternity, in fact," I declared to MacMore.

"You've written me down a villain, eh?"

I was able to meet that smile of his as I remembered some of the details of that border warfare.

"You won't deny that you work with El Tigre?"

"I deny absolutely everything—in court!"

"Three times I've seen the dead men after El Tigre passed," I stated. "It wasn't a pretty sight, either. And I don't want to see it again."

"Of course you don't! But I've never ridden with El Tigre in my life."

"I think that's a lie."

"A lie?" says he.

His smile froze on his lips, and I knew that he was on the verge of throwing himself at my throat.

"A lie," I repeated.

I was ready to send a bullet into his forehead if he stirred, and beyond a doubt, he knew it. He merely leaned a little toward me across the table, so that the lamplight fell more brightly on his face.

I saw a strange detail, then, which I would not have believed if it had been told to me by anything but my own eyes. It was a fairly warm evening, the sort of a time when the least effort makes a person perspire. For my own part, the job of facing down the man had me adrip and I was constantly afraid that drops might run down into my eyes.

But MacMore's face was as dry as could be. The lamplight modeled his skin, which was strangely pale for one who lived so much of his time in Mexico, and I never saw a handsomer face, if it had not been for that wild-animal look of the man who never has been denied.

Denied he was now, and thoroughly in my hands.

"I don't think that you could possibly hold me, if you carted me all that distance north," he suggested.

"We have good judges up there," I answered, "and they have a way of judging the crooks!"

He considered a little.

"Perhaps you're right, Warder. You're the sort of a fellow who generally is able to guess at the truth pretty accurately. But let me give you this idea," he continued, "which is that you may be wasting your talents up there in the cold North. There's a grand opening here for any one with an educated gun, my boy, and a few convenient talents along that line."

"Do you think I could make a living that way?"

"Beyond a shadow of a doubt," said he.

"In partnership with you, MacMore?"

"With me?" said MacMore. "Not at all! I'm a miner, you see."

15 ... Guns in Hand

MY FIRST idea was that he was a liar out and out; the second was that perhaps he told the truth, since there was no good reason why a confederate and ally of the terrible El Tigre might not actually be the owner of a mine.

70

Perhaps that was the reason at the back of the strange alliance—the white man's brains to furnish ideas to the bandit, and the bandit's long arm to protect the mine. I admitted that as a possibility, but still I was by no means sure. Whatever else he was, I could be sure that MacMore was a finished liar.

I probed him a little farther on the other side.

"But you think I could get an opening down here?"

"I know it."

"Because you're a friend of El Tigre?"

"That's it."

"I'm on the other side of the law," I told him finally, now that he had shown a part of his hand.

"I thought you were," he replied, "but sometimes a pillar of the church in Boston is a savage in Tucson. At any rate, I want to make some sort of a business deal with you."

"To save yourself?"

"Naturally. Let me see what it can be."

He raised his head and lowered his eyes, in the process of his thought.

"MacMore," I said suddenly, "why won't you let the boy see you?"

"What boy?" he asked, then added: "Ah, you mean Dennis?"

"I mean Denny," I said.

"Because he's young and the country is dangerous," said MacMore. "I walk here on the edge of a sword, myself. Do you imagine that I want Denny in this sort of a layout?"

"You can protect yourself, though," I returned.

"I play a double game," said MacMore, with the greatest appearance of frankness. "On the one hand, I am the friend and adviser of El Tigre, which is something like being a tiger tamer. One never knows when the big jaws will close on one's head! In the second place, I'm the miner. Now, then, I get on well enough with El Tigre and he's willing to give me protection from the Indians and the Mexicans. However, that protection is full of flaws. I don't even dare to let the location of my mine be known to every one. I have to keep it a half secret. I can protect myself, but I don't want the risk of protecting my brother, also. You've had a chance to see what sort of a headstrong youngster he is. He could easily pull both of us into the mire."

I stood back a little farther and studied the ingenuous face of Patrick MacMore. After all, it was exactly this sort of business that he would be apt to enjoy—playing one power off against another and gaining out of it a certain authority and also a certain amount of money. I began to lose some of my animosity and a great deal of my fear with it. You can't dread a man you commence to like.

"He has come a long distance," said I. "He rode through all sorts of trouble, as I happen to know. And if you send him away this time to New Orleans, you don't need to think that he'll stay away. He'll come back, and the next time, he'll either find you or die trying."

MacMore made a little gesture.

"No matter what you think, that kid is not a complete fool," he told me. "This lesson will be learned so thoroughly that he won't repeat it. He'll find a long letter from me when he gets back. That letter will tell him not to come to San Clemente again, and I think that he'll obey. Don't you?"

"I think that he might, if no one told him the truth about you and El Tigre and the sort of life you lead down here."

"Meaning that you may tell him?"

"If I get out of this country alive."

"Exactly," said MacMore.

He smiled at me, and the smile was a thing worth seeing and remembering. I thought of a cat licking its whiskers!

So I nodded at MacMore in turn. "We're dealing clearly with each other," I said. "You want my scalp."

"Not a bit. But my poor friend El Tigre does."

"And you pity him enough to help?"

"Naturally. He can't help being a brute. He was made that way, in the beginning. But he has virtues, too."

"Such as courage, et cetera?" I suggested.

"Exactly. And faith in his friends, unless he takes too much tequila on the way." He made a little pause and then added: "If I were you, Warder, I'd chuck this business. You're up against more than you possibly can handle."

It makes any man see red when he's told that he's up against the impossible, and like any one else, I couldn't help getting angry when I heard him talk.

At last I said: "Look here, MacMore, I've been given a job, and my business is not to argue about possibles or impossibles. I have to stick to the trail until I get him, or until he gets me."

MacMore smiled again, and I never saw a smile that I liked less.

"You amuse me, amigo," said he. "Here you are, a man of brains, courage, and virtue, plus a good deal of education. Where did you pick that up, by the way?"

"In prison," I answered.

"Ah, prison?" said he.

"Yes. I've spent enough of my life there. That's where I picked up a little bookishness."

"As good a way as any, I suppose. But all of your good qualities are tempered, stained I might say, by excessive virtue. I offer you a chance to play with El Tigre, but you won't be contented with anything other than a knife in your throat. Well, you are the chooser! I cannot help that."

"You can't help seeing, however," said I, "that before anything happens to me, a bullet will happen to you!"

"That may be true, but I'm only one hand of El Tigre. A right hand, if you will, but he has many others. People who would die for him, largely because he is apt to punish failure with something worse than death."

"You mean to say that you're a servant to El Tigre?"

"In a large sense, yes, that's true."

"I don't believe it," said I.

"Oh, you don't believe it?"

"I don't believe that you're a servant to any man in the world," said I, and looking him firmly in the eye, I was more and more convinced that what I said was true.

"Well," said MacMore, "of course, one might say that I'm a sort of junior partner in the firm. That's a pleasanter way of putting it, if you don't like the idea of a white man being the servant of an Indian."

"I've told you the truth," said I. "I'll tell you one more."

"I hope so."

"You're going to get up from that chair and come with me."

"Out of the house?"

"Exactly. Out of the house."

73

"My friend, you'll find twenty people to pick you off on the way."

"Not if you tell them to hold off."

"Shall I tell them that?"

"Yes, while you have a revolver pressed against the small of your back."

"A very cruel idea, Warder."

"I'm talking to a cruel man, MacMore," I answered. "You'll have to stand up."

"Very well," said he. "In that case I'll have to use my last argument."

"If you attempt any move, I'll shoot you where you sit."

"I know you will, Warder," he answered. "I know all about you, in fact, because we had to find out as soon as we learned that you were on this trail."

"How did you find that out?"

"There are leaks in any sieve."

"I suppose so."

I ran my mind's eye over the men of the marshal's office. It was quite true that half of them were capable of any kind of rascality, though I knew that the other half were pure steel.

"But knowing all about you," he went on, "of course we're afraid of you. You must have heard me giving the order that you're to die before the morning?"

"I heard that."

"It will be carried out."

"Perhaps."

"Without fail, whether I live or die. You've had the period put to your useful career, my friend. All of your robberies, gun fights, and then arrests on behalf of the law are at an end, no matter whether I leave this room with you alive or not."

"I hear you say that; in the meantime, suppose we start along."

"Willingly, but I haven't stated my last argument to you."

"Come then. I'm listening."

"This is the fact of the matter. You are a good hand with a gun, Warder. A great hand, some say; but you and I know better. You are no El Tigre, though a very sufficiently skillful practitioner. However, there is one circumstance under which your skill will be useless."

"I don't know what that circumstance can be," I retorted.

He had reached out a hand in the midst of his argument, looking at me fixedly in the eye, as a man does when a great idea is about to be brought forth by him.

"Darkness!" he shouted suddenly at me.

And with a side move of his hand, he dashed the lamp to pieces and filled the room with darkness.

I fired as the lamp went out. I fired by the last flash of it, as I saw him fling sidewise from his chair. I fired knowing that the noise of the shot would probably bring a rushing crowd which would dash me to pieces.

But, somehow, it seemed to me far better to shoot and take this clever rascal with me than to allow him to get off unharmed.

Yet, even as I pulled the trigger, I knew that I had failed. I shot again as I heard him strike the floor, and there was an answering crash of a gun, and the whir of a bullet breathlessly close to my face.

The battle was on.

16 ... Out of One Fire

WHEN I faced that man in full light, having him at an advantage, I have said that I felt like one caged with a beast. And now I was with him in the same room, with no advantage, and lost in the darkness! Besides, footfalls began to hurry down the hallway, but they were nothing to frighten me; I was almost glad of whatever might happen, so long as it took me away from the power of this superman. If this seems a strange reaction, then I can only say that I have not been able to convey the right impression of him in what I already have spoken about MacMore.

I know that I crouched down against the floor and glared about me into the blackness, with eyes starting from my head, moving a little from side to side as I strove to get a sight of MacMore against the faint moonlight that showed outside the window and always backing toward the door.

Up to that door, in the meantime, the footfalls and the voices came rushing, paused, and burst it open. All at once I saw several faces, and above all others, the towering, huge shoulders of Gualtero.

A terror behind me and a terror before, as you might say!

I heard MacMore shouting in a terrible voice for them to look out, because I certainly would try to break through them; before he had the words well out, I plunged at the legs of the men, driving myself forward with all the speed and the strength in my body.

A man will remember things with a wonderful vividness at such times. I have heard people say that they had seen the whole course of their lives when in danger of death, but of course, I am not a tender or imaginative soul. At any rate, all that I have seen was the face of the danger, and that with a wonderful clearness. For instance, if I were a painter, I could show you every detail of the faces and the men who now stood before me, and above all the bare knees of a long-legged *mozo* at which I threw myself.

I thought I had broken both his legs when I struck them with my shoulders, they gave so before me, and he went down with such a dreadful screech. I tumbled on top of him, but without losing much motion.

So I pitched to my feet again, with half a dozen hands reaching after me. Why didn't they shoot? Perhaps because the game seemed so entirely in their hands. You don't waste powder and shot on the wild bird when you have it in the room with you. At any rate, I did not keep a straight course ahead of them. I remembered the long legs of Gualtero and knew that I could not outrun him, whatever I could do with the rest. On the left hand I saw an open door, and I rushed through that in time to jerk it shut in the faces of those yelling man hunters.

One sweet moment of hope was that when I heard them shouting away with the thickness of that strong door behind me. Heaven bless the carpenter who framed that door, the locksmith who made the lock, the stong-hearted tree which furnished the wood! I heard them fling their shoulders against that barrier, and with their bullets they crushed out the lock itself, but in the meantime I had a second of respite.

Of course, I was at the window. It looked down into the courtyard, and there I saw five or six horses, all with empty saddles, except one, where a man sat with his hands ironed together behind his back.

When he looked up at that instant, I recognized young Denny MacMore, and he, it seemed, recognized me as I hung out from the window into the cold light of the moon, for he shouted hoarsely.

It was a friend's face, and it gave me heart, no matter whether the hands were ironed or free. I shot myself through the window. There was below me the narrow ledge of the eaves that projected above the window of the ground floor. If I missed that, I would carom onto the cobbles of the patio pavement, and that would mean a broken head or a snapped leg bone, at the least. However, there was only that chance.

Inside the house, already I heard the thunder of heavy feet on the stairs as they rushed to cut off my escape in exactly this manner, though others remained above, battering in the door. So I loosed my hold. My feet struck the ledge, fair and true; but the sagging of my knees forced them against the wall, and this shock slipped me off the ledge as quickly as I landed at it. However, the force of my fall was decidedly broken, so that I landed in the courtyard of the house on both feet again, well shaken, but without a broken bone or even so much as a bad bruise, except where my knees had struck against the wall of the house.

I could have stood worse pain than that, however, at that moment, for the hope which I had felt as I got a door between me and my enemies was a thousand times stronger now that I was under the open sky. I shouted, without knowing at the moment that I did so.

I remember that within the house the voice of some one running rapidly toward the patio shouted with an enormous strength something about the gate, and a *mozo* scurried toward it, leaping out from the shadow.

But by this time I was in the nearest saddle. I scooped up the reins of MacMore's horse while, as only he could have done, he shouted at me to go on and save myself and not worry about him.

The brute of a horse pulled back—for how long? Oh, half a second, perhaps. But half a second is enough when a bullet, say, is tearing its way through your body, and no bullet could have given me more exquisite pain than the fear of Gualtero and the older MacMore running out toward me from the house.

The pull on the reins and the thumping of Denny's heels at last got the stupid horse in action. He trotted, then lunged into a gallop with a suddenness that almost jerked MacMore from the saddle.

Before us, the *mozo* was leaning back with all his weight, forcing one panel of the patio gate shut, but we went through the other with a rush and turned our horses in the open street, poor Denny reeling in the saddle and almost going out of it as we straightened away.

We turned the next corner, and I sent the horses headlong into the trees. Then I pulled rein.

For one thing, I wanted to get Larry; for another, that street was scoured clean of people, and I was fairly sure that our exact course had not been marked. The pursuit might run on past us in this hiding place which they would hardly think we would resort to. Frightened men with horses under them are more apt to trust to the spur, and I hoped that the pursuit would count on this.

Well it turned out that I was right. I heard a vicious roaring of many hoofs that turned the corner and then bolted past the trees, with some one shouting commands in ringing Spanish. I shuddered a little as I listened, for I recognized that voice!

Here we were then, with three horses, but MacMore's hands ironed behind his back, while we listened to the pouring hoofbeats turn distant corners and then suddenly diminish to nothing, so that we could hear the sound of the music in the Plaza Municipal soaring softly and sweetly in the distance. It brought violently into my mind that all of these things had happened in a single evening, and that we had twice come out of the teeth of death in almost exactly the same manner. From that day to this a quiet little patio has never seemed a place of peace to me, but rather like a lion's mouth.

Young MacMore offered no suggestion, did not speak a word, in fact, of thanks or of praise, but simply waited at my disposal while I stared at the moonlight that filtered through the trees and wondered what I could do next. But at last I climbed into the saddle on Larry and guided the horses straight through the little wood, and out onto the street on the farther side, leaving behind the animal which I had ridden from the house of Cantaras.

I was cursing to myself, because my bruised knees had begun to ache terribly; and that faint muttering of my own voice raised my heart a good deal. As a matter of fact, I had no idea what we should attempt to try next. All I knew was that we were free for the instant, and all I saw before me was inescapable danger. Before long, every street of San Clemente would be filled with busy man hunters, if I guessed rightly at the power of MacMore, or of his barbarous chief, El Tigre.

In the meantime, it was better to go slowly and attract little attention. So we kept the horses not even at a trot, but walked them down the dusty street.

Children were playing in it! It was as strange to me as anything I've ever looked at to see them at their games in the soft dust, tumbling, wrestling, racing when there had been such happenings a single square away from them. The light from windows and doors, also, touched on us like quiet, unseeing eyes, and let us go by unchallenged. In the middle of the next square I heard the rapid chinking of a hammer upon an anvil, and turned at once toward it.

Young MacMore guessed my intention and for the first time tried to oppose me since we had started from the house of Cantaras, for he cried out softly to me: "There's no good in this, Joe. Every minute that you lose now is giving them a chance to guard the roads out of San Clemente. No matter about my hands. No matter at all. Let's get out of this."

The answer I gave him was a shock to me. Perhaps you have done the same thing yourself, mulling a matter over in your mind and yet hardly knowing what the effect of your thought was until suddenly your own voice put it into words.

"We're not leaving San Clemente," I told him. "We're staying right here inside the town."

I heard MacMore gasp. There was about as little fear in him as in any man I ever knew or heard of. But this decision was a shock to him, and no wonder. It was a shock to me, also, as I spoke.

But what else was there for us to do, except to adopt the strong policy and face the danger?

I was at least inside the walls of the enemy, at this time. Once outside of them again, I never would have a chance to get at the mystery of El Tigre. I had seen Denny's brother face to face—and luckily brought my life away from that encounter. And although I had bought these two gains at the expense of a great deal of danger, still they were something in pocket. And no matter how thoroughly El Tigre searched the town where he seemed to have such power, at least there was some chance that we could hide here for a while longer. It was no small village every nook of which could be combed. We might lurk in a corner.

That single gasp was all the protest that the boy made. He remained silent as before, while we headed down a little alley and so came to the hammering which we had heard in the distance. A greyhound stood up at the open door and snarled at us; and by the light of a pair of smoky lanterns we looked in through air streaked with curls of smoke and saw inside the blacksmith at his forge fire, where he was working the bellows with one hand, the other resting on his hip. He was as grim a looking man as I ever laid eyes on, but I was resolved to use him for our purpose, so I dismounted at once.

17 ... Into Another

ALL MAKERS with brain and hand should be cheerful people, because there is nothing so contenting in the world as to make beautiful or useful things out of plain wood and from solid iron. But above every one, I think, the blacksmith is the good-natured man. His work keeps him in muscle, which gives him a sense of important superiority to his fellow men. Usually, he is a fellow of some tonnage, too, to balance the weight of a twelve or fourteen-pound sledge. He is the perfect combination of brawn and brains, and such a thing as a stupid blacksmith, I dare say, never was seen on the face of the earth. By that, I don't mean the people who work in big factories, going through a few mechanical maneuvers which machines will eventually replace, but I mean the man who stands by with raw iron and ventures to make to order with hand and fire. Having such powers, and yet without a craft which can lead them to wealth, no wonder that they are found to be contented people as a general rule.

But one glance at this man in San Clemente was enough to tell me that he was of a different nature. He was a lean, time-dried man of more than fifty, who looked over-matched by the ponderous sledges that leaned against the wall, so meager were his arms, though they were strung with narrow sinews of muscle. He had a leather apron around him for protection against the stinging showers of sparks, but there was no shirt beneath the apron, so that I could see his ribs and count them one by one. The cords of his neck stood out like fingers, and his chest still was heaving from his last bout at the anvil. To crown his appearance he had a lean face with a hawk nose, and a smudge of soot over one eye gave him an expression of sinister whimsicality. His glance, almost as a matter of course, was thoughtfully resting on the ground.

I remained in the shadows by the door while I tested him with words, in spite of his gloomy appearance. You can't tell even a mustang by the mere look of him.

"Señor," said I, "you are a good example to us all."

He merely raised his eyes from the floor and looked at me with a glance which, I knew, pierced the shadows and read every line of my face. I was sunburned till my skin was even darker than his, but I saw his brows lift a trifle and knew that he was saying to himself, "Gringo."

A bad start for me!

"Because," I explained myself clumsily, "you show us how to make the working day longer."

He worked the bellows automatically while he answered in a voice much pleasanter than I had expected:

"You know, I am only a poor slave, señor."

"I would lay a bet," I answered, "that you are no slave. You own the whole shop you work in, I should say."

"And, therefore," he answered, "I have to pay taxes on it. I have a house, also, and that is worth taxing as well. So that I am twice as much a slave as if I were hired."

"Then the richer the man the more he is a slave?" I suggested, managing a smile.

"Slaves are well treated," he replied. "Suppose I am a *hacendado,* I treat my peons well because a fat peon makes a good worker, and a sick one is something out of my pocket. That's a simple thing to see."

"Then why not sell your shop and your house and go to work for another man?"

"Because I am proud," said he. "Pride is the whipstock and the lash, and the hand that swings it. I worked for forty years to get a house and a shop, and after getting them, how can I give them up?"

"You talk like a tired man," I told him. "After all, a few taxes are for the good of the country and don't make you a slave."

"I am a slave, nevertheless," said he. "Why am I here to-night?"

"For the sake of money," I suggested.

"For the sake of the Donna Alvarado," he answered, and sneered at the thought.

"Well," said I, "she will appreciate the quick work."

"She will appreciate nothing," said he. "I never work to win good praise, but to keep away bad talk. You are never praised unless you have been a fool and gulled out of any good measure. She will pay for the work, look three times at the andirons, wish that she had bought old ones, and then forget the andirons and me, and everything except the price that she paid for them. However, sparrows should not cheep when the hawk is in the air."

"That," said I, "I cannot follow."

"Do you think there is no hawk in the air, hanging above San Clemente?" he asked. He sneered again, and added: "Or I might say, something that prowls and hunts?"

I was surprised to hear him. It seemed clear enough that he was referring to El Tigre, and that was a thing which I had understood no man in San Clemente dared to do.

"Señor," said I, "you are a brave man."

"For what reason?" he asked.

"Because you, at least, say what you please."

"I pick out a safe listener, however," answered the blacksmith. "It can never be said that Enrico Orthez speaks to the dumb or pats the neck of a tiger!"

Now that he had become as open as this, I felt encouraged to take a step into the shop. He turned a little from me to gather the coals above the flame of his forge; a puff of thick, heavy smoke instantly jetted out from the sides of the new fuel. It rose in a cloud and enveloped Enrico Orthez in the fumes.

"How do you know that I am a safe man to talk to?" said I.

"Well," said he, "a man who is under the paw of the tiger is not likely to tell him that a mouse is nibbling at his hind foot."

"I am under the paw of El Tigre?" I asked, stepping instantly into the full sense of his talk.

It was enough to chill any one, the calmness with which this man told me such a thing.

"Ah," said the blacksmith, "perhaps you have been climbing walls and shooting guns for pleasure, and nearly breaking your legs as you jumped? Perhaps that was not because of El Tigre?"

"Why do you say these things?" I asked him, curious.

"You have nearly rubbed through the cloth over your knees; the skin of your finger tips is rubbed to the raw, and there is a streak of red on the butt of your revolver," said he.

"I stumbled in the street," I answered, beginning to feel that this blacksmith was an evil bird in more than his lean looks, "and I fell on my hands and knees. The red on the gun butt came from a touch of my hand."

Enrico Orthez yawned. "And when you stood up," said he, "you found that your friend was in handcuffs. Is that the story?"

It made my head spin, and I must have showed my astonishment in my face, for Enrico permitted himself the faintest of smiles.

"So you have come to the poor blacksmith to ask him to put his own life in danger by cutting off the irons which the Señor has put on your friend's wrists? Tell me, my friend, if you think that I am only a blacksmith, or also a fool?"

"I think," I said from my heart, "that you can look through walls, see in the dark, read men's minds, and foresee the future. How in the name of fortune do you happen to know all these things?"

"There is a certain cat," he replied, "that purrs in San

Clemente, and whenever it purrs the entire town listens. When it sharpens its claws, the people grin with fear. Now, the whisper came through San Clemente that two strangers were coming to our town, and that the noble Señor wished to see them. I see these two on the very night when I already have heard the sound of guns a few squares away. I see two strangers who come to my shop and speak good Mexican with strange faces. I listen to them, and in spite of myself, I cannot help hearing chains on the hands of one of them, though he has kept a distance away."

He ended his explanation with a wave of the hand, his arm looking skeleton thin as he extended it.

"You see that everything is plain and easily understood," said he. "There is no mystery about a poor blacksmith."

I laughed aloud. He had looked through and through me and my poor little affairs, and so easily that I almost forgot to be afraid. If he could see through me so easily, I was hardly the man to be considered worth hunting to death by the terrible Señor. And yet I could not help remembering that the Señor with his own lips had pronounced me dangerous enough to be worth killing at once!

Now the blacksmith, in my estimation, grew greater and greater. He seemed like a seer, or a wizard.

But young MacMore stepped readily into the light of the lanterns, and turning his back to the anvil, he held out his locked hands.

"You know everything about us," he said, "but perhaps you don't know that we are honest men. Look, Joe. We are in his hands. If he so much as whistles, we're done for. Señor, will you make me a free man—for five minutes before I die?"

I was surprised to hear the little dramatic flourish in the voice of Denny, but it had its effect upon the sardonic Orthez.

He nodded and grunted. Then he said: "I have seen handcuffs once or twice before, in my life. Let me see those!"

He leaned over them for a moment, grunting again with satisfaction. Then, with a short piece of watch spring, or something that looked like it, he worked for a moment at the lock, and was rewarded almost at once by a distinct click. The cuffs opened, and young MacMore's hands were once more free!

He had turned to thank the blacksmith when we heard the horses in the street. I whirled to get at Larry, when Orthez broke in with his usual calm:

"There is nothing to do by running. This is a blind canyon that you have ridden into. The street is closed, and you cannot get through, my friends!"

Actually he stood there leaning one hand on the handle of the bellows and looking as though he were greedily devouring our fear.

Then he grunted, as the noise of the many riders grew. "Let them stand where they are, and come back through my shop."

18 ... In the Garden

For an instant I hesitated, staring at Denny to see if he shared my suspicion that the blacksmith might be playing us false; but Denny seemed incapable of thought. He merely stared back at me with strange, wide eyes, as though he saw no way out of this danger, but was willing to trust in me blindly. It may make some men proud to be so trusted, but it did not have that effect on me. I prefer to do my work alone and have no skin but my own to answer for in the end. I had to make a decision by myself, and make it in half a second. What I decided was that there were two chances out of five that the blacksmith would be honest, and those two chances were worth taking.

I nodded to him, and Orthez motioned us through the back door of the shop, set in close to the forge itself. Passing through this, we found ourselves in a small garden sweet with orange blossoms and fenced in by a wall except where the blacksmith shop itself was standing, and where a house appeared just opposite it. I could guess that that was the house of our friend Orthez.

What was clearer than anything else was that we were neatly trapped here. The wall was high, and with one gesture, the blacksmith could send the hunters in to catch us. Everything now depended upon Orthez himself. So when I found a chink of light that pierced through the wall of the smithy, I put my eye to it. I was lucky to find such a spy hole, because the wall of the shop was made of thick adobe, but here one of the bricks had crumbled in part. There was a mere chink on the outside, but this opened like a funnel within and allowed me to take a view of the greater part of the shop.

I was kneeling, with MacMore close beside me, and even the fear of El Tigre's men and the Señor was not enough to keep another fear out of my mind. For the soil of Mexico is fertile in something more than plants and trees, and through my brain went all the stories I had heard of vipers, striped, and coral-colored with black heads; of the *vinagrillo* which trails a strong poison wherever it goes; of the lizard from whose bite no man can recover; the *eslaboncillo* which dies of anger if it fails to bite; the *cencoatl* which shines in the dark; the black-and-red spider whose sting fills your bones with agony which cannot be driven away until you have spent five days in a room filled with smoke. And all of these dangers leave out tarantulas and scorpions! Perhaps the poison of snakes and insects is not as deadly as the fear men have of them; but the terror and the venom together have killed many a fellow who had laughed at guns. At any rate, I was shivering like a child as I kneeled in the soft garden mold, until with a rush of hoofbeats, the men of the Señor arrived.

He himself came first, springing from his horse and into the shop, where that good fellow, Orthez, was now working away at the iron which he had taken from the fire, bright red showers of sparks squirting out under his hammer strokes, so that the shop was filled with a pulsation of ruddy light.

He kept on his hammering in spite of the appearance of the Señor with big Gualtero behind him, and others pouring in as well.

"Orthez!" said the Señor.

The smith made his hammer hang in the air for the next stroke, but instead of answering with a word, he merely stared back at MacMore. I knew enough about the position of the Señor in San Clemente to feel the daring of such an attitude on the part of Orthez.

86

"Where are the men who rode those horses?" asked the Señor.

Orthez waved slowly the hand which was heavy with the hammer.

"They came here and asked the way."

"What way?"

"The way of this street."

"Quickly, Orthez! Where did they go?"

"I told them it was a blind alley and they would have to turn back. They did not do that. They jumped from their horses and went on."

"Went on where?"

"Down the street."

The Señor turned on his heel and leaped out through the doorway, singing out a command to Gualtero and one or two others to keep watch upon the blacksmith shop while he was gone. Twelve or twenty men may have followed him; others swarmed across the alley to examine the walls on that side and see where they could have climbed.

It gave me an odd chill, as though somehow one part of me were fleeing out there before the hunters, while the rest of me kneeled there in the garden muck and, looking through the chink, saw Gualtero stalking up and down through the shop. The two peons who remained there with him looked as savage as any one could wish to see; but they remained back near the shadows of the entrance, and looked at nothing but the giant, as though he were made of fire and might burn them.

Says Gualtero presently: "Orthez!"

But Orthez was hammering again at the iron, which now had cooled to a dark red. He toiled at the work, and perspiration dripped from him.

"Orthez!" bellowed Gualtero, when his first hail was not answered.

He made a great stride forward; he extended a huge hand that looked able to crush the skull of the blacksmith like an eggshell. Then the blacksmith looked up, but only for one glance. He continued his hammering, merely grunting out with the strokes: "Get out of my light, you great hulk! You are only big enough to cast a shadow."

It was rude talk to six feet eight or nine of powerful muscle and bone; and I saw the two fighting men at the doorway draw a little closer, their teeth and their eyes flashing in savage expectancy, so that I could guess they had seen the monster at work many a time before this. But I was surprised to see that Gualtero's big hand remained suspended in the air for a moment—and then actually fell to his side.

And Orthez went on hammering, turning the iron with his tongs and criticizing it as a hawk might turn a small prey and eye it. He seemed totally indifferent to the presence of the others, and taking the iron up, at last, he brushed close past Gualtero and gradually dipped the forging into the tempering tub. It entered with a mild and then a loud hiss that cast up a cloud of steam, through which Orthez went back to his forge.

"I have turned into a fat-brained fellow," declared Gualtero, "or else I would crack your head for you, or dash in all your teeth with one blow."

This unusual blacksmith answered:

"You are afraid, Gualtero. As a matter of fact, you would rather put your hands on a nest of rattlesnakes than to touch me. Because if you rest a mere finger on me, I'll be the death of you!"

He had been pushing a fresh piece of iron into the forge, but now as the smoke began to gush out while the bellows worked, he lifted his head and looked at the giant steadily, eagerly, with a dreadful greed in his eyes.

Gualtero went half a pace backward and then steadied himself; but he had to grapple at the handle of his revolver before he felt himself once more. And a wonderful thing it was to see that monster, that professional man crusher, recoil before the lean blacksmith. Gualtero blinked like a man come from darkness into light.

"You would use poison," he said. "There is no evil in San Clemente as bad as you are, Orthez."

The blacksmith passed the red tip of his tongue over his dry lips, while still he stared at the big man.

"There are poisons that rot a man slowly, from day to day, Gualtero, and you would last half a year, as a slow fire eats up a big tree!"

I never saw such venom in a man's face, and it fairly made the eyes of Gualtero roll with fear. He turned his back on Orthez, muttering something about a dark night and a knife in the back, but I had a very distinct impression that he would leave this dangerous blacksmith alone forever. I was of the same mind, until I saw the ghost of a smile flicker on the lips and the eyes of Orthez, and I knew that he had played a small game, and played it for the benefit of Gualtero. If it were acting, I never saw better in all the days of my life! From that moment I put down Orthez as one of the most remarkable men I ever have seen.

The shop was half filled with smoke when the Señor came back from his vain hunt.

"Search the shop!" he said curtly, and added: "Orthez, you have been lying to me!"

The thoughtful eyes of Orthez rose from the ground and fixed upon those of the Señor, but here he had met his match. There is a saying that no wild beast can bear the eye of a man, but I have tried to look down the black panther, where it lay in a cage like a pool of shadow in which floated two shining yellow orbs. I looked long enough to bring him with a snarl to the bars of his cage, but I could not make his glance turn from mine, and it was I who looked away and went off with a chill down my spine. There was a good deal of the same expression in the eyes of the Señor, now. And the blacksmith looked down to the ground.

They were searching the shop in detail, tearing open the tool chest in the corner, and opening a big box that stood by the entrance, but they did not find what they looked for, of course.

Finally, Gualtero found the door to the garden and thrust it open.

He stood there not two paces away from me, and stared about him at the trees and the walls. I had my gun on him, taking aim at the ridiculous small head that was the chief feature of his ugliness.

"There is a garden here, where they may be hiding," said he.

"Search it!" called the Señor.

Gualtero strode off among the trees, while I flattened myself against the foot of the wall.

The moon shone with what seemed to me a terrible brightness, now, touching all the trees in the inclosure with silver, and gleaming on Gualtero as he disappeared; but its brightness merely helped to thicken the shadow that covered us at the base of the wall. So I still hoped. In the meantime, I heard Patrick MacMore speaking again inside the shop, and saying: "Orthez, five years ago you were a fat, good-natured man. What has happened to you?"

"Five years over a forge fire will dry the pitch out of any man," said Orthez.

One of the party, however, now broke in: "He had a son called Juan who was killed five years ago. Some people say that he was riding with El Tigre."

"And some say," said Orthez in a low voice, "that he was stabbed from behind."

At that moment I heard the crunching of the soft soil under the foot of Gualtero, and the monster came looming toward us.

19 . . . Whom the Tiger Has Bitten

I COULD forget the Señor, and the blacksmith, and everything under the sky, at that moment, except the great bulk of Gualtero as he came striding among the little orange trees. He carried a naked revolver in his hand, but the gun looked as tiny as a toy, rather than a full-sized .45—such was the hugeness of Gualtero.

Just by the wall of the smithy he stopped again. In two steps I could have reached him, and I sheltered the barrel of my gun under my arm, for fear lest he should see it glimmer. I can swear that he looked straight at us, and that was the moment when he stamped his great foot with impatience. Then he went hurriedly on into the shop.

Another year was taken from my life! I still stared to the side where the form of the giant seemed to be glimmering in the moonlight. It was a full minute before I could fully realize that he was gone.

I could listen to the voice of the Señor as he was talking to Orthez inside the shop.

"Now, then, amigo," said he, "it is true that El Tigre is my friend, and that I love him because of the good he has done for me; but it is equally true that when men ride out with him they are rough and wild and likely to follow their own pleasure rather than what is right. I don't believe that your son could have been killed while—"

"El Tigre gave the order, and the thing was done," said the blacksmith. "People do not carry tales for nothing, about El Tigre."

The Señor was quiet for a moment and I studied his face through the chink in the wall. He was very thoughtful, but he made up his mind in an instant.

"Whether you are right or wrong, you think that you have been harmed," he said. "Therefore, I shall do what El Tigre himself would have done. There are two horses. Take them with their saddles. They are yours."

"Are you the alcalde to make such judgments?" asked the blacksmith.

"They are yours and no man will ever ask them of you," said the Señor. "Gualtero."

The giant had just come into the shop.

"The garden is empty," he said.

"We must have more men. We must scatter them," said the Señor, "and see that every man, and woman, and child in San Clemente knows that the two are here, and who they are. The small one is to be taken alive. There are five thousand pesos for him living, and a bullet through the brain of the man who kills him. For the older man ten thousand pesos, and living or dead makes no difference."

While he talked, three or four of the crowd who seemed to be lieutenants had come forward and listened respectfully, and one of these I thought to be Cantaras, though he was back among the shadows so that I could not be sure.

These words MacMore poured out so rapidly, then fairly ran from the shop and jumped upon a horse. The whole gathering scattered at once here and there.

And all the scene had dwindled to the thin blacksmith, patiently clinking his hammer on the ironwork. Finally, he put out one lantern, and taking the other one, he first paused to close the front doors of his shop and then came back into the garden.

He went slowly, like one who suddenly has become very old and weary. Then he stood beside us in the garden, where the lantern feebly invaded the moonlight.

"There are two things you can do——" he began.

"We can thank you for our lives," said young MacMore.

"There are two things you can do," broke in the black-

91

smith harshly. "One is to take your horses and ride out of San Clemente if you can. The other is to put your horses in my stable and wait to be captured later on, while I am shot as a traitor for housing you."

He said this so dryly and deliberately that the suggestion he was making entered my mind with a start of wonder. That he, old Orthez the blacksmith, should take us in and hold us as his guests against the town! That he should make his house a fortress against the rest of the city, where every hand, most likely, would be ready to strike on behalf of El Tigre or the Señor.

"Man, man," said I, "are you suggesting that we should come and live in your house in spite of El Tigre?"

"I suggest it," he said.

"Although you know that we are bound to be captured?"

"I think you will be captured, but that I cannot really know. When two men stand together, why, sometimes a whole world of others can't hold them!"

He had thrown back his head a little as he said this, and there was a ring in his voice which I, turning my head, seem to hear again at this moment, so that the same thrill runs through me that ran through me then.

"Out of this, no good in the world can come to you," I told him.

He laughed, the first real laughter that I had heard from him, though it really sounded like the barking of a dog, far away.

"If there is anything that harms El Tigre," said he, "do you think that I cannot gain by it? If I could know that you are going to strike one blow against him, don't you see that I should be repaid? Aye, if I were to die the next moment—with the andirons for the Donna Alvarado uncompleted."

He laughed again, as he made this whimsical close.

I began to shake my head.

As a matter of fact, I had been so nearly mauled so many times in that one night by the claws of El Tigre, and I had had such a close rub with his men on the way south toward San Clemente, that by this time I was ready to throw up the sponge and admit that I was beaten. I was about to say so, and declare that we would slip out of the town, as well as we could, when young MacMore replied to Orthez for me, saying: "It is almost as hard to get out of the town as it is to stay in the place. Of course we'll stay."

"I've decided to leave," I told him curtly, because I was angered that his patient courage should make me look so like a changeling and a coward.

"You may leave when you wish to leave," said the boy, "but I have to stay here." He added to the blacksmith: "If you will let me, señor."

I could tell how the old man's heart leaped when he heard this calm, brave voice by the sudden stir of the lantern in his hand, which he held now in such a way that he could look more clearly into the face of my companion.

"You are welcome to stay with me," said he. "You are as welcome as if you were a blood brother of my own dead son. I would take in a dog off the street and care for it, if it had so much as bared its teeth against El Tigre! Come, come! Go get the horses and bring them around to the garden gate. I shall have it open by the time you get there. Or take your horse, young man, and let your friend go where he will!"

I hesitated, drawn by two ways as rarely a man ever can have been drawn. On one side my duty, my promise to the marshal, my hope of some great reputation taken out of this thing, drew me toward staying; and, besides that, it would be a sad thing to leave young MacMore after we had gone through so much together. But, on the other side, this affair seemed to me more and more hopeless. A man only needed to take a pace in San Clemente before seeing the fangs of El Tigre bared or being raked by his sharp claws; and the longer I stayed in that place the sweeter the life in the northland seemed to me. No matter how short a time spring lasted on the desert of Texas and Arizona it was of that spring that I thought, when the hills turned moss-green, and the flowers made all over the earth a dainty mist which was soon burned away. The men I knew there seemed stronger, wiser, braver, better, truer than they had been; and fried bacon, pone, and bitter black coffee appeared delicious food. I wanted to get back to those places and those men, when I heard my voice betraying me suddenly by saying to young MacMore: "If you want to stay, I'll stay, also."

I went with him through the shop, took Larry and the

other horse, and we glanced up and down the street. No one stirred in it, near us, but at the farther end, where it ran into a small plaza, I could see three horsemen pass at a gallop in the moonlight.

A door in the wall near by opened with a creak, and there we found the blacksmith waiting with his lantern. We led the horses in through the gateway, and after Orthez had jarred home the bolt behind us, he showed us into his stable.

It was a very small barn, in which there were two she-goats, together with a little tough-looking mule for all-around work or the saddle, even, to judge by the marks on its back; but there was also room for the two horses, and these we unsaddled and fed, while our host bore the lantern here and there to give us light.

At this time he said nothing, but watched us caring for the horses until we had ended, when he merely remarked: "Fat horse, wise master," and took us up from the stable toward his house, leading the way close under the garden wall, for the obvious reason that this cut off the chances of his neighbors spying upon him.

We were almost at the rear door when it opened suddenly before us, and this gave me an uncanny start.

"Your wife?" I said to Orthez.

"My wife is dead," he said shortly.

We went in behind him, past an old Negro with a withered, ugly mask of a face in which the eyes appeared as dead as the eyes of a statue. He closed the door behind us and stumped along afterward on a wooden leg which made very little noise because it had been secured with a thick pad at the end.

We came into a cool room of rather a good size for such a tiny house, and there our host motioned us to seats on chairs covered with flossy white goatskins. He asked if we would eat, while the Negro brought a lamp and put it on a side table. I was hungry enough, and so was MacMore, so Orthez told the servant to bring what he had, and that turned out to be cold roast kid, tortillas, cold beans cooked with plenty of pungent peppers, and goat's milk for a drink. MacMore could not help making a face over this, but I had grown used to it long years before, and accepted it gratefully.

94

Orthez noted our anxious looks at the Negro and he put us at rest by saying simply: "El Tigre bit off the other leg."

That was enough to make us feel sure of the man, and it began to appear that the entire life of the blacksmith was organized for the purpose of opposing the great bandit. Otherwise, Orthez did not talk while we ate, but sat at one side smoking cornucopia-shaped Mexican cigarettes and watching our appetites.

As we ended, I said softly to the boy in English: "Denny, you know what great danger you are facing by staying here?"

He looked squarely at me, which was his custom, and answered: "The man they call the Señor is the man I want. He is my brother."

20 ... More of the Tiger

IT WAS what I had hoped he would not understand. There was no way in which he could have seen Patrick MacMore except through the chink hole which I had constantly been occupying, but the mere sound of the voice had been enough for him.

What would the reaction of Denny be? Why, his face was as hard as the face of a fighting man, and his eye was a steady light. He looked older than he had been that morning—and no great wonder—and there was more man and less boy to him.

It made me hurt to think of the pain he had been enduring all the while, without saying a word. But I blundered on, saying: "Why didn't you let him know you were here?"

"What would have happened to you, in that case?" asked Denny.

"Why, you could have protected me with your own brother!" I suggested, to bring him out.

He didn't hesitate, but answered like a flash: "I used to know him pretty well, but I never knew him well enough to change his mind. He wants to kill you, Joe. You know it, and I know it, too. And nothing I could say would change him!"

"Do you think, Denny," said I, "that all things considered, it might be a wise thing for you to get out of this town and stay out? If he will pay five thousand pesos to get rid of you—unharmed—it means that he doesn't want to see you!"

"Of course he doesn't. It would be almost as bad as seeing one's conscience face to face. His gold mine!"

He laughed a little, hollowly, and the pain that the boy felt made his eyes waver from side to side.

"Well, he may have the gold mine. He probably has."

"El Tigre is his gold mine!" said Denny bitterly.

He had hit on something close to the truth, I felt, and so I couldn't very well argue with him.

"Then," said I, "I don't see what your business is here."

"Don't you?" replied Denny darkly. He burst out. "D'you understand that we've been living on the money that he sent us from his 'gold mine'? We've turned it into clothes, and house, and food, and education, and pleasure and everything. We owe all that to El Tigre—who stabs men in the back and—bites off their legs at the knee!"

He laughed a little, saying this, and his laugh was a snarl.

"Are you going to take him out of Mexico and make him pay back what he has sent you, or help to pay it back?"

"You sneer at the idea," replied Denny with the quiet of a deep resolution, "but out of Mexico he has to come, and I'm the only one to take him—with your help, perhaps, Joe."

I rested my chin on my hand and grinned at the boy because he was so full of hope and of fire. Every time we had come near to the Señor, it had been like catching a galloping horse by the tail—we had been knocked head over heels. But still he kept up a confident spirit. He would have raised the heart of a wooden image. He would have put hope into a leaden statue.

"All right, Denny," said I, "when I'm through taking El Tigre and shipping him north—express—then I'll come over to you and give you a hand with your brother."

The blacksmith then broke in suddenly: "Two men can stand against the world!"

96

He had not been able to understand our actual words, but he had sensed our strife and this was his comment. Denny smiled at him, and I shrugged my shoulders. For my part, I felt as though I were trying to walk on the verge of a precipice with my eyes blinded. I wanted light to see so much as a possible way out. Then, by scheming and using all the might in our hands and our hearts, perhaps we might accomplish something.

I put a point-blank question to Orthez: "How much power has the Señor?"

He replied with another question: "How much power has that same El Tigre?"

"But he can't have as much."

"He has more, in a way. Some people say that El Tigre is only the knife, but the Señor is the hand that uses it."

"I believe that!" broke out Denny. "Patrick never would be the man to play second fiddle. He would have to lead!"

"You'd rather have him a great robber than no robber at all?" said I.

And Denny blushed and hung his head a little. He could not help that blind pride in the prowess of The MacMore. I suppose that that was natural enough.

The Negro was taking off the dishes now. We sat back and smoked. It was the cool of the night. We had escaped from so much danger in the last hours that with food inside us, and smoke in our lungs, and a quiet place to sit, our spirits could not help but rise a little.

"The Señor," said Orthez, after he had patiently listened to our comments in a strange tongue, "is such a man that nobody but El Tigre could make him second."

"I have seen the Señor," said I. "But I've never in my life heard El Tigre described."

He nodded. "You have come a long distance," said he.

"I come from a country where El Tigre has made a great many raids. Almost enough to cause a war. I could name seven banks he has looted, Señor Orthez. But we don't know much about his looks."

"Why not? You have surely captured some of his men."

"We have. But most of them fight like wild cats, so that they're already dying before we take them; and the ones who live to be hanged are more afraid of El Tigre than they are of death."

97

The eyes of Orthez flashed a little. "El Tigre is a great man." said he.

All at once he had almost forgotten his hatred of that man in his pride that the Mexican race could claim such a hero! I hardly blamed him, because that name El Tigre was beginning to haunt me like a legend of a dragon and giants.

"I can tell you how he looks," said Orthez. "He is pure Indian. And like an Indian he looks!"

He said that with pride, also, and again I did not blame him. For no matter how King Alcohol and adopting some of the ways of the white man had spoiled the Indians, I've known a score of them, or a hundred, worthy of meeting the finest white men in the world on even terms.

"I've heard that, of course," I answered. "He even has the old fashion of very long hair."

"It falls down past his shoulders," said Orthez. "And when he is on the warpath, he is dressed like an Indian, too. That is, he wears a loin cloth, leggings, moccasins, and a light robe which is more often off his shoulders than on them. In his hair he wears eagle feathers because he is a chief in his own right, as I have heard."

"He is a big man, and very strong," I said. "That much I have heard."

"He is a very big man," said the blacksmith. "You have seen this Gualtero? The people here in San Clemente are apt to say that he is the strongest man in the world, but the men of El Tigre say that he is even stronger than Gualtero."

I blinked a little at this. However, that might be something that had been stretched a little in the making of the legend.

"There is something terrible about his face," I suggested, "or is that only a story?"

"His whole face is twisted to the right side by a great scar," said Orthez. "But no matter what men may tell you, it is not the scar that makes him appear terrible. It is the eye and the voice of El Tigre."

"You have seen him?"

"No. But my son saw him, and told me. He had joined the band. He was young and foolish and in love. I begged him to stay with me, but he wanted a great deal of money quickly. He had fallen in love with a woman who was beyond his reach. But he would not believe that. He thought he could make a ladder of gold and climb to her. So he rode with the men of El Tigre. I know that they went a great distance to the north, and that when they had come to the right place, they met together on the soil of the gringo."

He grew excited as he talked.

"They had ridden north in little groups. They crossed the Rio Grande and met together at the appointed place. It was night, and over the hill they saw an Indian chief riding, with the starlight glistening on his naked breast. His rifle was balanced across the pommel of his saddle. He rode a great horse with a savage head. And my son, who was a brave man, said that he knew this man could not fail. When El Tigre came closer, he saw the long hair, and the twisted face, and the eyes under heavy black brows, and he knew there was no other leader in the world like this man.

"All that night, wherever danger was, there was El Tigre also. They came back loaded with gold and with American money. My boy had his share. That one share was almost enough to make him rich, as riches go in San Clemente. He could have bought a house and land. But when he went to talk to the lady, she only pitied him. Although she liked him very much, too, because he was a handsome man. There was no handsomer man in all San Clemente."

He made a little pause, here, as his eyes rested on the young listening face of Denny MacMore, and I knew he was saying to himself that Denny, even, was hardly a finer-looking fellow than his dead boy.

"But he was only the son of a blacksmith, and she, of course, was an Alvarado. Then he received word that he was not to trouble the lady any more. He received word from one of El Tigre's men. He was furious and cursed El Tigre and all his ways. The next day he saw he had done a foolish thing. He told me. I ordered him to ride as fast as he could, but he was overtaken and killed in the road."

He made an end to his story, saying simply: "That is what I know of El Tigre. He stays off in his wilderness and makes the Señor organize everything for him. El Tigre lays the great plan, and he comes down to command in the midst of the raid. But the Señor is his lieutenant. You have seen the lieutenant, so you can imagine the captain."

I had, as a matter of fact, seen the lieutenant, but I could only dimly imagine what the captain might be, because The MacMore fairly well filled my mind.

However, I could make a wild mental picture of the scarred face, and the sweeping, long, black hair, and the glistening coppery shoulders of El Tigre as he rode into battle. It was almost enough to make the Señor seem the lesser man; almost, but not quite!

21 . . . "La Carmelita"

WE TALKED no more that night, for we were enormously tired, though it was not too late for the band to be playing in the Plaza Municipal. I listened to it when we lay on mattresses laid down in the second story of Orthez's house. There was nothing to upset me except one of the boy's attacks of conscience just before I got to sleep. He was in a fury of trouble because he felt that perhaps we were not doing right in staying on in the house of Orthez, and thereby drawing down some degree of trouble on the head of that good man. I asked him if we should go out and ask for rooms in a hotel, and when this did not pacify him, I pointed out what was the simple truth, that the blacksmith enjoyed nothing in the world so much as the thought that he was sheltering men who might eventually do some harm to El Tigre or the Señor.

This had enough weight to stop Denny's chatter. And in ten seconds he was sound asleep. His emotions could be turned off as suddenly as they were turned on, if one only knew the proper way to use the key. I fell asleep myself, listening to the far-off strains of the band as it swung into the eternal "La Paloma."

I was awakened by a touch on the shoulder. It wakened me from what had become my usual dream of the man tiger. This time it was a tiger I shot, but the dead tiger turned into a living man and caught me by the throat.

"You sound as if you're choking," said Denny, as he woke me.

He looked as fresh and as cheerful as could be, smiling down at me while he asked his question.

"I was choking," said I, "but that was only in a dream, and I expect we'll be choked by a real rope before the day's over."

"Hanging is an easy death," says the boy. "But there's trouble started already."

That had me out of the bed in an instant, and I was soon dressed. I asked him what he thought the trouble might be?

"They've found out that we're in the house, I guess," said Denny.

I got to the window in a step, and looking down to the street through the shutters, I saw fifty people milling in front of the blacksmith shop and around other parts of the property of Orthez. They were talking seriously together, with a great many gesticulations and a good deal of excitement, but I noticed first of all that very few of the men carried weapons. At least, none were displayed.

"They're not after us," I said to Denny.

His face altered. I had not noticed how strained it was before.

"Then why on earth are they out there as if it were a promenade?"

"Why, because we've been there."

"Have we made it holy ground?" says Denny with his grin.

"That or the reverse. It doesn't make much difference."

"Nothing to do but come and waste time over us?"

"You can put up all your money that San Clemente is talking about nothing else this morning. You can trust that this town leads a quiet life most of the time. There's not much to talk about."

"How do you know that?"

"Where El Tigre keeps his lair, do you think that lesser crooks are going to try their handiwork?"

"I suppose not," says Denny.

"You can bet your boots on it. San Clemente is thrilled up to the top of its collar because something has happened in the town worth talking about. They've come to beg old

Orthez to let them look at the horses. He'll tell them he has the horses to sell and not to look at. He's a hard one!"

"He's one of the finest men I ever met!" said Denny, breaking out into one of his enthusiasms. "Some day I'm going to do something for that man."

"I'll tell you exactly what to do," said I.

"Yes, tell me, Joe."

"Cut El Tigre's throat," says I.

He was able to laugh at that, but not loudly. And we went down hunting for food as quietly as mice.

The Negro had breakfast waiting for us. He went about serving us with a wonderful smoothness and agility, considering that wooden leg of his. Afterward, while we sat about and smoked Mexican cigarettes, he told us how El Tigre had "bitten that leg off at the knee."

In a northern raid, he had been present in the vault room when a safe was cracked, and the force of the explosion had toppled a section of the outer wall, and pinned him helplessly under some large fragments. They could not pull him out, his foot was so caught; but one of El Tigre's chief principles of action was to leave no prisoners behind him. Therefore, the brute with his own hands had amputated the leg at the knee, gagging the poor man to prevent him from screaming. With a fiendish ingenuity so horrible that it made one gasp to hear José tell of it, this monster in human form stopped the bleeding, wound a bandage hastily around the mutilated limb and forced that poor José to ride with them twenty miles to a place of safety across the Rio Grande! It took him three months to recover—and he had one deep hunger left—which was to give El Tigre one per cent of the agony which he had suffered. He was not half so old as he seemed. That terrible experience had turned him into a white-haired mask of a man at a single stroke.

Well, I had heard sufficiently horrible things about El Tigre before this, but nothing that rubbed my nerves raw quite as badly as José's story. As for Denny, it made him faint. He sat afterward with his head in his hands.

"And to think that my brother knows such things as this and still keeps working for El Tigre!" said he.

Gradually it had dawned on me that nothing much mattered to the boy except his brother and his brother's place in the world. It was not simple love; he had worshipped

Patrick MacMore, and now the head of the family was the servant of a human monster. I thought that if he had ever seen in Patrick's eye the look that I had seen there, he would not have been surprised to hear that cruelty did not upset The MacMore a great deal.

Orthez came into the house at noon for his lunch.

He was greatly changed. It seemed to me that there was a glow of light in his eyes and of color in his cheeks. He seemed younger. His step was light and he actually smiled without sarcasm as he talked. What I guessed was the truth. All of San Clemente was buzzing about the two gringos who had invaded the town hunting for the Señor. No, it was El Tigre himself that they wanted. They had come. They had twice slipped out of the hands of the Señor and his servants. It was said that the Señor himself had for a time been helpless before the gun of one of them! And then the prisoner, the younger one, had been snatched away by the other, and the two of them had disappeared from the ken of man!

Put in that way, it was enough to excite the townsmen. It was fairly determined that the strange pair had not left San Clemente. No matter how cunning the two gringos might be, every road out of the town had been kept under a strict watch, and a cordon, in a sense, had been flung about the place. The two desperadoes were on the inside, but where could they be hiding? Of course, in a day or two the searchers would discover them, and San Clemente then would have a chance to enjoy something more than a bullfight!

I could agree with that part of the news.

Orthez was quietly on fire with pleasure. The man seemed to care nothing at all for his own life, so long as he might have the exquisite pleasure of doing some harm to the slayers of his son.

"But the Señor," says he, "will have punishment enough. For him, I wish nothing but a long life!"

We asked him what he could mean by this and he exclaimed through his teeth that the same woman who had sent his own boy to his death would be able to plague the Señor. For he was to marry her!

It was another shock for young Denny. Moisture rolled down his face, and I could see why. Already this evil life

103

had a sufficient hold on his brother, but if The MacMore married into the country, nothing would get him away.

He wanted to know who the woman could be, and he was told that it was the Señorita Alvarado, who was better know by reputation through San Clemente as "La Carmelita." She was the flower of San Clemente's beauties but she had reached the advanced age of twenty without ever marrying or considering marriage. She had broken hearts without number. And it was on account of her, of course, that poor young Orthez had started on the wild career that so quickly ended in his death. The face of the blacksmith wrinkled with a sublime hatred when he spoke the girl's name, and I could hardly blame him.

He went on at a great rate, to prophesy what would become of the Señor. Eaten with a terrible jealousy every instant he was away from his wife, devoured by suspicion, which would all be lulled to sleep again when he was in the presence of the beauty, he would alternate between heaven and hell until at last his life was no longer worth living. His temper would break. He would be despised by those he had commanded; fall from his position; be cast from the band, and at the moment of his downfall she, waiting for the moment to hurt him the most, would promptly abandon him.

Let him live, then, until from a broken heart and a wretched soul, he took his own life.

When Orthez had carried on for a while like this, I could not help breaking in: "Your countrymen are great lovers of beauty, Orthez, but we from the North are a good deal colder of blood. I don't think that the Señor is apt to break his heart about the woman, no matter how pretty she may be. And if she's a great flirt whom he can't trust, he'll simply get rid of her and never see her again!"

Orthez heard me out with his sinister grin, to which I was beginning to grow accustomed.

"Señor," said he, "you are a man who has traveled a great deal?"

"That's fair to admit," said I.

"You have seen many beautiful women?"

"I've seen a few," said I.

"However," says he, "you never have seen La Carmelita, and, therefore, you have seen nothing."

He went off for his siesta, as soon as he had said that, and I smiled at young Denny.

"That's like a Mexican," said I. "There isn't a town in the country that doesn't contain the most beautiful woman in the world!"

But Denny was not smiling at all; he was looking at visions through the ceiling.

22 . . . In Borrowed Plumage

WHEN WE SAW Orthez after his nap, he told us that we ought to remain quietly in his house for several days, during which the excitement about us would increase for some time, and at last would die down as people took it for granted that we had managed in some manner to escape. In the meantime, he would open negotiations for the sale of the horses, but would prolong them without coming to an actual sale. These negotiations would free him from any suspicion of harboring the mounts for our advantage.

This seemed to both Denny and me the height of common sense. I knew that in Mexico sensations die out almost as quickly as they spring to life, and I could fairly hope that within three or four days our story would be forgotten in San Clemente. When that time came, and little crowds ceased buzzing around the spot where the strangers had disappeared, then we could attempt something of importance. In the meantime, we could map the town in our minds and lay our final plans with the greatest care.

I was in a state of composure, therefore; but Denny was far from that condition. He kept moving restlessly about all day, and in the late afternoon he told me that the story about La Carmelita had completely destroyed all his hopes. The excitement of The MacMore's business with El Tigre would in itself be almost enough to hold Patrick; but a woman he loved would make a bond which no amount of family persuasion could dissolve.

105

This was clear enough, but I was not prepared for the point to which it led Denny.

"Very well," says he, ticking off the points on his fingers. "If I can't persuade Patrick directly myself, then I have to persuade him through somebody else. Who could that be?"

"Me, perhaps," said I, laughing at him. "Listen to me, old son. There's nobody in the world who is going to persuade your brother. He's his own master as much as any man I've ever heard of or ever seen. Now I'm going to tell you the exact story of what happened between him and me."

I did, too, exactly as I've written it down, and throwing in a few extras that didn't make the picture of The MacMore in action any gentler. He listened to me as though he were hearing the Bible read aloud. It never occurred to him to doubt anything that I said, but I think his grief because of the grim nature of his brother was about fifty per cent offset by his pride in the strength of The MacMore.

"Even you were afraid of him, Joe?" he asked me half a dozen times, and then he pondered on the answer, when I said yes.

Then I finished by asking him if that was the sort of a man who could be persuaded away from his own inclination, and Denny shook his head stubbornly.

"He's no longer his own master," he insisted. "Who is his master, then?" said I.

"The woman he loves," said Denny.

I threw up my arms. "His only master is the monster he works for!" I told Denny from my heart. "But even if the woman he loves commands him, what good does that do you?"

"Suppose she could be persuaded that Patrick has to be taken away from Mexico and El Tigre? Why, then she would beg him to go, and he would do it, and there you are!"

He finished off this explanation with an exclamation of pleasure at his own cogent reasoning, and I laughed to hear him.

"Who is to do the persuading?" said I. "Who is going to tell La Carmelita that little story and decide her to leave her native country? Great Scott, Denny," I ended, "you talk like a crazy man, if you'll excuse me for saying so."

106

"You don't think it could be done?" says he, his face falling.

"Never in the world."

That threw him into gloom which lasted the rest of the day, but toward the evening I found him talking to the Negro, José, and asking questions about where the house of La Carmelita stood. I saw at once what that was driving toward, and it frightened me. If he exposed himself, I felt that he was a gone goose. It was true that the reward the Señor offered for the apprehension of Denny was a reward offered for his living body; but it would not be so easy to take a wild cat like Denny alive. If they tried to lay hands on him, he would force them to give him his quietus.

That was what was in his mind as I listened to the talk with José. Finally, I broke right in and said, "José, tell this young fellow if he possibly can get into the house of Alvarado?"

José opened his eyes as if I had asked if a man could jump to the moon. Then he pointed out that the Alvarados were extremely wealthy, kept a house filled with faithful *mozos* who would like nothing so well as knifing any intruder, and that, besides, the house was under the eye of picked men of the great Señor.

That was as convincing an answer as I could have wished for.

But the Negro went on to say that there was only one way to see the girl, and that was at the promenade on the Plaza Municipal in the evening, when every one went there. There she could be seen accompanied by her mother or her duenna.

I was relieved by this, too, because no one could be so reckless as to undertake to accost a woman on the promenade in the plaza. That is, a woman of the upper classes. Of the lower orders, it could not be said, because among them it was a sign of bravery for a fellow to break in among the girls and walk with his sweetheart for a round, in spite of the jeers and the mockeries. But among the upper orders, there was no offense as great as that of interfering with the ladies. In addition, by exposing himself to the eyes of the crowd, young MacMore was sure to get himself recognized.

I was not so sure of that dare-devil, however, as to let the matter drop here, but I explained everything to him, exactly as it was. He listened to me, and assured me that he had no such wild impulse in mind.

I believed him. How could I help believing that he had at least that much common sense?

Well, the end was that at supper we sat a long time over the food with Orthez, and afterward he brought out some abominable red wine, which he considered delicious. I added two parts of water to mine, and so managed to stand it and remained sipping the stuff and talking to Orthez and to José, who came back into the room familiarly after he had cleared up the dishes. But young Denny declared that his head was ringing, it ached so badly, and he went off to his room to lie down, he said.

I had a grand talk with Orthez that night. The old fellow was a well of wisdom. He knew his own nation, for one thing; the weakness and the glories of the Mexican, and he was as willing to criticize as he was to praise. I remember that he made one very good point, which was that the ideal of the Mexican was still the old ideal of the Indian—the warpath and the glories of the warpath. Nobody could blame them very much for wanting to show their courage, and show it they did; but it would be infinitely better for the nation when it settled down to work as large sections already were doing. He told me a great deal about his own experiences as a blacksmith. He was one of those naturally cultured men who are able to judge the whole world by the small section of it that passes through their own lives.

It was very late before I decided to go to bed and said good night to Orthez; but when I got up to our room and entered softly to keep from waking the boy, the first thing I saw was the white moonlight falling on his empty bed.

The sheepskin had not been at all disturbed!

I stood there dazed, for a moment. Then I noticed a heap of clothes in a corner, and when I examined them, they turned out to be the outfit of Denny.

That was another facer to me.

I stood with those clothes draggling down from my hand to the floor and feeling that the world was at an end. I had not realized before how fond I was of the youngster, but now it came over me with a rush that, in spite of his headlong foolishness, in spite of the fact that he could not ride, rope, shoot, make a camp, cook a meal, or so much as sharpen a knife without turning the edge of it, he was the cleanest and straightest and bravest lad I ever had run across.

I went down to Orthez, half staggering, and he met me at his door with his sardonic eyes glittering with excitement.

"We shall see," said he, when I told him briefly what I had found.

We went rapidly through the other parts of the house, thinking that he might possibly have left our room to find some cooler place for sleep; but there was no sign of him, and at last we went into the apartment which had once been reserved for Orthez's son.

Then he opened a closet and showed me that there were clothes thrown into disarray.

I did not see the meaning of this for a moment. I was too stunned by my fear for the boy to make head or tail of it.

But Orthez said quietly: "He has dressed himself in my son's clothes and he has left the house."

I repeated the exact words after him, like a parrot.

"And of course that," said Orthez, "is the end."

"That is the end for poor Denny," said I. "They will surely skewer him if he tries to speak to the girl."

I had told him beforehand of the talk about La Carmelita, so that he understood what I meant.

"They will take his skin off and hang it in the plaza as a lesson in manners to other foreigners," agreed Orthez.

"I've got to get there and stop him," said I.

"Do you know what time it is?" said Orthez.

That stopped me in a flash.

It was late, and of course Denny had left long before. When he got up from the table, he must have started his preparation and have slipped out through a window immediately afterward. Whatever mischief he could get into, he had landed in it by this time.

"It is time," said Orthez, "that you and I should look to the safety of our own scalps. Because the boy is taken before this, and being taken, they will follow his back trail to my house."

"If you think that he'll tell where he was hiding, you're wrong," I assured him.

"I don't think that," said Orthez, "but they will have his

clothes to go by, and from them and the marks of the tailor, they will surely be able to trace the clothes back to my house.

"After that, amigo mio, we are dead men!"

I stared at him, realizing that what he said was undoubtedly true; and as we stood there motionless, looking at one another and seeing our fears, I heard a hand tap softly at the street door—or was it a sound made in testing the fastening of the shutter on the street?

23 ... A Gallant Youth

FOR WHAT immediately follows, I have not the narrative of Dennis MacMore, though it is about him and his strange adventures that I have to speak. I have not his version, for a reason that will soon appear; but all that I describe is substantiated by my knowledge of San Clemente and of the boy himself, by certain eyewitnesses, and by a mere use of sheer logic, from time to time, to fill in the interstices. All that I wish to assure you is that what follows is no more a fiction than what has gone before, and I am as convinced of its reality as though I had been an eyewitness of every act and the auditor of every word.

To begin with the moment when the boy left the table.

All that day he must have been grubbing over and over again at the problem of his brother.

He had come to Mexico leaving a promise behind him to take Patrick back to his family in the States. He had come to carry word that now Patrick actually was The MacMore, a title which seemed to carry such an absurd amount of significance to that family. And between that good news, an appeal to him for the family's sake, and soon, he had hoped to get the missing member back. The entrance of La Carmelita into the case changed everything. Behold, Dennis would sally forth and find her and persuade her.

I've heard of fools and their folly before, and I've seen a

good deal of it; but, drunk or sober, I never heard of such a crazy performance as this one of Dennis MacMore's.

For that very reason, if for no other, I am trying to put down every detail of the expedition in black and white, though there are some things which, of course, I cannot tell, because I was no eyewitness to everything. How much I wish that even the least things could be narrated here, because they could not help but make the story more wonderful!

To begin with, then, when he went upstairs into the bedroom, he already must have had some scheme in his mind, but vaguely, as I believe. He had indistinctly determined to leave the house, but before he had looked twice at himself, he must have decided that his "gringo" clothes would instantly attract too much attention to him.

His first step was, therefore, to look for other equipment, and he must have begun a search. Probably he looked through Orthez's bedroom in the beginning, and passing on to the room where the dead boy had lived, he found there the gala suit which poor young Juan had bought with his hard money five years ago.

The clothes fitted.

However one looks at it, it seems a strange fatality that Denny should have donned the very clothes that the other had worn when he went out in search of this same woman. Orthez had died because of his effrontery in daring to lift his eyes to a woman above him. Now Dennis MacMore started on the same terrible adventure.

Look at him as, at last, he takes stock of himself. He makes sure of a handkerchief, of polished boots, of the fit of the coat, of the elegance of the stick which had provided the finishing touch to the costume of Orthez. But he is not farsighted enough to take with him a knife, which could easily be slipped in unobtrusively under his tightly fitting clothes. Certainly he does not consider carrying a revolver as he issues out into a city filled with enemies!

Fully dressed, now, it seems that he went down again to the ground floor and took the window at the farthest corner, fronting on the street. Why he did this, we could never tell, unless it was that the poor boy already had tried the other windows and found them with their shutters so tightly lodged that he was afraid of making noise enough to attract the attention of Orthez and me as we sat in the other room and gabbled together like a pair of geese.

The shutter he selected must have opened freely enough, because certainly I did not hear a murmur from its hinges, and my ears are as sharp as most.

Then he slipped out onto the sill, stepped to the street, and closed the shutter behind him, as we found it afterward.

The folly of selecting this window was that in issuing from it, he came within the view of the two streets which forked out from the alley at this point, and, therefore, ran three or four times as much danger of being seen, as in fact he was seen.

But of that and the results of the discovery, more must be said hereafter.

We know this, moreover, that having left the house, poor Denny stood in the full moonlight at the triple corner and hesitated there, as though wondering which way he should go. Perhaps, just then, the music of the band had ceased, or if it was sounding, he could not find the direction from which it came, for a moment. But when he finally felt that he had located it, he took the left-hand street and walked down it.

Another man would have skulked and kept to the shadows, for any other would have been oppressed by enough fear to have bowed the heart of a giant. Not so Dennis! I knew him too well to guess that.

Undoubtedly, the instant he had taken two or three steps and fairly committed himself to the adventure, his heart was high, he whirled the cane in his hand so that it flashed like a sword in the moonshine, and he was singing under his breath one of his foolish songs. Aye, or singing it out loud and never thinking whether it were a song in English or in Spanish!

He was enough to take the eye of a whole army! Let alone his good looks and his youth, that gala dress he wore was as bright as a canary's plumage and streaked with silver and gold work. Besides, the short jacket was cut away a little to show to advantage the gorgeous sash which was knotted around his waist.

There was as little vanity in Denny MacMore as in any man who ever trod this planet, but I suppose that even he could not have failed to know that he cut rather a fine figure as he stepped daintily through the dusty streets of San Clemente.

I wonder how many eyes peeped out at him from behind half-opened shutters, that must have opened wider still as the watchers stared after the brilliant figure?

On he went, still swinging his stick, still singing his song, and unaware of the follower who skulked behind him, after pausing for an instant to take note of the blacksmith's house and of the very window from which the bright apparition had appeared.

At the corner of the Calle de San Martino, we know that he paused while a *carreta* went screeching and groaning past on its wooden axles, making a twisting, jerking course down the street; for there was the witness of the peon who drove the cart, afterward, that he had seen the gay young gallant at this point. Then he went on toward the music and the meeting with the unknown beauty on whom he never before had laid eyes!

Well, I think of it with a swelling heart. Such men as Denny have made up the soldiers who march in lost causes from the beginning of the world.

At the bridge over the San Clemente, I know that he must have stopped again, not from fear, but because he would have leaned there over the parapet of the bridge to look down at the great water lilies that grew in the sluggish shallows of the stream with pads six or seven feet across— capable of holding up the weight of a man like a boat, for a few seconds. He would have leaned there, and breathed of the fragrance which forever in their season rose up from the lilies as they opened their great yellow hearts to the air. Perhaps he watched the dark swirl of the central current, and listened for an extra moment to the whisper of the water against the piers, for his mind was ever open to every pleasant thing that the world affords.

Then on again, and over the arched crest of the bridge, and on to the farther side, with the sweet music from the Plaza Municipal now stirring his blood.

In five minutes more he was on the edge of the big square itself, inhaling the breath of the orange bloom and the sharp sweetness of the lemon trees. Black myrtle grows in the plaza also, and throngs of the alamos. You must not have in mind a park made up of smooth lawns, dotted primly here and there with fine trees, and neat rows

113

of shrubbery, for the Plaza Municipal of San Clemente is like a bit of wild forest, with certain paths cut regularly through it, and from the center of the space comes the sound of the unseen band.

It is a very pleasant idea. There is nothing in the world more delightful than to shake off the heat of the day, and the memory of its labor, and its grime, and to walk out into the delicious air of the night, cool, touching the face like ghostly currents of water. For light there were the rows of lamps along the paths, like a display of dull yellow moons. For one can hardly tell, looking at them, whether they are placed here more for ornaments or to give light. There is enough of this beneath each lamp post, but in between is a region of pleasant misty light so that faces and forms are continually passing into ken and out of it again. That is one satisfactory feature of such light, and the other is that there is never any dazzle or glare about it. It cannot be called a modern illumination.

In fact, there is little to take the mind away from what this scene must have been when the conquistadores laid out the scheme of it three-hundred-odd years ago.

No doubt that young Denny thought of them as he stood there at the entrance to the Plaza and breathed of the blossom-scented air, and picked out the music, dissolving it into its component parts.

For he never could have been close to such music as this before. There was above all the piccolo carrying the same weird, high, tenor note which runs into the very voice of the Mexican. There was a bass viol, too, mumbling and rumbling, and yet played with a good deal of sweetness. Guitars, of course, had to be thrumming to make up the rhythm and give it a strong dancing beat such as the Mexicans love to have pulsing at their ears, and finally the sound was sweetened by the strains of the violin.

It was not a large orchestra, and it was a strangely consorted one, but nevertheless, it achieved certain things in its own way that no other musicians in the world could have accomplished.

I think I know what it meant to Dennis MacMore as he loitered there that last moment on the corner.

It spoke of love, love, love, until his head tilted back and joy and sadness filled his throat.

Then he would have given one of those slight shrugs of

114

the shoulders with which he generally prefaced his wildest actions, and away he went to enter the crowd.

He could not have seen that the spy who followed him now hesitated an instant, marked the course of the brilliant youth, and then turned and ran skulkingly but with speed down a side alley.

24 ... On the Plaza Municipal

As I THINK of Dennis MacMore on that night, I can see every step that he took into the Plaza Municipal, and how his feet strode from the hewn rock of the curb to the street itself; and I watch him pass under the big alamos, growing dim in their shadow and being washed with the silver of the moonlight in the open places between. He comes to the canal, in which there is always running water, whose current is, nevertheless, so extremely slow that it can only be seen stirring now and then. Thin slime forms on its surface and in the mire are the gigantic water lilies and worlds of watercress. So he comes to the promenade proper and sits down for an instant on one of the benches of blue-black limestone, polished till they looked almost like black glass.

Here he can watch the circling of the plaza by the crowd, and he finds that all goes on with a great deal of merriment, and of order also, such as he hardly had imagined, in spite of what I had told him beforehand. In four streams the promenaders move. The lower classes are occupying the inside paths, a current of men flowing in one direction, of women in the other; and in the two outer paths the superior parts of the San Clemente population stroll. Here Dennis MacMore takes his seat for a moment to observe, and to study faces.

It was some sort of saint's day, and the result was that about half the costumes were gala affairs, very much like the borrowed one which he was wearing. He saw the same tight jackets and many of the broad, gay sashes; white silk shirts worn with neckties, or often, like his own, open at the throat; tight trousers, buttoned with silver down the sides, but flaring bell-like at the bottom.

He was conscious, now, that he had come out without a hat on his head to a crowd where the hats were the most important article of dress, for the gallants wore huge sombreros with silver plaited around the brims, silver bands two inches wide around the head, and on the crown four rosettes of the same metal. But presently he forgot his bare head and all else as he watched the ladies pass. Oh, the ladies of San Clemente! Never had he seen such beauties before, and never would he see such beauty again, because everything, for Dennis, was touched with magic, was dreamlike, fragrant, and ravishing to his soul. How could it be otherwise when he looked at that scene for the first time? I had seen it in other cities, but San Clemente has a special air of miracle, and above all the beauties, as they pass along the promenade with their mothers and their duennas, their little narrow shoes tapping on the great limestone slabs which pave the way, and their heads covered with mantillas.

Why should one say covered? Spider webs silvered with dew would be gross and heavy work compared to the texture of some of that black lace. Gather it in a single hand, and opening the fingers, it floats out a dozen yards like smoke, stirred by the slightest breeze. So through these films, or framed by them, the dark-eyed ladies pass by, and the boy watches them in rapture. He has not been, he really has not lived before.

In the plaza at San Clemente the girl you love goes by three times a minute, and each time she wears a different face. She is Castilian pale; she is the stern Indian type; she is tall or small; she is regardless as a statue, or winning as a child. But as she walks, she shows how amiable she can be to her duenna. If she cannot smile at the gallants, she can let them see how well she knows how to smile by practicing on the old dame who escorts her, the angel of the flaming sword in that garden. But, above all, there is not one woman in Mexico, old or young, who does not know how to look at a man with a special look, meant for a man alone. Not one of them does it in the same manner. Some flash the glance quickly to the side as they are almost past, so that the startled and delighted fellow who has been favored sees only the smiling curve of the cheek as the girl passes on; and some, with lowered head, cast the glance upward. These are the specially coy ones, apt at blushing, excellent in dropping their heads again and hurrying on, only to half turn their heads again, at a little distance, as though desperately tempted to glance back over the shoulder. There are other ways—hundreds and hundreds of them, in which the play of head, and shoulder, and smile, and cheek, and hand, all have their part, varied into an alphabet from which an infinite language can be evolved, of countless words, and the greatest miracle of that language is that every syllable of it is instantly understood by the most ignorant young man in the world. Do I say young men alone? But all men are young in San Clemente; otherwise it is better to be dead at once.

"Great heavens," said the boy to himself, "how can so much beauty be poured into one city in the world! It is a feast day, and all the beauties of Spain, and the Indies, and Mexico, from Panama north, and all the fairest from the Argentine and Rio de Janeiro, and the blond girls of Chile have been sorted and judged, and the very most lovely have been permitted to walk here in the plaza at San Clemente!"

He says it to himself, but not entirely. His voice is a whisper, and his fervent eyes are turned in worship on that stream of faces. How could they help but look back at him? There was that handsome bare head of his, and that worshipping look which must have seemed to each of them specially poured out to her. How could they help but look back at him and give him notice? Of course they did! There was not one girl whose heart did not leap as she looked at the gaudy jacket of the boy; there was not one young matron who did not wish that she were free; there was not one duenna, even, who did not groan to be young again for such a prize as this!

How was he to tell the Carmelita in such a crowd as this? She was supposed to be wonderfully beautiful, but here there were a hundred deserving the same name. It was typical of Dennis that he did not hesitate. He turned to a man who sat on the bench beside him and said: "How could one tell the Señorita Alvarado?"

This bench companion was soberly dressed in black. He was tall, thin, with a very long jaw, and a yellowish complexion.

"You will know her when you see her," said he, and he actually smiled a little at young Dennis.

What is more, he was right. But Dennis, after another half-anxious and half-delighted glance at the promenaders, turned back to his companion and went on: "I would as soon try to find a needle in a field of straw."

"Suppose," said the stranger, "the needle gave off its own light?"

"She is very well known in San Clemente, then?" said Dennis.

"We have a blue sky over San Clemente," said the stranger, "and we have La Carmelita in it."

He was not a boy and he did not look romantic, so that his words carried a redoubled weight in the mind of Dennis MacMore.

Then he saw her!

It seemed to him that the crowd was scattered before her and behind, though, as a matter of fact, the people walked as thickly around her as around others. Only the very prettiest girls avoided that nearness, because there was no one of them so foolish as to wish to come too near the sun and so be passed over, though they might be very lovely stars.

The mantilla did not cover her face, and through its dusky film he could see a white flower in her hair, but she was dressed like a dozen others. It was not that which made her different, but there was pride in her; and, as the stranger had said, she seemed to Dennis to shine by her own light.

He stared, of course, with his soul in his eyes. And as she differed somehow from all the others, so did the look which she gave him. Her head was frankly turned toward the youths who promenaded, but her eye was blank of all thought for them, as though they were mere silhouettes flickering over a distant hill. Then she saw Dennis, and suddenly she glowed.

I know, for I myself have seen that look, and I understand how the eyes widen and brighten and the smile begins faintly, and dwells.

She went on, and Dennis stood up to look after her. No, not her face alone, but by the carriage of her head and by her walk he could tell her thereafter in a crowd of ten thousand. He could paint the truth of her, if he had been a painter, after that single look at her.

Then Dennis sank slowly back upon the bench.

He had no thought of her wisdom, her virtue, her truth. He simply knew that she was beautiful. He passed his hand over his forehead, for he was stunned.

"She does not need to have a lantern carried before her, eh, my friend?" said the sallow-faced man beside Dennis.

"She needs no lantern," said Dennis feebly. "I should think," he went on in a burst, "that men would be killed because of her!"

"Plenty of them," said the other. "Of course, plenty of them have been killed, and still others will be, before the end. Though just now they are kept off by the shadow of the tiger's head!"

Dennis glanced sharply at him. That look was not returned, for the sardonic eye of the stranger was fixed upon the passing crowd.

"However, when she is tired of the Señor, then the same old story will begin over again. Like the story of poor young Orthez."

"You're not afraid to say what's in your mind," commented Dennis.

"I dare say that the same thought is in yours," went on the stranger. "You know Orthez well enough to have a good deal of sympathy for his dead boy."

A chill went through the marrow of Dennis as he listened. He suddenly felt an eerie lightness and uneasiness of spirit.

"Are you the evil one?" he said. "What do you know?"

"That the clothes of young Orthez fit you well."

"You are the evil one," said Dennis.

"A friend of his, at least," said the tall man.

At this, he managed to take his eye from the crowd, and he deliberately fixed it upon Dennis, probing him not curiously, but as one who previously had read that page of humanity. Dennis met the glance straight and fair, but he grew hot with the effort.

"You say that I am a friend of Orthez and that I am wearing the clothes of a dead man."

"You are," said the other. "But they are still in fashion, and I hope it was not a contagious disease which carried him off."

Dennis twitched his shoulders. It was as though the point of a knife had pricked his back at that instant.

"You seem to know a great deal," said he. "What else do you know about me, señor?"

"Why," said the other, "I know that even without the clothes you are worth five thousand dollars to any man."

25 . . . Man of Mystery

IN SUCH A CASE what would you have done?

For my part, I should have liked to have a gun under my hand. But young Dennis, meeting the keen, sardonic smile of the stranger, merely relaxed more completely against the back of the bench.

"You know all about me," he said quietly, "but you don't mean me harm, so what do I care for your knowledge?"

The eye of the other lifted and returned to the faces of the drifting crowd.

"You don't care a great deal," he remarked, "but perhaps I could teach you to care more."

"In what way, señor?"

"By reading a little more of your mind. That is usually what surprises people, in my experience with them."

"So?" said Dennis.

"Why yes. To prophesy when the movement of a certain star will wipe out the earth and human civilization is dull news; but a man is always astonished if he is told what he had for lunch yesterday and what the meat course will be to-morrow at supper."

"Then I suppose you know a great deal about me?"

"Well, as much, I should say, as the Señor."

"Ah?" said Dennis, who was determined that no matter how he was shocked, he would not betray any emotion in words.

"But hardly as much as your companion on this adventure. I mean Señor Warder."

In spite of all his good resolutions, Dennis jumped. He

stared at the sallow-faced man as he never before had stared at any human being, and if the man had turned into a puff of smoke with a strong smell of sulphur about it, I don't think that Dennis would have been very much surprised. Certainly he would have been relieved.

There was nothing extraordinary about the man except the keen and rather cruel brightness of his eye. His appearance was a little odd, to be sure, owing to the bigness of his hands and the narrowness of his shoulders. He wore a rather threadbare black suit with a bow tie, which looked out of place beneath the usual towering sombrero. He took off the hat, now, as though to let the boy take a fuller stock of him, and revealed a narrow forehead which sloped rapidly back and made his head seem small.

"Go on," said Dennis. "And tell me what I am doing here?"

"Waiting to see La Carmelita, of course."

"Are you sure of that? But, of course, you heard me ask about her."

"You didn't tell me, however, that you were going to upset the rules by stepping into the promenade and accosting a lady you never have been presented to formally. And even if you had been, that would make the breach no less."

"I believe now that you are the evil one," said Dennis.

"Thank you," said the stranger. "I've been told that before."

"Why do you thank me?"

"Because you flatter my pride."

"Will you tell me how you know these things?"

"By reason of a peculiar gift."

"Of course."

"I read the mind, in fact."

As he said this, he favored Dennis with one of his dry smiles.

"I almost believe you," said the boy.

"Thank you again," said the stranger. "Is there anything else about yourself that you wish to know?"

"A great deal. When I speak to the lady, what am I about to say?"

"Very little. You will beg an interview."

"And what shall I say in the interview?"

121

"That's another point. Now you wish me to stop reading the mind and become a prophet."

"Is that too hard for you?"

"Not at all. To a man of my gifts, the future is only a little more dim than the past."

He spoke, as usual, with a slight, dry touch of mockery in his voice.

"Then what do I wish to say to her?"

He leaned forward a little, certain that this question could not be answered, and feeling a rather childish satisfaction in the opportunity to put down the omniscient stranger.

The other half closed his eyes and was lost in thought, or pretended to be. At last he said slowly: "You will tell her that your brother's future depends upon his removal from Mexico, and you will beg her to influence him to leave the country."

That was the real staggerer for Dennis MacMore, and he gripped the edge of the bench, glaring at the tall man in dismay.

Finally he managed to say: "What answer will I get, then?"

"You will get an answer," said the stranger, "that is not at all in your mind at present."

"Do you mean that she will put me off?"

"In a sense, that is exactly what I mean."

"Tell me," said Dennis, "what her words will be."

"Ah, my friend," replied the other, "even the evil one himself cannot tell beforehand what words a woman will use!"

At this Dennis was able to laugh, but only very shortly, and he continued to stare at his bench companion in bewildered excitement.

"You're a detective," he said at last.

The other merely smiled.

Then Dennis said: "But I don't think that I'd ever have the courage to bluntly break in upon Señorita Alvarado in the midst of her promenade."

"You will, however, when she passes us the next time," replied the man of mystery.

"You are prophesying again?"

"Yes, and as a matter of fact, I wish you well, and there

is nothing that you could do that would be more to the point."

"Will you tell me for what reason?"

"Willingly. All my stock of information is at your service."

"Thank you," said Dennis. "Then tell me why it would be opportune for me to break into the promenade and speak to La Carmelita when she passes us again?"

"Because in that way, facing danger in the front, you may escape from danger from the rear."

"Danger from the rear?"

"Yes."

"What danger, if you please?"

"When you left the house of Orthez, you were followed."

"Ha?" exclaimed Dennis.

"Exactly. You were followed, and you were trailed to the Plaza Municipal. Then the fellow who shadowed you so far hurried to give information to the police. They at once dispatched four gendarmes and two men in civilian dress to effect your capture. If you turn your head a little, you will see two of the gendarmes walking now at the edge of the promenade, yonder."

Dennis followed the suggestion, and he saw two gendarmes sauntering, as had been said, under the bright glow of one of the oil lamps.

"You are right again," he said to the other. "If they really mean to attempt to—"

"They will wait for the other two to come up to them. Neither of that couple are very brave, and they want numbers. You can see the plumes of the second two coming up through the crowd there in the distance. Do you spot them?"

"I do!" said Dennis, craning his neck. "But if I start now—"

"That is the worst thing you could attempt, because on the far side of this promenade there are two police in civilian clothes, and one of them is a ruffian with a grudge against the Señor."

"What do you mean by that?"

"If you give him a good opportunity, he will surely shoot you down and say that it was done in the line of duty. That would not save him from the revenge of the

Señor, but the brute is too short-sighted and hot-hearted to look very far into the future."

If a very sign of fire had been placed upon the forehead of the stranger, the time had come when Dennis could not have believed him more implicitly.

"I'm to bolt through the promenade, therefore?" he suggested.

"Exactly."

"What shall I do then?"

"You will do the only sensible thing. You will probably run straight through the plaza and past the grand stand. On the farther side of the square, you are sure to find saddle horses, carriages, and what not. In one of these you will ride off and, after turning a few corners, the police will be dropped."

Dennis wiped his forehead.

"My friend," said he, "this is the strangest talk I ever have listened to."

"It is nothing more nor less than the saving of your life," declared the man of mystery. "However, I don't expect gratitude. Now I must leave you. I am sorry if I have stolen some of the sweet of the evening; but you will recapture it in a few seconds after I'm gone. She is coming now through the crowd."

He stood up as he spoke, and the boy beside him.

"Shall I see you again?" asked Dennis.

The mockery and the sardonic look faded out of the face of the tall man, and he regarded Dennis with a sort of weary pity, like one who knows too much about the great sorrows of the world.

"Young man," said he, "you will see me again—and Heaven help you in the meanwhile!"

That was his only farewell, and turning from the bench, he walked off with a rather shambling, long stride that seemed wonderfully deliberate, and yet that carried him rapidly away in the stream of the promenaders.

Dennis looked after him.

No man on earth ever was more bewildered and confused than Dennis was at that instant. He told himself that the fellow was a faker, a sham, a pretender who could not possibly know, but only guessed. And yet as he told himself these things, and tried to rub away the sense of mys-

124

tery, his very heart rose up in him proclaiming the truth of the man in black.

He had something else to occupy his attention an instant later, for he saw the two gendarmes on the right turning back against the stream of the strolling crowd, while from the corner of his eye he made out two more approaching rapidly from the left with the current of the walkers.

He was about to be seized, exactly as the stranger had declared. Then, turning back, he saw La Carmelita coming once more toward him through the crowd.

26 ... A Lady Speaks

Now, with the law closing its hand upon him from both sides of the promenade where his bench stood, and with not a hope in the world of really escaping from the mysterious man in black, in spite of his kind suggestions, Dennis did not try to make himself small and skulk away, as I should have done. He did not pull a gun, for the simple reason that he was not carrying one. But he spun his cane until it flashed, and raised his head a little higher, while his lips wore that faint smile of a brave man endangered, and loving the peril in which he finds himself.

So he stepped straight forward toward the slow-moving throng of the ladies.

They saw him with pretended horror, and with real amazement that even a foreigner should dare to break such an ancient and sacred convention as this. They shrank from him with little squeaking cries, hurrying ahead, or to the side, or drawing rapidly back; but every eye was turned in a vast deal of curiosity to find out what was the goal of the handsome young stranger with the lighted eye.

The gendarmes should have rushed at once to seize on him and reduce him to order with a few good thumps; but they knew, of course, that he was wanted for more serious things than this. Besides, perhaps they were charmed by the boldness of the man. People who love to see the courage of the matador would not fail to appreciate the serene manner of the boy as he stepped on among the crowd, the cane still swinging in his fingers.

Who was his goal?

They could guess at once, perhaps, who distinguished La Carmelita approaching. She had inspired enough follies before this, and yet none exactly like this. To her that promenade must have been like a field where battle never ceased, and she a general who always had won; and when she walked on the promenade, she must have seen many a ghost and many a fine figure of a man beside those who actually were strolling in the moonshine and in the pale lamplight.

It was wonderful that her family had not disposed of her long before, considering the richness of the offers, but that mystery was easily explained. Her mother had suffered from a loveless marriage, and she had vowed that the wedding of her daughter should be one of love, or not a wedding at all. So the youths had come in a great procession and, what was not often seen in Mexico, they had wooed her shamelessly, openly, in the eyes of the whole world.

It was no guilty thing or ridiculous thing to have loved La Carmelita. She was merely fifteen when poor young Orthez went to his death in his vain effort to make himself a great enough figure to take her eye. In that same year, Gil Fernandez, with all his wealth, and his estates, and his youth, and his ancient name, and his cultured manners, and his five languages, and his noble future just opening before him, saw her on this very promenade and went mad about her lovely face. For a whole year he besieged her. His friends came down from Mexico City and begged him to stop making a public spectacle of himself. They could not stop poor young Gil Fernandez until he was toppled over by a fever and got out of bed thin, and gray-headed, but able to leave the enchantment of La Carmelita at the last. Since then people said that he had been as grim and grave and stern as he had been gay and cheerful before.

At one step, this episode made the fame of La Carmelita. She had been noticed before, in San Clemente, of course. But now she was as celebrated as could well be. More people tried to see her on the promenade in the

Plaza Municipal than ever stopped off to see the cathedral, in spite of its miraculous tower and its well of holiness.

Gil Fernandez was not the only one to appear on her list of celebrated victims. There was Montessi, the general. People even said that the reason he started his revolt was because he hoped in the ensuing confusion to be able to seize San Clemente, and the beautiful girl within it who had refused him. The next great man's story had a touch of comedy in it. He was Pablo Ducone, who had lived for ten years in Denver, and had raked in a vast fortune from his silver mines. He was fifty when he saw Carmelita Alvarado, and he went limping on his rheumatic feet to see the señora. Without preamble, frankly, bluntly, he had attempted to buy the girl from her. Other men had done exactly the same thing in the past, but Ducone was worth remembering because of the vastness of his offers. The señora had listened and smiled. He disappeared for a week and then called on her again. Two men came with him and carried up a heavy satchel. When he was alone with the señora, he opened the satchel and took out stack after stack of paper money and piled it on the table. Then he stood back and waved to it in triumph. There were a million and a half pesos in these stacks of money, men said. But the señora, of course, merely smiled. She was an Alvarado.

After that, Lord Wycombe came to Mexico in a trip around the world seeking adventure. When he reached San Clemente, he decided that he had gone far enough. And he labored for nearly two years, off and on, to try to win the heart of La Carmelita. It was said that her mother almost forgot her vow and used her maternal authority to force her daughter into this desired match, for Wycombe was not only a great old name in England, but he was rich, intelligent, a keen sportsman, a perfect gentleman. However, La Carmelita would not listen, and, therefore, she remained absolutely free.

There were others as great in the world as Wycombe and Gil Fernandez. La Carmelita had walked through a crowd of worshipers all the days of her life. And Dennis knew it, without knowing the names. She carried an air of authority that was little less than queenly. No woman could have it who had not been obeyed by men, feared by men, served loyally and with a desperate hope by them.

Only at last it appeared that his brother had won her. Even she could not resist The MacMore!

That made him smile a little more, as he advanced straight toward her with his handsome head so high.

Her mother was not with her, or undoubtedly the incident would have been stopped before it well began. There was only the duenna who had seen her beautiful mistress adored by men these many, many years, but never had seen one make such a rashly daring step as this toward her.

The duenna cried out that the man was mad, and was so thoroughly frightened that she bundled up her skirts and fled back into the crowd.

That left Carmelita alone. The conventional ladies had drawn back or hurried ahead on every side, pausing to gape at the scene. The officers of the law, though they were at hand, looked with amused excitement and delayed their interference. She was left alone, but she was not a whit dismayed. She went straight on, her head as high as ever, until Dennis stepped straight into her path. There she paused, and Dennis bowed before her. She was not tall. I doubt if even high heels could raise the lovely head of La Carmelita more than five feet five inches from the ground. But she looked a little more than queenly. Her hauteur was not that of an aristocrat, though an aristocrat she was. It was rather the pride of a goddess to whom life can give all human joy, but no human stains and defilement. She was not timid or shy, but gentle, instead, and her eyes as straight as the eyes of any man.

Otherwise, I suppose there was not one woman in all of Mexico who would have dared to outface public conventions by speaking to that bold intruder while hundreds of shocked and curious spectators looked on. The rest would have gathered the thin veil of the mantilla across their faces and hurried on past him, or turned hastily back to where the duenna had fled. She merely paused and waited for him to speak.

It was only a moment.

He said: "I am Dennis MacMore. I want to speak to you about my brother, but I am a hunted man. They are ready to catch me now if they can. But if I escape from them, tell me when and where I can see you?"

As readily as though these were words out of a play to

which she knew the answering speech by heart, she replied: "I will be in the river garden behind our house after midnight."

She said this, and smiled a little on him. She was seen to speak, and she was seen to smile, and the heart of San Clemente thumped in its breast when it heard the tidings later on.

That was all there was to this famous interview, of which I myself heard twenty legends later on in Mexico. It was exceedingly brief, because it had to be. As she spoke the last words, the gendarmes were already hurrying up from behind him, and in another instant they would have had their hands on his shoulders, but Dennis, bowing to her again, stepped quickly on across the promenade.

The gendarmes called out after him, one of them running in pursuit, and the other drawing a revolver with a good deal of bravado. So Dennis MacMore leaped away at full speed.

He could not use a knife or gun; he was like a loose sack in the saddle; to him a hatchet was a problem and an ax a mystery; but, nevertheless, young Dennis MacMore could run, and he fled now like a deer.

The second gendarme fired wildly over his head a couple of times. He dared not shoot closer for fear of striking some innocent bystander among the crowd of the lower classes who filled the inside promenades across which Dennis was now bolting. But the two officers in civilian clothes who had been mentioned by Dennis' bench companion were also in pursuit, and one of these, exactly as the stranger had declared he would do, began to fire well-aimed bullets with the purpose of winging the fugitive.

Those shots did not go home, though one of them grazed the hat of a peon, and Dennis MacMore got safely into the brush and among the trees that filled the center of the park. After him went the six men of the law, yelling and cursing. But even on fair ground they would have had the handicap of their heavy weapons against them, whereas Dennis was light, and running for his life.

He shot past the band stand with the last strains of "La Paloma" hanging sadly in the air; he plunged through the greenery on the other side of the stand; he bolted across the four promenades at that side of the Plaza Municipal, and so gained the main street itself.

He gained in the race, but it was not yet won. The fellow in civilian clothes who had done the shooting with intent to kill was an athlete, and he was still distinctly in the run, swinging his revolver with every stride to pull himself forward.

Dennis had a glimpse of him across his shoulder, and seeing a fashionable victoria driving by at that moment, he did not hesitate, but leaped into it.

27 ... Heaping Up Trouble

IN THAT victoria there was a very rich, very fat, old general. His name was Alfonso Pinzon. He was stuffed into a heavy uniform coat, loaded down with vast epaulets, and stiffened with gold lace, and brightened with stars, and ribbons, and all sorts of decorations. You could have clipped enough metal off of that gaudy old rascal to furnish a throne room. He had a sword between his knees, so that his gloved hands could rest on the hilt of it, as he reclined against the cushions and looked from under the golden rim of his uniform cap to the right and the left, greedy for praise and notoriety as a cat is for canned fish. Beside General Alfonso Pinzon was his wife. She was as little and shriveled as her husband was fat and puffed. And in front of them sat their daughter, who was getting ready to promenade and preparing to shine among the smaller stars. Even a mantilla could not make the Señorita Pinzon a beauty. Not even a mantilla and the moon of San Clemente.

Of course, the general had two men on the driver's seat. They both sat up as straight as carven images. They turned their heads neither to right nor left, for the good reason that the high collars of their service coats gripped them beneath the jaw and kept them immobile.

This was the outfit that Dennis jumped into!

If he had had any luck, he might have taken to something a good deal easier to handle. If he had had any sense whatever, he would have seen the glitter of the general's gold lace and hunted easier grounds; or he might have taken notice of the two men on the driver's box.

He noticed nothing, however, except a vehicle that could go faster than he could run. So straight into that victoria he pounced like a wild cat.

The señora shrieked. The señorita yelled at the top of her voice and probably also had time to tell herself that this was the most handsome and delightful young bandit in the world. But the general only snorted deep in his throat. He had a perfectly good little bull-nosed revolver in his hip pocket, and what was more, he knew how to use it, if he was the General Pinzon I heard of afterward in the revolution. But merely pulling a revolver and shooting a robber was not enough. It would do for open country, say, but not for the Plaza Municipal of San Clemente. I suppose the general instantly conceived the idea of himself standing proud and lofty, boldly swinging his trusty sword and cleaving the scoundrel in two.

At any rate, that old man draws out a yard of steel. It was no toy sword. Down there in Mexico they understand how to use a saber, because most of them have worked with a machete, at one time or another. This was a sort of wide-bladed scimitar, and it was heavy and sharp enough to carve Dennis in two from the shoulder to the stomach. That was what the general heaved up into the air, but just then the victoria struck a bump, and Alfonso Pinzon lost his balance. He had time to strike a blow at the air that missed Dennis a mile and nearly split the skull of the señora. He also was able to shriek out "Treason!" a couple of times, and then he whanged the pavement full length and went to sleep.

Dennis looked back at the gold lace flattened on the street, and at the same instant, he saw the leading officer jump into a carriage immediately behind them, standing up and shouting at the driver, who put his whip to the span. In the meantime, these things had happened pretty rapidly, and the two men on the driver's seat were just pulling up the horses and trying to turn around, which was a job their strait-jacket uniforms made hard to do. Dennis was there, mind you, without a weapon in his hands, but he simply taps one of the men over the shoulder with the cane he had stuck to when he ran, and then he sticks the point of it into the driver's back.

131

"Go on," says Dennis excitedly, "and go fast!"

I suppose they thought that the ruffian was ready to pistol them both from behind. At any rate, they gave the horses the whip, lurched the victoria into rattling full speed, and turned out of the Plaza Municipal on two wheels, while the señora's shriek sounded like the squawking of a rusty axle.

The daughter was enduring the shock pretty well, only crying now and then as a matter of form to show that she was upset, but the rest of the time centering a lot of attention on Dennis. I suppose that by this time the moonlight was shining in his blond hair and flashing in his eyes, and he must have been pretty easy for a girl to look at.

At any rate, a moment after this, as they scoot around another corner, while the general's wife moans part of an Ave and a phrase of an evening prayer, the girl stands up and calls to Dennis: "I know that span of blacks. They belong to the Jefe Aloyado. We're sure to beat them! We've beaten them twenty times before! What have you done?"

She had forgotten about screaming, and about coyness and about maidenly timidity, and all that sort of stuff, and she stood up there and whooped for Dennis' escape. Four or five centuries of etiquette had been dumped off her shoulders and what was left behind was simply the right sort of a girl. She was a good sport!

I wish I had met that Señorita Pinzon. If she could have put up with forty-two years and a broken nose, I would have taken a chance with her even if she wasn't a beauty. She had enough of the right stuff in her heart to do me proud!

They won the race, all right. They pulled away in fine shape, with one coachman handling the whip and the brake; while the other worked on the reins. They drew off in such good style that the murderous policeman in the carriage behind them opened fire with his revolver and succeeded in cracking two holes in the back of the victoria and spilling the señora in a dead faint. Her daughter paid no more attention to her than to a sack of straw. Which is another reason I would vote for her.

They had rushed out into the river boulevard by this time, with the policeman and his gun out of range behind them, and now what does our friend Dennis do?

You won't believe it. I can't believe it myself, but I have to write down what I've heard for the facts.

It is hard to think that any sane man would really have intended to visit the river garden of the Alvarado house at midnight, or at noon—no matter when—unless he had a letter of invitation from the head of the house. I have seen that garden myself, and I know the sort of a household staff the señora keeps. There's not a *mozo* of the lot that wouldn't die with a smile if his mistress asked him to. And he wouldn't even stop for the asking.

It was crazy enough to intend to go to that garden, but even after he had determined to show up for the appointment, what idiocy caused Dennis to let the rest of the world know all about it?

At any rate, he says: "Which is the Alvarado place?" when he sees the river flashing under the moon.

The girl froze up.

She thought she was dealing with a romantic criminal— a political refugee or something extra-specially scented and sweet, like that. But instead, she now figured that this was a guest of the high and mighty Alvarados, who thought very little more of a general than they did of a chimney sweep, and who needed an adding machine and several languages to tell the names of the counts, and grandees, and won battles, and sacked towns, and commanded ships, and castles built or blown up, and all the history that went with the ancient, and musty, and glorious name of the Alvarados. So the poor general's daughter merely sighed and pointed across the river.

I know what Dennis saw, because I've stood where he must have been then, across the river, and I've seen the front of the old house standing up like a jail, or a post office, or something like that, looming behind the great cypresses that walk along the edge of the river.

Go into that garden uninvited?

I would like to know exactly what passed in the heart of Dennis then, and whether or not he did not, at this moment, feel a touch of fear, and a little faintness of heart, and dizziness in the head.

"Thank you," says Dennis, as they thunder along close to a bridge. "Thank you very much. I'll get out here!"

They stopped the carriage. He handed the drivers some money and got a pair of wide grins in exchange. I suppose they really loved Dennis like a brother when they saw the old general and all of his medals flattened out and ironed smooth on the pavement, and if they could have seen another carriage bump a tire over his fat stomach, they would have been still happier.

The girl was pretending to be too busy reviving her mother to hear Dennis' adieus, so off he marches across the bridge, a free man for the moment, at least, but with trouble coming up behind him as fast as a great thunder cloud.

Because what happened?

Why, exactly what any three-year-old child could have imagined!

The instant that the señora was recovered from her faint and had finished her second screaming fit, she begins to talk over this whole brilliant affair with her girl while they drive back to the Plaza Municipal, inwardly hoping that old Alfonso has broken his neck, and outwardly praying that he has not been seriously injured.

The girl immediately broaches her idea that this is simply a guest of the famous, elegant, socially hundred-percent Alvarados, and that the young fellow is out on a wild fling and has stepped on the toes of the police—a newly arrived guest who doesn't even know how to find his way back to the house.

Perhaps that was a good deal to make out of a simple remark such as Dennis had let fall, but at any rate, he was a fool to mention that name, since he intended, actually, to fulfill his engagement with La Carmelita.

The señora and her daughter arrived back at the plaza in time to be met by the general himself. He had been pried up from the pavement and brought to his senses, but he was now almost out of them again. He did not mind the bump on his head, but his sword was broken, and his best uniform dress coat was split up the back. That gave him breathing space to curse and rave, and when he heard the stranger's name linked to that of Alvarado, he swore he would find out the scoundrel and make him smart for this outrage.

So Dennis heaped up trouble on the way, as a loaded barge heaps a bow wave on its own course.

28 ... Youth in Gardens

Now THAT Dennis was over on the right side of the river—having already left behind him the clue to his destination for fear the legal authorities might miss him—he used a surprising amount of good sense in his further maneuvers. In this section of the river the best of San Clemente's homes were backed against the bank, where enormous cypresses, centuries old, were standing. There are no cypress trees in the world like those of the San Clemente River; they are giants, and they screened from view the houses which lay behind, except a few monstrous old palaces like the Alvarado place. And Dennis got a boat at a mooring up the stream, managed to climb into it without turning it over, and then drifted with it down the edge of the current so that he could pass on the Alvarado place more carefully and at close hand.

There was a great river wall to secure the land when the San Clemente rose, and lest any uninvited eye should enjoy the garden, that river wall was raised so that it sheltered the garden as well. Enough to make you swear, to see such a thing, but a Mexican loves privacy. He can't live without it. The aristocrats, I mean to say.

The landing from the river at the house of the Alvarados was a double flight of stairs that dropped down to the water's edge, but when Dennis was about to touch with the boat there, he saw a man at the head of the steps looking down at him, and Dennis felt discouraged, particularly because the man at the head of the steps was carrying what looked like a double-barreled shotgun with sawed-off barrels. That gun looked big enough to rip a dry crossing through the San Clemente, and young Dennis let go of the mooring ring with a shudder and floated on down into the great round shadows of the cypresses that were cast on the water by the moon. Before he got out of sight, he saw a second man with a second riot gun walking up and down along the front of the Alvarado garden.

135

It must have seemed strange to the boy that a garden would be so guarded, but then he was forgetting the Mexican psychology, which would never allow a garden and the young beauties who might walk in it to go unwatched.

Two men—two riot guns—and now, of course, he turns back.

Ah, not Dennis MacMore! He is only beginning to get thoroughly interested, as a matter of fact. He tells himself that nothing could bring him to speak to the fiancée of his brother except a natural family interest, and also for his dear brother's sake, but by this time, what with rivers, and guards and shotguns, between him and his goal, Dennis is getting a little dizzy with the excitement, when he thinks of facing La Carmelita in person. The more barriers, the keener he is to overleap them. He was all Irish, was Dennis, and the more lost a cause appeared to him, of course, the more attractive it was to his Irish heart.

He pulled his boat across the river and rowed it up the moon mist on the farther bank; then, when he was a sufficient distance above the Alvarado house, he recrossed the stream and dropped as slowly as before along the edge of the current, studying the landing steps one by one. He had decided that he would try to land just above or just below the house of Alvarado, and then work in across the wall to get into the right garden.

Two houses up, he touched the steps, secured the boat and climbed the steps to the top. He barely had passed through the river gate of the garden when a burly Mexican in a ten-gallon hat came up and wanted to know his pleasure. That Mexican was a walking arsenal, and to make matters still more uncomfortable, he had a pair of dogs that looked as disagreeable as a toothache. All that Dennis could think of saying was to ask if this was the house of Señor Oñate. The guard melted a little, particularly when he saw the gold lace of Dennis' short jacket; and besides there was an Oñate who lived a little further down the stream.

So he told Dennis which house it was, and MacMore got away, glad to have his skin intact.

A moment later he was passing the Alvarado steps for the second time, and he ground his teeth impatiently as he did so. At the very next landing of the house adjoining that of Alvarado, he deliberately pulled up to the landing

136

ing, stepped out—merely barking his shins as he did so—and kicked the boat out into the current once more. Then he turned and started up the stairs with the idiotic determination of fighting it out on those lines, if it took him all the evening.

He should have walked straight into trouble, but he did not. Trouble still was postponed for him on this night, though he was headed surely for it.

At the top of the steps he found the gate closed and locked and he scrambled desperately over the iron spikes. In doing so, he sat down on one of them, which made Dennis swear a good deal, and hop around in circles when he got down to the ground inside. He hardly noticed that the garden was overgrown, wild, unoccupied, and that all the windows of the house beyond the garden were closely shuttered. But finally he realized his luck. He had walked into a deserted garden and he was as safe there as could be.

Why should he have had such luck? Well, he was young and handsome.

He decided that the tide having turned in his favor, he would take advantage of it, so he went straight at the adjoining wall and swarmed up its side; but near the top his hand caught in a bad adobe brick that crumbled under his weight, and down went Dennis with a crash to the bottom, where he landed in a berry bush that filled him fuller of prickles and thorns and stings than any porcupine's skin.

As soon as he got his breath back, he started to untangle himself from the long, snaky, octopus arms of that bush, and while he was picking his way free, he heard footsteps come running on the farther side of the wall; then the voices of the two guards began, and he heard one telling the other that from the noise he had heard, some one certainly must be in the adjoining garden, and they had better take a look.

He remembered those riot guns, and even Dennis had sense enough to know that a riot gun won't fail of its mark at any reasonable distance. He writhed out of the thorns, therefore, as rapidly as he could, leaving a few pieces of his trousers and a good many patches of his skin behind him. He just managed to get into the shadow of a great bush as the two guards mounted the wall. He was in the shadow, but his gold lace betrayed him.

"It's the same one that I saw going down the river a while ago," says one of them, and hoists his gun to his shoulder.

Dennis was making tracks to get out of sight, but he never could have escaped from the charge of that gun if the second guard had not knocked up the muzzles, declaring that the young señorita had just come home and must not be disturbed and alarmed; besides, the neighboring garden was no affair of theirs.

It was the narrowest escape that Dennis had had, not even excepting the one at the hands of that Oñate in the north. But he did not stop to give thanks to luck or fate; he simply turned back through the obscurity of the brush and went at the Alvarado garden wall again.

This time he got rapidly up to the top. He could squint down the line of the fence and, in spite of some intervening and overhanging branches, he could make out the two guards still in their place and still wondering whether or not their duty led them to investigate the stranger in the adjoining garden.

While they talked, the marauder was no longer in the adjoining grounds, for he had dropped down to the ground, giving his knee a bad bump on the way.

He was now hot, tired, sweating, dusty, thorn-raked and thorn-beset, with his clothes pretty badly torn, and a good many pieces of skin lacking from his anatomy.

But he was in the garden of the Alvarados, and the next moment he was passing the Pool of the Three Graces. All of San Clemente referred to that group of marble in capital letters, because once upon a time the great Don Hernando, the brotther of the ruler of Parma, had said that the group was charming. Perhaps it is. I've seen it myself, and the three girls have their arms around one another, and they are all smiling a little cockeyed, which is true to nature, because that is exactly the way young girls act when they're together. One of them held a cornucopia out of which a shower of water spurted up into the air and fell back on their heads. I must say that in hot weather they looked pretty cool, and I suppose that in the moonlight they looked even better.

I've gone to a lot of trouble and detail in describing this group of the Three Graces because it comes in again pretty strong, not so far from this point. I said that Dennis was passing the Pool of the Three Graces, and deciding that there was no sense in his remaining in the garden until after twelve o'clock, when her ladyship had promised to appear. He had heard the guards say that she was already back at the house, and so long as she was there, he would go to find her.

That had always seemed the crowning effrontery of that young man. He already had had enough trouble with Mexicans, and he had escaped from being blown into his next life with a charge of buckshot and iron scrap only five minutes before, but he was not contented; he actually had to invade the house of Alvarado itself, though he knew that it was garrisoned with devoted *mozos,* as the stranger in black had told him.

That man fascinated the mind of the boy more and more, it seems; and no wonder, for at that time it seemed as though he did have some sort of mysterious insight into the minds and affairs of other people.

But he had apparently foreseen this meeting; he had given it authority, as one might say, by forecasting its occurrence, and Dennis actually went ahead as though the thing were decreed by the books of Fate.

He found another obstacle almost at once, which was that the house was surrounded, on the garden side, by a sweep of beautiful lawn that received his footfall in silence and softness like a most exquisite carpet. But this open lawn made it easy for eyes to spy on him from the windows of the house. To be sure, most of these windows were heavily shuttered and all of the lower ones were secured, as usual, with heavy iron gratings. Dennis moved along in the shadow of the trees, staring up at the few lighted windows he passed; and finally, in one of them, he saw two girls, and one of them laughing in the delightful voice of La Carmelita.

29 ... Youth and a Maiden

He could not fail to know that voice, though he never had heard it in laughter before, but only in the speaking of a few words; however, Dennis was a musician, as I've said before, and therefore he had a well-trained ear in some ways.

Now he had seen her, and he could hear her words, now and then, but how was he to get in touch with her? He could have climbed up to the window, perhaps, and undoubtedly he would have taken that means of breaking his neck; but then there was another girl in the room with La Carmelita—some favorite *moza,* perhaps, or a guest. They sat there at the open window, breathing the cool of the garden and the river, and very gay because they bubbled continually with laughter.

How was he to reach her and bring her down to him?

Just then an owl hooted a long, booming note, and I laugh when I think of what Dennis did. Perhaps you have seen that he was a fellow who would attempt anything not out of vanity but out of sheer ridiculous courage. I suppose that he had read a good deal about imitations of bird calls, and now, never having practiced one in his life, he tried valiantly to hoot like that same owl.

The laughter at the open window simmered out and grew still at once, while the companion of La Carmelita leaned out from the window and said in good Spanish but with a trace of a foreign accent: "There is surely some one down there, my dear."

"It's one of the guards, I suppose," said La Carmelita, coming closer to the window also. "The impertinent—"

"Are they calling to you?" said the companion.

"Calling to me? Conchita, what are you thinking of? Calling to me, indeed!"

"I do believe," said Conchita, "that I see a man under that big tree."

The mantilla dropped suddenly over the head and face of La Carmelita.

"No one would be so impertinent!" said she. "Close the shutter, Conchita!"

The first wing of the shutter was, accordingly, drawn in, and the second was about to follow when Dennis—

But no. It's impossible to believe that there could be such effrontery in any man! But the fact is that when he saw the window's shutter about to be closed across and he, accordingly, cut off from the girl, he stepped out from his tree and into the full silver of the moon.

"Ah," says the girl, "Carmel! Carmel! There is a man down there on the lawn!"

La Carmelita was at the window in a flash, thrusting the first wing of the shutter out. So she leaned and saw beneath her that same handsome young madman who had spoken to her in the promenade.

"Great heavens!" says La Carmelita. "You're not really here! You can't be unless you've flown with wings! Go away at once!"

"I came here by appointment," says MacMore, getting angry. For he was none of your soft-hearted idiots who will not stand up for their rights against a woman.

"There are two other windows looking out on this side of the lawn!" cried La Carmelita, trying to guard her voice, and yet make it carry to the stranger. "You must go, go! Great heavens, they'd tear you to pieces!"

"Are you coming down to me?" says Dennis MacMore.

"Of course not," said she, and she turns and murmurs something to her companion.

"You gave me your word," says Dennis.

"I never dreamed that you would break in here—Will you get out of sight?"

"Not till you promise to come down here."

"Close the shutters, Conchita!" says the girl.

"I'll climb up and tear them open," says he.

Now, at that, she came into the window once more and measured the distance to the ground, and the reckless attitude of Dennis. Perhaps she knew in her heart that instant that he would certainly attempt to do as he had threatened. Perhaps she also guessed that he would fall and break his ridiculous neck if he tried the climb.

However that might be, she was in great trouble.

"Do you believe what I've told you?" said she. "Your life is really in danger. Dear Mr. MacMore, I do beg you to leave the garden at once!"

"Dear Señorita Alvarado," says this young rip, "I believe every word you say. I only ask you to believe me also, when I say that I won't stir a step till I've talked to you."

A shutter creaked in a near-by room just then, and the noise finished the girl. She made a gesture of surrender, waved her hand, and drew back at once.

Even then Dennis would not jump for safety. He was too filled with dignity by this little victory of his, as he turned and strolled back into the shadows, only just in time to escape from the sharp stare of two or three pairs of eyes now unmasked above him by the opening of another window.

That shutter, however, very soon closed, and Dennis stood in the thick shadow waiting until—after what seemed a great space—he saw her slip around the corner of the house, and go covertly from shadow to shadow until she was before him.

"I wanted to talk to you alone," said Dennis, as blunt as a sledge hammer.

"I have only come down, Mr. MacMore," said she, "to tell you that whatever may be in your mind to say to me about your brother, this is not the time or the place. There are men here who would shoot you on sight!"

"I know it," says Dennis. "They nearly have already."

La Carmelita is a steady-nerved sort of a girl, but she was a little staggered by this.

"Do you mean that they saw you enter the garden?" says she.

"They saw me maneuvering next door," said Dennis. "And if they have enough brains to put two and two together, they may spot me here soon."

La Carmelita, after all, was no hysterical young fool. When she saw that Dennis was so rash that he really preferred gambling against buckshot to giving up his stubborn will, she merely replied: "If we have to talk, this is not the place."

She took him to the pool in order to keep away from the house. For a Mexican house never sleeps, but keeps a least one ear and one eye awake both night and day except in the siesta hour.

They went to the pool, which was surrounded by a tall hedge of flowers, with three benches of stone to match the Three Graces, and the Graces themselves looking very simpering and silly, touched as they were by the running film of water, and the silver of the moonlight as well.

La Carmelita had her temper well up by this time, but she controlled it very carefully, and spoke in a level tone to Dennis.

"You know that my reputation would be killed if people knew about this meeting, señor."

"Señorita," says Dennis, quick as a flash, "if people knew about this meeting, I would be dead before your reputation."

There was enough impertinence in this to make her smile. I suppose she had feared that he was a young madman, wild with romance.

"At least," said she, "we can be brief."

Dennis drew himself up stiff as a board; he looked down at her from the height of his twenty-two or three years. "My dear child," said he, "I am trying to consider my brother and his affairs, not my own."

It was the first time in her life that La Carmelita ever had been patronized by a man. No matter how old or important they might be, she had always been able to "cut them down to her own size." I think it took her breath to hear him talk, and see him frown.

She did not even answer for an instant, but stared at Dennis almost as though she were afraid.

"How have you come here?" says she then.

"It would take an hour to tell you," says Dennis, "and you had better sit down."

La Carmelita looked into the sky for advice, and the sky seemed to agree that it was all right. She sat down.

"Every second you spend brings danger closer to you, and of course you know that?" says Carmelita, speaking truer than she knew.

"Of course I know that," says Dennis in a very superior and indifferent manner.

"Are you going to remain standing, Mr. MacMore?"

"I can't sit down," explains Dennis, "because I sat once

143

before this evening, and that time it was on a spike on the top of the garden gate next door."

La Carmelita allowed a smile to creep into her eyes.

And Dennis at this went and sat down, gingerly, on the arm of the stone bench, close beside her.

30 ... The Señor's Methods

"AFTER you left me in the plaza," said La Carmelita, "tell me what happened to you. I thought for a moment that they would run you down, and shoot you, and tear you to pieces."

"So did I," agreed Dennis, "and that made me lighter than gunpowder. I ran across the plaza ahead of them all, jumped into a victoria a general was riding in, and made him so angry that he stood up and fell out on the other side, making a swipe at me with his sword. Then we galloped like mad, came to the river, where I paid the coachmen, thanked the ladies, crossed the bridge, and got a boat; and since then I've barked my shins, sat on a spike, fallen into a patch of thorns, and nearly been shot with a riot gun. But finally I reached the tower, from which I drew down the lady and she sat with me in the moonlight and laughed at Dennis MacMore."

She was laughing, to be sure, by this time, and then Carmelita wanted to know what really had brought him here other than the sheer love of trouble. It was a very good, proper question, except that she knew one part of the answer beforehand, and Dennis did not leave her in any further doubt. His frankness with women was always a thing that made my ears tingle.

He said: "Well, you know a good reason for my hunting you, and that was because I couldn't keep away."

Says she: "A man stops me in the middle of the promenade! A thing that no one in San Clemente ever had heard the like of!"

"To notice me was one thing," said Dennis MacMore; "but to glow at me was another; and to smile at me was nother; and to soften and melt at me was another still; nd you knew perfectly well that you were sending cold ipples down my spinal marrow and darkness over my yes, and tremblings through my heart. You knew all hose things well, but you enjoyed making the poor young tranger suffer."

"I had better go in!" says she.

"I won't talk any more about that," said Dennis, "but vhen I'm asked to explain an axiom by the inventor of it, t's pretty hard to avoid the truth. However, I didn't come ere to talk like a romantic fool. I came here to talk about 1y poor brother."

La Carmelita straightened a little.

"You say that you are the brother of Patrick Mac-Aore?" said she.

He was thoroughly amazed that she doubted this.

"If I were not, why under heaven should I be here?"

She considered both him and his amazement.

"Why," she said, "you could be here for a whole crowd of reasons. You could be here to pass the time; to flirt with . poor girl in the moonlight; to see the garden of Alvara-lo; to bait the guards; to drive my mother frantic; to con-inually enjoy the thrill of risking your life; to win a wager; r simply to give yourself something to talk about for the ext week."

"Do you think," said Dennis, "that I could be such a ellow as that?"

And suddenly she could see that under his gayety he vas a simple and serious boy, and from that instant she 1ust have begun to like him a great deal.

"No, no," said Dennis, "I came to you because I had to ome to you, and all for the sake of my brother. And if ou doubt that—why, look closer at me, and I think you'll ee some resemblance, though, of course, I'm not a uarter of the man that he is!"

She looked closer and saw the resemblance, clearly nough. Like the resemblance, let us say, between a house at and a panther. However, it was there. Besides, I sup-ose he looked formidable and manly enough to La Car-1elita, who had seen him dashing through the whole Plaza Aunicipal and creating furor and a scene in her honor.

"I believe what you say," admitted La Carmelita, "but vhat could I do for the Señor?"

"You could do this. You could take away that title and give him back the one that really belongs to him—The MacMore!"

"You mean that I'm to persuade him to leave San Clemente?"

"Yes," said he, "of course. I came down here all the way from home. Mother isn't as well as she used to be and there were other reasons for getting him back; but when I learned that he—that he—"

He paused. It tormented him to speak of it to the girl.

"When you learned that he's El Tigre's right-hand man?" she helped him out with her little smile.

"Well," said he, perspiring, "when I found out about that, it was a pretty bad moment. I would have tackled him about it, but when I learned about you, I knew that I couldn't do anything. It would have to come from you. I wanted to offer you reasons—"

"But," said she, "you don't have to offer me any. I've tried a hundred times to get him away from San Clemente."

"You have?" groaned Dennis, clasping his hands together in a strange, childish fashion which he had when he was greatly upset.

"Of course I have," said she. "You don't suppose that I want to marry him, do you?"

That was such a staggerer that Dennis almost fell off the arm of the bench; but he recovered enough to stand up before her and say that he hoped she was not making a joke of him, for that really he had taken his life in his hands in order to see her.

"But I tremble every time I see him," said she. "And if I were not so afraid of him, I would certainly never see him again."

"I don't know what you mean," said Dennis, who began to tremble violently, so that his knees were perceptibly sagging; "but I hope you don't mean to suggest that my brother—would—would—I mean, that he would try to influence you—through fear?"

It was plain to her that Dennis was in an agony of shame, but of course she could not realize how great that agony was. She would have had to know what I knew about Dennis' worship of The MacMore, the great and faultless hero of the family. Now to hear that that hero ac-

ually had been using the point of the gun, so to speak, on
the woman he wanted to marry—

"I certainly do suggest that he would try to influence
me," said she. "I certainly do mean to suggest that there
isn't a soul in the Alvarado family who wouldn't be in
danger if I were to make him angry, to say nothing of the
Alvarado estate."

Poor Dennis laid a hand upon his heart, because in fact
he was stifled by its furious beating.

"Do you know how the Señor paid his attentions to
me?" said she.

Dennis was silent.

"He sent his hideous giant to my mother, and announced that he would come to see her the following day.
We stayed awake all the night, trembling, and the next day
he came and announced further that he would be pleased
to marry me, and would call on the following day to talk
to me. And on the following day he came and had me
brought in before him, and condescended to tell me that
he would take me as his wife!"

"Oh, Heaven forgive him!" says Dennis half under his
breath, and half aloud.

There was such stricken horror in his face that suddenly
La Carmelita forgot her own trouble and was filled with
pity for the boy.

"Ah, Dennis," said she, "didn't you know about those
things?"

He held out both his hands and then let them fall back
heavily at his side.

"How could I dream of it?" groaned Dennis. He added:
"You were my last hope. Now I've got to go talk to him
myself and persuade him if I can."

"Dennis, he'll simply send you packing out of the country. I've begged him to give up this life, and if he com-
passes that marriage with me, I've implored him afterward
to take me away from San Clemente, but—the truth is,
Dennis, that no matter how the rest of the world fears Patrick MacMore, just that much he himself fears El Tigre!"

But now the point had come when the affairs of his own
life and that of The MacMore meant nothing compared to
one thing to the boy. He pressed his hands against his
face. When he could look at her again, he begged her to

147

tell him once more that his brother really was marryin
her by force.

"I didn't laugh at his first threats," she answered. "N
one in San Clemente really could laugh at the Señor. Bu
suddenly my uncle and his two boys disappeared on th
road to Vera Cruz. And at the same time a bank close
here in this town—the bank where my mother's mone
is—and I saw that these things could not have happene
by chance. I sent a note to the Señor. Suddenly it appeare
that bandits had carried my uncle and his boys off—by
mistake, and they were put safely back on the road! Th
bank opened. There was no harm done. And I learne
what I could expect from the Señor!"

"Horrible, horrible!" says Dennis softly. "You have t
be saved from him!"

"Saved from the Señor? I wonder if even the Seño
might not be shamed if he met his brother face to face?
she said thoughtfully.

"He might simply ship me out of the country," sai
Dennis.

"And that would be the safest thing," said La Carmeli
ta, "that possibly could happen to you in San Clemente."

31 . . . Advance of General Pinzon

IT INTERESTS me to guess how much the beautifu
daughter of the Alvarados, the last of that long line, wa
able to look into the mind of young MacMore at thi
point. How far did she see the truth about him, and hov
clearly did he show that he was losing his mind about her
How much was she upset, and how much amused, by th
abrupt way he talked to her, as though she were anothe
man? Well, however she felt, one thing is sure, that sh
never before had met another like him. I think that hand
some head of his must have carried some weight with her
but still I really believe that she was more amused than i
earnest as she sat there talking to earnest young Dennis
Women are apt to adopt that attitude toward men, thoug

148

why, I should like to have the lovely ladies tell me. However, it's a superior attitude—to sit back and smile. Even the gods can do no more, and even the gods cannot be more irritating than pretty girls. For my part, I'd like to see them spanked and sent back to school to learn manners.

So this charming Carmelita sat back on the bench and her laughter rippled softly up to Denny, as though there were something mysteriously absurd about him.

Poor Denny was as willing to laugh as the next one, but he had one of the shortest tempers in the world, and he showed it before long by leaping up from his place on the arm of the bench and standing in front of her.

No matter how she smiled, he told her, he would guarantee to bring his brother to time and end his persecution of the señorita in five minutes, if only he could get to the Señor.

"But," said La Carmelita, "I have a magic ring that will take you to the Señor at any time!"

"Am I such a joke to you?" says Denny, hot in the face.

"Not at all," said she, "but the fact is that your brother isn't above a little swagger. He gave me a ring and told me never to be without it, because he said that it would help me in any trouble, and it would certainly be a passport to him whenever I had need of him. I never expected to have any need of him, but I took him seriously enough never to leave that ring lying around! If you think you can help me, suppose you try if this will take you to him?"

Now, as she said this, she drew out by a thread-like golden chain that looped around her neck and fell into her bosom, a man's ring with a great flat-faced emerald set in it. She unclasped the chain and gave the ring to Denny.

Then she repeated what the Señor had said when he gave her the ring: That one man out of every ten in San Clemente would know that ring; that they would be the wisest, strongest, bravest, and most determined men in the community; and that these men would certainly obey her in any way, help her in time of danger, and willingly go so far as to lay down their lives for her. For her own part, she had accepted both the ring and the speech with a grain of salt. You could see she was no romantic young fool. However, now she handed over the ring to Denny and made him welcome to use it as he saw fit in getting to his brother; though she said she dreaded lest it might carry him into a trap.

"Do you think that I fear my own brother?" cries Denny to her.

"Hush!" says she, jumping up. "I hear people coming! Hush! Don't you hear them, too?"

There were people coming, right enough, but in order to explain who they were and why they were there, it is necessary to go back to General Alfonso Pinzon, and Denny's asinine speech to the Señorita Pinzon.

When the general recovered himself a little, the first thing he did was to rush home and put on his second-best dress uniform. He did not feel at all well until he was incased in it, though it was at least two inches smaller around the waist than the last coat, and accordingly put him into a bad state of mind immediately. His wife wanted to put some liniment on the bump on the back of his poor head, but he gave her a terrible glare, and told her that he was a soldier, and that he hoped that fact was known to the rest of the world, though he couldn't expect it to be remembered by the weak wits of his own household!

Then he clapped on his head his second-best military cap, groaning when he saw that some of its metal braid was the least bit tarnished; he jammed his second-best sword into the empty scabbard; he ordered out his wildest, tallest, most prancing and dancing parade horse; and on its back he dashed and crashed and skidded through the streets of San Clemente until he came to the house of Alvarado, where he threw a *mozo* the reins and an oath, and then at the front door gave the house *mozo* his card and a message for the señora that he wished to see her at once on a matter of life and death.

It has already been made clear that the Pinzons and the Alvarados were not on the same social level. When the señora was waked up and given the card and the message, she yawned a few times, and gritted her teeth. She vowed that the Pinzons were social climbers and that she would not see the general or any one else of that contemptible name at that hour of the night. However, "life and death" means something, even in Mexico, and so she finally got out of bed, and two maids were scared into her presence and scolded as they dressed her in her blackest gown and shoved only seven or eight rings onto her bony fingers, and looped a necklace or two around her skinny neck.

Then she descended to the room where the general was sitting on the edge of a chair, gripping the hilt of his sword nervously, and wondering if he were not going too far.

He got a good deal more nervous when the Señora came stalking into the room. She stood off among the shadows. She did not need close range in order to freeze a guest, and she froze poor General Alfonso Pinzon until his tongue was as thick as a day and night of tequila could have made it.

He had to look down twice at the rows of decorations that were strung across his chest before he decided that, after all, he was somebody, even though he was not an Alvarado. Then he got back the use of his tongue and asked her point-blank if all was well with her and her family, and to assure her that the only reason he called was to inquire if she needed any help—since he had authentic word that the villain who had accosted her daughter in the Plaza Municipal had still further designs in the way of making mischief. He prayed that they might be foiled!

He got that far when the señora interrupted him. Her skinny chest heaved three or four times, and then she squeaked at him:

"Accosted my daughter? In the Plaza Municipal? I thank Heaven there is no man in the world who dares accost my daughter—in the Plaza Municipal!"

The general bowed. He bowed because he had to conceal a grin, and he grinned because of the exquisite pleasure which he felt in putting the Alvarados, and the very head of that clan, in their proper place.

But he told her in his next breath, when he had regained control of his facial expression, what the whole town knew —amazing that the señora had not heard!—how a young gringo actually had broken into the ladies' promenade and had spoken to her daughter before the eyes of all men— and all women as well.

The señora almost dropped, but remembering that she was an Alvarado, she declared that madmen cannot be prevented from mad actions, but the important thing was that no daughter of hers could notice such a creature under such conditions.

151

"On the contrary," says the general, "she was seen to speak twice to him!"

It was a great blow for the Alvarados. A thousand of them must have stirred in their graves, and a thousand vases of ashes must have grown hot as the general said this.

The señora would have dropped, I think, if she had not managed to get a hand on the back of a chair. From this position she waved off the general as he came hurrying to offer his assistance.

"This disgraceful—" said she.

She remembered she was speaking of her own daughter and set her teeth over the rest of the sentence. Then she said that she would have both her daughter and her daughter's duenna down to be examined—in the general's presence, so that he would be able to set right any misapprehensions among the townspeople if they dreamed that a daughter of the Alvarados would speak to a madman on the public promenade.

The general protested his entire willingness to utterly disbelieve such a thing even if a thousand eyewitnesses lived to assure him. He was tickled to his backbone. He was almost glad that he had fallen out of his carriage since he was now able to humiliate the Alvarados so thoroughly.

The duenna was sent for by one *mozo,* and the daughter by another. And before the duenna could appear, word came scurrying back that La Carmelita was not in her room.

That unstarched the pride of Señora Alvarado on the spot.

She crumpled up in a chair and clasped her hands over her faded face. She had been a beauty in her day, and now terror and despair and grief—all founded in a ready imagination—made her great dark eyes almost as speaking as ever.

The general assured her that there must be a mistake; at such an hour, of course, the girl was in her room—in the house at least!

But a hurrying brigade of servants presently announced that La Carmelita was not there.

"The garden—at least—" says the general.

"The garden!" says the señora in a husky, broken voice.

"I shall look for her myself," says the general.

Micronite filter.
Mild, smooth taste.
For all the right reasons.
Kent.

America's quality cigarette.
King Size or Deluxe 100's.

He steps close to the lady of the house and bows: "Command me in everything," says he, "and particularly in silence!"

That touched the poor lady. She gave him one look of agony and appeal, to which he answered with another bow, his hand on the hilt of his sword, and then she gave him command of the searching party.

A dozen of them marched into the garden, with the general at their head.

Frankly, he never had marched in a more important cause, though he was as hardy an old campaigner and loved a fight as well as any man in the world; but now he saw before him a great triumph, and his family raised to the social level of the Alvarados. He saw his foolish wife seated in the Alvarado carriage, chatting carelessly with the Señora Alvarado in the open light of day! He saw his daughter arm in arm with La Carmelita herself!

That made him a little dizzy as he walked out into the garden, but dizzy as he was, he had not taken twenty steps from the house before he recognized the tactical possibilities that lay in the possession of such a point as the Pool of the Three Graces. So he spread out his followers in a broad circle, and with one other man he boldly advanced to beat up this covert.

Their footfalls were what Carmelita heard. Then through a break in the hedge, the two were plainly visible.

It was bad enough for a girl to be found alone, in the middle of the night, even in a private garden—social rules are strict as steel in Mexico. But of course, the presence of the man was the thing to be avoided. One wave of the hand was enough to warn Denny and tell him to get out. He sneaked off on the opposite side, and as the general came up from one direction, Denny bolted off in the other as fast as he could leg it—and fell crash into the arms of a pair of broad-shouldered house *mozos!*

32 ... When MacMores Meet

IT'S HARD to say exactly what that capture of Denny in the garden meant. In the States, it would be a thing to laugh about for a day or two; in Mexico it could be built up into a scandal as virulent as a plague. And the people of San Clemente were just the ones for the job of course. They feared and looked up to the Alvarados as to a species of social deities, and when they had a chance to drop on them with such a social breach as this, it would have been more than human nature to fail to talk.

The general knew this.

He knew that he would be able to make the Alvarados his slaves. As for the house servants, they probably were as devoted as servants could be. They would not talk. Or if they did, servants' gossip was not greatly considered by the elect. All rested upon the silence of his own tongue, and he would undoubtedly have made every concession if it had not been that, in the person of Denny, he recognized the scoundrel who had caused him to miss a saber stroke and fall flat on his back in the middle of the street in San Clemente.

That was too much for Alfonso Pinzon.

He saw Denny; he uttered a roar; and then he charged to exterminate him. Poor Denny!

He was perfectly willing to fight till he dropped, but he hadn't a chance. He was held as helpless as a child by two iron-handed *mozos* and this in the presence of a girl! He wriggled, writhed, and cursed, but he could not budge away from them; and now the general came at him with a regular war whoop. He wanted to scalp Denny, but he knew he could not do that. He would at least, however, manage to spoil the gringo's face.

So he gripped Denny by the left wrist and poised the saber to bring the hilt fairly into the boy's face. That stroke would have smashed nose and bone and spilled teeth like water. But just as the general drew himself up on tiptoe, to give extra force to the smash, he caught sight of the emerald ring on the left hand of his victim. The face of that ring was as broad as the finger that wore it, and the moonlight shone so clearly on the jewel that even the first glance showed him the eagle with spread wings that was incised in the face of the emerald.

When General Pinzon saw this, the breath went out of him almost as swiftly as it had left him when he whanged himself on the pavement earlier in that same evening. The sword actually fell out of his hand, and instead of throwing himself at Denny, he lurched back so rapidly that he almost lost his balance and fell.

He recovered himself enough to scoop up the sword. Then he glowered at Denny like an eagle at a hawk which is too fast for him on the wing. He had to explode in some way, or else choke. So he roared at the two honest *mozos* who had made the capture: "You thundering blockheads, what do you mean by interfering with this gentleman? Get out of my sight. Take your hands from him!"

He kicked them away with might and main. All in an instant Denny was free. Alfonso Pinzon, purple in the face, was swelling with emotion, and bowing to young MacMore, asking what he could do to serve him in any way.

"Get me away from this place, and the lady safely back into her room. Can you do that?" asked Denny, feeling pretty dizzy, but willing to take advantage of the situation before him.

"As you know, señor," said the general, "nothing is impossible to patience, courage, and brotherhood!" He said it significantly, with a great raising of his brows, and then fell to work.

After all, he was a general, and he whipped the situation into some sort of shape with amazing speed.

The two guards had come rushing up from the river wall. He sent them to the right-about with one roar of anger. Then he slid the lady into the house, saw her to her room, and was presently attending on the Señora Alvarado, who sat alone, with a sick face and a fallen head. Her he assured that the girl was treating herself to a scare by wandering through the attic like a romantic goose, and the señora thanked General Pinzon, and took his hand with a

155

warmth that made him understand he was lifted a whole dozen degrees in the social scale from that moment.

She did not tell the honest general that there was no attic in the Alvarado house!

He left her at once, because he had on hand something of more importance to him than even the pleasing of the Alvarados. This was to attend on the wild young man who had dumped him out of his carriage and then carried confusion into the Alvarado home. He found him near the street gate, surrounded by half a dozen of the suspicious servants who wanted nothing better than to cut his throat, though they dared not touch him since he had been shown so much consideration by the general in person.

Alfonso Pinzon scattered them like chaff and at once took Denny in charge. He was as deferential as though he had the King of Spain beside him, and at once began regretting that he had made the scene in his carriage. If only he had been given the sign at that time, the carriage and, in fact, all the general's men and all his possessions were at the service of Denny MacMore. What could he do for him?

Denny was not in a humor to protest that such service was not his due, that he possessed no sign, and that he was amazed by such subservience; but like a hero in a fairy tale, he calmly accepted the miracles as they hove above the horizon, and told the general to guide him instantly to the Señor!

For Denny had the tenacity of a bulldog, and though his teeth might be somewhat weak, he had all the will to hold on to his purpose, which now was to get at his brother and talk him back to sound sense, out of the disgraceful course of action to which he seemed to be committed at present in regard to La Carmelita.

General Pinzon was entirely agreeable. He actually insisted on mounting young MacMore on the big parade horse—I always wonder how he was able to stay there—and brought him straight to a house on the river not a quarter of a mile from that of the Alvarados. There was nothing extraordinary about this place. It was, in fact, a little smaller than most of the houses along that street, and it faced upon a garden which had been allowed to run down, but which had a small summerhouse in the center. The general presented his guest; was received by a *mozo;*

by a smiling youth of apparently good education, and finally by a scar-faced, surly fellow who seemed to have authority for the night. At least, he bluntly declared that, general or no general, the Señor could not be disturbed that evening on any account.

General Pinzon seemed more irritated than hindered. He turned abruptly on MacMore and asked him if he would speak the word.

"What word?" said Denny blankly.

At this, Pinzon puffed like an angry toad and suddenly pointing down to the broad-faced emerald, he asked the man of the scar if he were a fool or not?

That was the first time that Denny observed the magic effect of the ring and was able to guess that it had accounted for Pinzon's own sudden change of front. The man in charge of the house turned from yellow-brown to yellow-gray, and begged Denny to go with him that instant!

Pinzon said good-by, received a smile and a cordial handshake from Denny, and went home, probably thinking that this world was a place of strange fortunes and of still stranger gringos. But Denny himself was conducted straight through the house and into the garden.

Two riflemen rose from the brush and closed the path.

"Patience, courage, brotherhood!" said the guide rapidly, and the two melted back into the shadows from which they had risen.

Then Denny saw before him a little round house overwhelmed with a wave of climbing vines, a light showing dimly inside it. To this he was taken. Another guard stepped up before them, was passed with the same watchword as a formula, and eventually Denny and his companion stood before a door upon which his guide rapped, waited, rapped again, and straightway opened the door without waiting for any response from within.

They came into a little antechamber where in one corner they saw the wide-shouldered giant Gualtero. He lurched to his feet, and his own shadow behind him looked like that of a half-shaven monster.

"Domingo," says the monster, "you are a ten times greater fool than I thought! The Señor will have your hide off and tanned for disturbing him tonight!"

"Will he?" said Domingo. "Suppose you—"

Here Gualtero broke in with a low mutter of joy: "This

is the man! This is the man! Aye, Domingo! You've brought him to claim the reward?"

"Reward? What reward?" says Domingo. "Look!"

He pointed out the ring as he spoke. Its effect upon Gualtero was less than its power over the general or Domingo.

"I thought he was outside of us!" says Gualtero, with a bitter scowl at Denny; but, without making any more resistance, he raps on an inside door, then pulls it open, and waves Denny through.

In went Denny; the door closed behind him; and he sees the Señor seated at a table with a small lamp on a stand at his left, writing with the rapidity of a strong-handed man whose mind is full of thought.

He did not look up. He merely said, without ceasing from the scratching of the pen:

"If you ever give me such pulpy paper again, Gualtero, I'll wring your thick neck for you. I'm not writing. I'm plowing a furrow on the page!"

Because, as you might imagine, he bore down heavily, and the point bit deeply into the soft paper.

"Do you hear me?" says the Señor, with the same purr in his voice, I suppose, that I had heard before in it.

"I hear you!" says young MacMore.

At that, the Señor looked up, and for the first time in eight years he looked at his brother, and his brother looked at him.

33 . . . They Talk

I KNOW what Dennis saw, and I can imagine what he had last seen in his brother. Eight years must have made Patrick MacMore a little fuller in the face and squared his jaws a trifle. The Señor was a handsome man, as all of San Clemente would have been willing to admit; but there was something about him that made it entirely possible to forget all about his good looks, as I had been able to feel on that occasion when I first met with him. I suppose, eight years before, his eyes had been as bright as they were now, but the brightness must have been a little less hard. He had looked into the souls of many men in that interim; those eyes of his had the terrible calm which comes of handling death. Sometimes you will see that look in the face of the murderer, when he has been condemned and no longer cares to wear a mask. So he relaxes and allows the world to see as much of him as it will.

What the Señor had last seen of his brother must have been a mighty attractive lad of thirteen or fourteen, quick, bright, keen, and gay. No matter how often he had told himself about the changes in Denny, no matter how often he had looked at the pictures which his mother sent to him from time to time, still I suppose that the real image in his mind's eye, when he sent back an installment of money, was that picture of the young lad as he last had seen him in the flesh. Cameras never can substitute for the feel and the grip of a human glance. What he saw now was a thing that he could have crushed with one hand. Certainly, Denny was no duplicate of the Señor, and the only resemblance between them was a certain measure of good looks. One would have to be told, in order to feel the relationship in any degree. For, above all, their expression was different, and the feline look of the Señor had nothing in common with the wide-open cheerfulness of Denny.

I dwell on the physical appearance of the pair and how they seemed to one another because the other things are too hard to handle—I mean the heartache that must have been in each of them, and the anger rising in the Señor, and the scorn and pity in the boy.

If you had been the Señor, how would you have acted, what would you have said?

What he actually said after the first long look was: "Won't you sit down, Denny?"

And half rising from his chair, he rested one hand on the paper on which he was writing, and extended the other. Gently he clasped the fingers of his brother, with only one slight pressure of the thumb which showed him with an accurate gauge the physical weakness of poor Denny. But certainly the Señor could have felt no real pity as he stared at Denny a second time, more closely. For if his younger brother was weak in muscles, he had the eye of a fighter, and a world of spirit.

Denny sat down and clasped his hands around his knees. It made him look smaller than ever to sit in this attitude, but he never was one to seek for dignified positions.

"I'm glad you're safely here," says the Señor, nodding and smiling a little. "This is a rough town."

Denny waved his hand and brushed all such casual talk aside, as much as to say that he knew enough about everything in the town and didn't care to listen to half statements and fairy tales. If the town was rough it was because the Señor and his terrible employer, El Tigre, willed it so!

"Patrick," said the boy, "how long can I talk to you?"

Patrick half closed his eyes. "For half an hour," said he.

"Tell me about mother."

"We don't have to waste time on that," said Denny, "because I'm going to take you home to see her."

The Señor shook his head. "I'm involved here in very important business, Denny," he said, a trifle grandly. "There are some mining operations which will take time to complete—and then of course, I'm coming home forever."

"I thought," says Denny, "that you did your mining with revolvers and rifles."

And he looked the Señor slam in the eye, of course.

"I don't understand," says the Señor, "what you think or what you know."

"I understand," says Denny, "that the money you've been sending, the money mother's lived on, and I've gone to college on—has all been stolen money, got with bank robberies, murders, and all that sort of thing."

This he said with a good deal of restraint, but the cold statement made the very neck of the Señor swell with rage. He started to say something about gratitude, but stopped himself short; he was the last man in the world to use a platitude.

Then he said: "That's untrue. All of my money is not stolen money. I have an honest mining business, as well."

"What percentage do you get out of honest mines?" asked Dennis.

Again the Señor flushed. For eight years he never had heard a man speak to him like this, and it hurt!

However, he was made of the same sort of metal from which Denny was fashioned. I would have given a lot to be present when their wills clashed.

When the Señor did not answer at once, Denny went on in the same brisk voice: "You'll think that I'm not grateful. Well, I'll show you some day that I am. With love—and with interest!"

The flush of the Señor grew hotter. He was being offered interest on the money he had sent home. And the sending of that money, beyond a doubt, had been the one great redeeming feature of his life. It was his hold upon a vanishing decency. Now he was to be repaid—with interest!

"You're going to repay me, Denny?" he repeated. "And the money that I sent our mother, too?"

"Either that, or else tell her the truth about the origin of that money."

That was the spur that sank deep, but the Señor knew how to use self-restraint and diplomacy, even if his younger brother did not.

"You put everything in the harshest possible way, Denny," said he.

Denny jumped out of his chair, and ran to his brother and caught at his hands.

"Oh, Patrick," said he, "all my life you've been a god to me. I've been on my knees worshipping—"

He stopped simply because his voice had choked, and the tears brimmed his eyes and then ran in a torrent down his face. The Señor said nothing, did nothing. He was above taking advantage of the emotional moments of others, whatever his faults may have been.

After a while, when he had blown his nose and shaken the tears out of his eyes, Denny went back to his chair and sat down, adding to his last words: "I'd die for you right now, Patrick. I'd be glad to! Do you doubt that?"

"No," says the Señor. "I don't think I can doubt that!"

"Thanks," says the boy, "but as long as you're doing what you are, I'm going to fight against it! Oh, Patrick, how under heaven did a brute like El Tigre get control of you?"

"He saved my life," says the Señor—and this is a part of the conversation which I like to remember, because there was so much truth brought out here, and nowhere else by the Señor. "He saved my life, and got control of my body and brain by degrees."

"Good Heaven!" sings out Denny. "A red Indian? A wild man?"

"A wild man," says the Señor, "but at the same time, a remarkable man. If you ever meet him, Denny—which I hope most devoutly you will not!—you'll understand perfectly why he's almost invincible. He would tear you to pieces."

"He's a fool then, because I haven't harmed him."

"If you persuaded me away from him, you would do him the greatest harm in the world," says the Señor.

"That's a thing he couldn't know. He never could learn that!"

The Señor lifted a hand solemnly. "There's hardly a thought in my brain or a word I speak that El Tigre doesn't know!" says he.

And Denny breaks out: "Does the red master keep you so surrounded by spies? Patrick, Patrick, are even these brutes you keep around you not your men, but his?"

"My men?" said Patrick, drawing himself up a little. "Do you think that I would have such swine around me—if I could help it? No, no! They really have nothing to do with me. They belong to El Tigre!"

Denny leaned back in his chair with a groan of relief and of despair—relief because he saw a flash of the old Patrick in this man, and despair because he did not see how the battle would end in his favor.

Then he said: "Tell me one thing: You have no real affection for the red beast—that El Tigre?"

"Affection?" cries Patrick. "Why, I loathe him from the bottom of my heart, and if I could be rid of him—"

"Ah!" says Denny, "then I know the very thing. Go meet the brute, and put him out of the way!"

"He would crush me with a gesture!" said the Señor, and he dropped his face in one hand as he spoke. He even shuddered a little, his strong shoulders quivering.

"Even you are afraid of him?" says Denny, incredulous.

"Aye," says the Señor, "I fear him more than all else!"

It must have given Denny the cold horrors to hear it, for he knew that his brother was as close to a fearless man as there was in the world. What was El Tigre? That began to be the great, controlling question. No mere red-handed Indian, no mere pirate of the trail, but some one who exercised a subtle and sinister influence over MacMore.

"Patrick, I think he's hypnotized you!" he cries out.

"Aye, perhaps—hypnosis—I don't know what! The old

162

fable of Circe keeps running in my brain when I think of him, Denny. If ever you see him, then you'll understand—and Heaven help you!"

"What is it that he gives you, Patrick?" says the boy, eaten with grief and with curiosity.

"Power!" says Patrick in answer. "He fills my hands with it. There's hardly a man in San Clemente who doesn't jump when I speak. I can sit here in this room, Denny, at my ease, and look out through those open windows at the river. If I give one word, there is music. And dashed fine music it is. If I give another word, lights flash on certain house-tops, and as fast as light leaps, the word jumps into the mountains, where twenty well-armed and strongly mounted men jump into the saddle and spur away. That's power, Denny! El Tigre gives me that, and I love it!"

"You could revolt against him!" said Denny fiercely. "These people of yours like you better and fear you more than you think. I'll help you and, I can show you a man ten times as strong as anybody you know, when it comes to gun work. Almost as good as you yourself can be, Patrick!"

"That's your friend who's riding on the El Tigre trail, is it not?" says the Señor.

"That's the man, Joe Warder!" says the boy. "I'd be a dead man if it were not for him."

"Really dead?" says the Señor.

Denny told him about the affair with Oñate, and the Señor set his teeth and looked black.

"But what will you do? And how can I help to get you out of this land and go away with me?" said Denny finally.

"I can't leave this land—not this year. Go back home, Denny. Next year I'll surely be there."

"You don't mean it at all, even while you're saying it! You never will want to leave. You'll never lift up your hand against El Tigre."

"I've done it before," says the Señor sullenly. "Three times I've lifted up my hand against him, and three times I've been beaten—like a dog!"

That got Denny on his feet, panting, and crimson with shame.

"You mean that he actually struck you, Patrick," says he, cringing at the thought, "and that you're still working for him like a—a slave?"

163

"Be silent!" says the Señor, looking sick and white.

And they were silent, you can be sure, for a moment, both of them filled with their own thoughts.

"Tell me," says Denny finally, "is it only El Tigre that keeps you down here?"

"Yes," said the Señor.

"Is that the truth?" says Denny.

The Señor frowns at this, bending his head a little.

"I mean—what about Carmel Alvarado?" says the boy.

The Señor blinked, and then moistened his lips: "The one you spoke to on the promenade?" says he, apparently fighting for time.

"Aye, and I've spoken to her again in her own garden."

"You have?"

"Yes!"

"Are you going to interfere in that?" says the Señor.

"Patrick, how can you go on with it, when you know that she doesn't love you?"

"She told you that, eh?"

"I'm your brother. I sort of made her talk."

"Let me tell you. Marriage is not here the way it is in the States. It's by arrangement between families. It doesn't always start on the love basis that you're so used to think of. I'm simply following the national custom."

"It isn't indifference with her. She fears you and hates you!" says Denny.

"Listen to me," says the Señor, leaning a little forward, and with a sneer that was directed at himself, not at Denny. "She is the hire that El Tigre is offering to me. She's the great reward!"

Of course, he was stating it as blatantly as possible, for the very reason that it tormented him to even think of such a thing. He even added: "Don't you suppose I know that she detests me, and that she would even be likely to tell a stranger how she felt about the marriage? In spite of that, Denny, I shall take what El Tigre offers me. Don't be fool enough to interpose!"

"And you—you," gasps Denny, gripping his hands and shaking with excitement, "do you think that you've a right to degrade yourself, no matter how much you may want a woman who despises you? Do you know that you're The MacMore?"

34 ... The Bargain

JUST WHAT the Señor said in answer to this, I don't know, because my report leaves that a blank. Whether it was little or whether it was much, it became plain a few moments later that Denny had cleverly saved his trump card for the right moment, and that when he played it he nearly took every trick in the game. There must have been some hasty inquiries first, and then after Denny had told what deaths in the family now made the Señor the heir to that family title as head of the house, the thing began to work hard on him.

He got up and made a turn or two through the little summerhouse. It had many irregular sides, and a window in every facet, and he stopped here and there, staring out into the night where the river ran with stars in its calm borders, or toward the big garden trees moving in the wind, and the façade of the house behind them.

Finally he came back toward the center of the room, where Denny waited in great excitement, cleverly saying not a word, but letting the poison work, as one might say.

"Suppose I chuck the whole wretched mess!" said he. "Suppose I clean out—what should keep me? I can take enough to care for us all. By Heaven, I could be a Mac-More such as never cared for the family before, since Roger MacMore of the old port-and-pistol days!"

"You could," said Denny, shaking with joy, and his hands gripped together, I suppose. "There's nobody that knows you who doesn't know what a leader you'd make for the rest of the family. What does it matter if you have to come back a beggar?"

"I don't," says the Señor. "I can take the ship with me even over dry land."

At that, he caught out from his pocket a little sack of thin gray chamois and I know what he spilled out on the table, because I have seen the contents with my own eyes. There were eleven jewels in that small sack, which one could crush into the palm of a hand, but every one was a selected prize, and I should say that that little treasure was worth at least eleven murders.

Perhaps it had cost that much.

There were two diamonds, very big and of a pure white water; they were cut in an old-fashioned way, but since that style was beginning to come back into fashion, their value was about twice what it would have been five years, say, before that moment. However, these diamonds were the least important of the lot. Four big pigeon-blood rubies, as fine as ever came out of Ceylon, I can remember as if I saw them one by one. I know something about rubies. Two of these were flawed, but the flaws were small, and it was almost a reward to look into the great red hearts of those stones and find some imperfection at the bottom. There was one pearl, too. It was pear-shaped, and big enough to have studded the hilt of the sword of the greatest rajah or shah in the world. I think there was something wrong with it, in color, or some such thing, but pearls are a subject that I never knew much about. The cream of that little collection were four emeralds. Naturally, the finest stones of the lot would be emeralds, considering that they had been all collected in Mexico. Four brothers, all of a bigness, green as eternity and filled with a twilight mystery. I have had them ranged in my hand, side by side, and each of them was a goodly fortune in itself.

As Denny looked down at the flare of those stones, he knew, even without knowledge, that he was looking at wealth, but he cried out:

"Leave them behind you, Patrick. For Heaven's sake, come home with your hands clean and we'll start life over again! Leave the jewels, and El Tigre, and all his miserable works behind you."

The MacMore gripped at the stones, and then pushed them slowly away from him.

"You're right," says he. "A boy leads me," he goes on through his teeth. "But what about Carmel?"

"Not a step with her!" cries Denny. "Oh, Patrick, that would be worse than all the rest!"

The eye of the Señor must have grown cold at that. "And perhaps you'd be willing to try your luck where the Señor failed?" says he.

There was the turning point. He got as pale as could be,

166

watching Denny, who says frankly, as he was always frank:

"I think I love her with all my heart! Why do you care, so long as she doesn't care for you?"

The Señor considered the boy a good deal as if he would like to cut his throat. Then he picked up the gems and thrust them back into the throat of the little gray chamois bag.

"We've talked enough nonsense and sentimentality," he says, as he puts the bag back into his pocket. "The fact of the matter is that I'm not a free agent, and never will be. Perhaps some time in the future El Tigre may let me go away for a vacation, but I know that there never will be a time when he can't overtake me and drag me back here. I'll never be my own man, but always a slave of his. And, therefore, Carmel is a part of my bargain. I want her, I will have her, and that's an end to it!"

"I'll prevent you in some way, if I have to die for it," says Denny.

"You're a child," answers The MacMore, "and I shall have to box you up like a pet coon, or a monkey, and send you out of the country."

"I'll be back again," says Denny, "and I swear I'll let the world know the truth about your career, and your marriage!"

"Sooner or later it would have to come out," says the Señor, now entirely calm and in possession of his self-control. "I only hope that you don't make such a trouble that El Tigre himself will break your back with a stroke of his paw!"

"Heaven forgive me if I am doing wrong," says Denny, "but if you attempt that horrible crime against Carmel Alvarado—"

"Be silent," says the Señor for the second time in that interview. "You're a light-headed child. In five minutes I shall have from you a solemn oath to leave Mexico, never to return here, and never to speak of what you have seen or heard in this San Clemente."

He said the words casually, without grimness, but Denny sneered in his face.

"I see," said Denny. "It's to be Indian tortures—fire, splinters driven under the nails, and all that sort of thing. Why, then, try your tricks, Patrick, and you'll see what it

167

is to be a poor MacMore, and not a poor, contaminated half-breed!"

That was strong talk to utter to the Señor, but Denny spoke the exact words that I have noted down. The Señor waited a moment.

"Are you sure," says he, "that nothing could persuade you to do what I wish?"

"Sure? Nothing under heaven could budge me!" said Denny.

"Very well," said the Señor. "In a moment or so we'll test you."

But here I must go back to that point so long ago—though it had happened on this very same night—when old Enrico Orthez and I, listening and staring at one another, heard the tapping at the door of the house.

"Wait here," he said to me at last. "I'll go down and investigate."

He went down. Just as I heard him sliding the bolt, I was struck from behind by two men who had come in catfooted, on naked feet, through the other door of the room. They slammed me flat on the floor, and by the time my wits were fully come back to me, they had my hands pinioned behind me with some hard-twisted cord, my weapons were gone, and every article, including my watch, was out of my pockets. When you're fanned in Mexico, nothing but the chaff of your possessions remains to you.

The pair who had done this good job were common peons, I saw, as they hustled me up to my feet again. I know I was probably close to my finish, and at that moment it irked me more than the thought of death itself to think that I should have gone down so easily, and at such hands.

They took me down to the street, where I found poor Orthez in the hands of just such another pair; a fifth of the same type stood by, and in command of the party was a tall man dressed in black, with a lean, ugly, long face.

He came up to me and looked me in the eye.

"Yes," said he, "this is Joe Warder."

Then he added in good English: "You led us on a long trail, my friend, but I think this is the end of it for you. However, the Señor will settle that."

I watched Orthez. He seemed entirely unmoved, and in

act, I believe that most Mexicans endure an unavoidable ate better than Americans. They possess a sense of fatalsm that is handy at such moments.

Two carriages stood in the next alley. I was put in one, with my guards beside me, and the man in black sat opposite me, smoking cigarettes, and looking lazily at the faces of the houses, as we jogged along the streets, rocking from one hole to the next.

Then we stopped and were taken into a house, where I remember that a barefooted *mozo* raised a lantern in order to look at my face. I shall never forget his hungry grin as he surveyed me!

After that, we were taken down a flight of damp, slippery stairs—cellar stairs, I suppose—and all seven of us went into a small room, with a single lantern hung on the wall to give us light. When I looked around me, I saw that escape was impossible. The walls were apparently strong —made of great blocks of stone fitted nicely together without the use of cement; our hands were tied; and four men guarded us silently, to say nothing of the leader in black.

There we remained, I suppose, the greater part of an hour. Once during that time a man came to the door and addressed a few muttered words to our chief captor, calling him "el colonel." And finally the same fellow reappeared and said we were to be brought out.

Up the stairs we went again, made another turn in the hall above, and issued out into a garden, where I could hear instantly the subdued voice of the river just beyond. I wondered if they would pass our dead bodies into that water before the morning came, or if they would even bother to dig graves for us.

At any rate, there we were, marched along a winding path and up to the door of a little octagonal summerhouse where the door opened to show us Gualtero, the giant, waiting.

He gave me a special grin, and we went on into another room, where I was not surprised to see the Señor seated at a central table; and where I was not very much surprised, either, to spot Dennis MacMore in a corner of the room.

But poor Denny, when he saw me, gave a wild, choked cry and struck his hands against his face.

"There," said the Señor, "is the price that I'm willing to

pay you. A very lucky thing that El Tigre doesn't know about this, or he would insist on wiping out the three of you. And when El Tigre speaks, I don't dare to intercede even for my own brother. But, as it is, I am willing to trust to your solemn word of honor that you'll leave Mexico and never return, under condition that I let the marshal have his life."

The eyes of Denny were bursting from his head. He was white, and looked drawn and ill. It occurred to me that he would not give the promise, and of course at that time, I could not tell why, so that I felt reasonably worried.

But then Denny said: "And Orthez, too?"

"Orthez is a dead man," replied the Señor. "He has had his chance before, and would not play the game fairly with me. No man gets a second chance with me, as I believe he knows. What, Orthez?"

The blacksmith shrugged. "Have I asked for anything, Señor?" said he.

But Denny was highly excited. "Both or no bargain!" he exclaimed.

"Are you such a fool as to try to bargain with me?" asked the Señor. "I am offering you the man who saved your life. Is that enough? It will have to be."

"Both of them!" cried Denny. "Orthez risked himself with us for the same cause. I won't abandon him now."

He said that in English, but the "colonel," as he had been called, seemed to understand, and he broke in: "Why not, Señor?"

The Señor made a little fierce gesture of abandonment.

"Very well, then," said he. "And now for your promise, Denny?"

The man in black spoke again: "He never will give it, amigo."

5 . . . A Chance to Escape

EVERY DETAIL of this extraordinary scene was printed on my mind before the end. In the first place, it was not a very large room, and I remember feeling that the Señor alone, and his anger, would have been sufficient to fill it. Most of the space upon the walls was taken up by the eight windows, though in addition to these the interals were decorated with weapons, mostly old. There were ld rifles, of the long, heavy-barrelled type that the plainsmen used, which they got from Kentucky, and with which Kentuckians always excelled all other people, I've been old by the old-timers. There were bowie knives, Mexican laggers, machetes, tomahawks, and even a few Indian lubs.

These things one could make out not very distinctly, for here were only two sources of light in the room. One was he shaded lamp on the central table where the Señor sat, with his rage growing, and the other was a holder containing a pair of lighted candles which were on a stand just beind me.

I had been noticing these things, of course, from the intant when I first entered the room, and I had made up my mind that, if the worst came to the worst, I would attempt o move back until my hands were close to the candles, and then use the candle flame to burn through the cords. But I had kept a high hope from the first words that the Señor spoke until this dry interruption from the man in black.

I would not have been so much surprised to hear him, if I had known at that time about his conversation with Denny on the promenade in the Plaza Municipal. But not knowing that, I had the full effect of his peculiar pretense at mind-reading conveyed to me at a stroke.

"He never will give it, amigo," the colonel had said, and the Señor burst out at him in an ungovernable rage:

"To the deuce with you and your prophecies!" he

shouted. "What do you mean by telling my brother what he will do and what he will not do?"

"Ask him again," said the colonel, "and you will understand."

Denny was looking at the man in black as though he were the Old Nick in person risen into the room; and now for the first time I really began to doubt how much Denny would do for me! Well, that was a shock, but it made me decide that I would have to make some step to save my own neck, depending upon no other man.

At that instant, before asking his brother the question which had been dictated to him, the Señor called to the guards to leave the room and wait outside. He kept in the room for the remainder of that scene only his brother Orthez, and me, the colonel in black, and that great mountain of a man, Gualtero. That made six altogether.

The Señor, except for certain moments of excitement when he sprang to his feet, generally remained seated at his central table, and never moved much from it. Gualtero stood behind him like a vast black shadow, set with a pair of eyes as glistening bright as pearls. Orthez was at my left. Denny was almost opposite us, but at such an angle that he could face his terrible brother; and finally, the man in black had removed himself to the farthest and darkest corner of the room, where he became more of a voice than a physical presence among us.

"Now, then," said the Señor to his brother, "will you tell me that you are sufficiently an ingrate to refuse life to the man who saved yours? Can you look at Joe Warder and say that?"

Denny looked at me with a tortured face and did not answer at once. But it was enough for me. Already I had been moving back, and now with a slight backward thrust of my hands, I was able to put the cord that tied my arms together in the flame of the nearest candle. I say that I put the cord in the flame, but, as a matter of fact, I put my own flesh in the fire, and scalded my wrist badly. I had to endure that without flinching or moving a muscle of my face, while I shifted my wrists to the side a little and hoped that the flame would strike the rope.

If you want to understand just how difficult a predicament I was in, try to work out the same thing with your hands tied fairly close together, and your back to the

172

ame that you are trying to hit. Then I was in terror lest
ome one should notice the diminution of light that came
t once, when the flame was involved with the cord. After
hat a rank smoke twisted up over my shoulder and almost
et me coughing, while I wondered whether I had set fire
o the rope or to my own clothes.

Denny, after staring at me for a moment, said:

"Somehow I think that I can stop that marriage if I
tick to the job. And Heaven forgive me if I wonder which
s my duty—to keep Joe Warder alive, or to save Carmel
rom such a ghastly misery. Joe, what shall I say?"

Of course, I knew nothing about Carmel Alvarado—
othing at all, and it merely seemed to me that Denny was
etting me down flat. I answered up brusquely that I would
ake care of my own life, that I never had owed it to an-
ther man before this, and that I didn't wish to commence
ow.

"More sentimentality," said the Señor, fixing his cat's
yes on me with a horrible fixity. "I can count on rational
uman beings, but I can't count on soft-headed idiots like
he pair of you! Do you understand me, Denny? Joe
Warder goes out here this moment to be shot, unless you
ntercede for him, and you know the price of the interces-
ion!"

"I'd like to ask one thing," says Denny, fighting for time
o think. "Who is the man in black, and why did you post
im on the promenade to warn me?"

"I did not post him there. Were you on the promenade,
Arturo?"

"I was," says Arturo, "until just before the romantic
meeting, and I took the chance to tell your brother a little
bout his future—and his past!"

"Instead of seizing him for me!" exclaimed the Señor, in
a great swelling fury.

"I haven't your power in the hands, Patrick," said the
man in black, entirely unmoved. "The result was that I
ould not take him for you without killing him; and I
new you didn't want that."

"Bah!" says the Señor. "Now, Denny, will you speak up
and tell me what you are going to do?"

That instant my hands were free. I shifted back a little
urther away from the candles and rubbed the glowing
ends of the cords—burning like fuses now—against the

173

wall, to put them out. At the same time, I looked from the corner of my eye at the weapons immediately behind me and the first thing I saw was a machete.

"Give me ten seconds!" said Denny.

"Ten seconds, then, and no more," said the Señor.

"There is something burning!" broke in the voice of the man in black.

"I wish it were you!" exclaimed the Señor savagely "You've put the idea of refusal into the head of this young fool."

He looked about him with one wild glance, at the same time, but he did not see the smoke, it appeared, and perhaps the smell of the burning had not yet reached him. At any rate, he did not stir to examine into the cause of the smudge which was still rank in my own nostrils.

I now was sneaking back my left hand and got the machete by the hilt, moving just enough to the side to place me close to Orthez and conceal the work of my hand with my body. I worked the machete off the hook that supported it, and then turned the blade, running the edge of it blindly down the arm of Orthez and feeling for the cord.

I wondered if I would slash the arteries of his wrist when I made the cut.

"The time is up!" said the Señor, and at that moment I jerked the edge of the blade down—the elbows of Orthez sagged wider, and I knew that I had made the right stroke! For the first time real hope rushed up in my heart.

"I've got to do it," says Denny with a groan. "No matter if she's an angel from heaven, I owe too much to Joe!"

That wall-eyed giant, Gualtero, yelled now in a thin, squeaking voice—because the natural roar was surprised and scared out of him: "Señor! Guard, guard! They have free hands!"

Free hands, aye, and something in them!

I had hoped that old Orthez would lift his own weight, but he lifted a good deal more. That fellow was a wild cat, and if he was past his athletic prime, the fine chance he had here of getting a whack at the Señor was oil to his joints and strength to his muscles. He took off the wall behind him the nearest thing his hand fell on—an old-fashioned Indian club with a couple of the original spikes still sticking out on it.

He did that as Gualtero yelled, and the next instant
174

Orthez had stooped forward and hurled that club over his shoulder as hard as though it were shot out of a gun. That thrown club did more mischief than you could imagine. In the first place, and most important of all, it went straight at the Señor, whose gun was coming into his hand as fast as the flick of a snake's tail. The Señor had to give half of his attention to dodging that club, which was the reason that he didn't sink a bullet into one of us, at least—and I don't think I'm too vain when I say that he would have put that shot into me.

But the big club went with terrific force, not whirling end over end, but true and straight. The Señor, as he pulled his gun, dodged the danger to the left. And huge Gualtero, with a knife already out, but no brighter than the flash of his grinning teeth, was ducking to the right and bellowing a call to the guards for help at the same time. There was no chance of the missile hitting either the Señor or Gualtero, and either one of them would have been enough to handle the three of us, I suppose. Instead, the club struck fair in the middle of the big blue porcelain bowl of the lamp. That lamp dissolved into a shower of powdered and splintered porcelain; shattered fine, chimney glass, and a stinging, blinding spray of the hot oil.

That spray struck into the faces of the Señor and the terrible Gualtero, and must have covered them with a double night, and left them blindly groping. There was still the light of a candle, the flame leaping and dwindling, and giving a doubly wild look to everything. But I was through with the picturesque effects in that room. I wanted to get into the dark of the night as badly as any small boy ever wanted to dive into the green cool of the swimming pool on an August day.

And dive I did. The machete I had picked off the wall had done its job in freeing Orthez, but I did not want to be encumbered by that great knife; I simply wanted the best speed I could get out of my legs. I dropped the machete and went through that window headfirst, rolled to my feet as I landed, and looked back in time to see young Mac-More scrambling up behind me.

I saw more than that, and the wildest picture that these eyes of mine ever rested upon, I think, was the sight of old Orthez, who had plunged straight on at the Señor, quite gone mad.

Gualtero had enough eyesight left to see the danger
What had become of the knife he once was armed with,
don't know, but he met the rush of the old man with hi
bare hands and a horrible yell in his throat. Well, I sav
the impact as those two met, and if I had had a gun,
think I would have been crazy enough to turn around and
go back into that room to help old Orthez.

But already it was too late for that, because I think on
grip of Gualtero's hands must have crushed the life out o
Orthez. It was too late, for another reason. The shoutin
and the uproar in general had brought every man on th
place toward the summerhouse with a rush. They came ir
regularly from all directions, with the dreadful roaring o
Gualtero still urging them on.

And that caused a strange thing. Or perhaps it was no
so strange, considering the dark of the night—the moo
being in such a position that all was now a dark shadow o
trees where the summerhouse stood. At any rate, those res
cuers, and soldiers, and good servants were in such fran
tic haste to get to the very spot where the voice of Gual
tero was roaring that they poured straight past the two o
us, blinded by their own excitement, and so we had ou
chance to escape.

36 . . . Hunted

I RAN as fast as I could leg it toward the river, bu
fast as I ran, young MacMore beat me out, and I hear
him making a little moaning sound of effort and fear as he
drew even and went past me. He could run, and that wa
the only thing he could do. He was a rabbit among men a
you might say.

When I got to the edge of the river, I hesitated for ar
instant at the side of Denny, before I set him the exampl
of heaving myself over the wall and diving into the stream
But just as I balanced on the verge of the wall I heard a
quiet, unhurried voice near by saying to me:

"You'll ram your head into a mud bank and break you

neck, if you do that. You have time to go down the steps to the boat which is tied at the landing."

It was the voice of the man in black, though how he could have got there before us I don't know, unless, unnoticed by me, he had slipped out of the summerhouse just before the crash came. What did he mean, furthermore, by giving us the hint on how to manage our escape?

Well, you can be sure of one thing, which is that though those questions occupy me now, they did not amount to a whit at the moment. All I knew was that I had received good advice, and I rushed to act on it, without stopping to pay for it even with thanks.

There was one thing that I doubted enormously, and that was that we would have time to go down that interminably long stairs to the river, and loose the boat, and push out into the current before we were overwhelmed with enemies, because well before this all the elements which had drawn in toward the summerhouse, attracted by the calling of Gualtero, had exploded outward again, driven by the frantic wrath of the Señor.

There was only one voice raised now, and everything else was utter silence, except for the stamping of heavily running feet. That one voice was from the Señor. He seemed to be standing on a high place, and the words rang easily and distinctly in our ears as we scurried down the long steps toward the boat which was tied below.

I heard him directing men to get to the river and get to the street, and to block each garden wall. And I heard him, distinctly, offer ten thousand pesos for either of us, alive or dead.

For either of us! For his own brother's head!

It made me feel faint and dizzy, and I dared not so much as look at poor Denny.

We got to that boat and found that the painter was tied in a hard knot—and there were two of us without a knife between us! I ground my teeth until the edges of them got hot, and pushed Denny out of the way so hard that he almost toppled into the river; then I fell to work on that knot.

I worked until the sounds of running in the garden came out onto the edge of river wall. Then I heard the voice of the man in black—Arturo, the Señor had called him—speaking to the searchers, and saying with its usual calm:

"You ought to go down the steps and look into the boat. They might have tried that way out."

The next instant I could hear the slipping of bare feet on the wet river stairs and, looking up, I saw them come in a strange, hopping procession against the stairs. And there we sat, helplessly cowering in the boat, tugging at the twisted knot of a painter!

That instant the knot gave, and immediately I felt the skiff lurch away as Denny leaned on the oars. I must say that on this occasion he was ready-handed in doing the right thing. He did not back her into the current, either, where she would have been instantly visible, but slid her down along the wall, where the steep shadow, contrasted with the brightness of the moon upon the river, covered us with a cloak.

We must have gone two boat lengths when the hunters reached the water's edge.

"There's no boat here," I heard one of them say.

Then another broke out sharp and quick: "There! There! Who goes there?"

I said in my most colloquial Mexican: "Bad luck and small fish goes here, friends. All the cursed fish have gone down to the sea and left nothing for San Clemente and Friday!"

"That's a fisherman," said one of the hunters.

I had stepped on Denny's foot and got him to rest on his oars when we were hailed, and now we were drifting slowly along in the little eddy that worked next to the retaining wall. Every moment was bringing us to a greater hope of safety, when the mischief possessed that young fool of a Denny.

You'll not believe it, but what he did was to show how nonchalant and perfectly at ease we were by singing a song—a Mexican song, of course—and "La Paloma" was his selection.

It took ready wit, courage, presence of mind, to sing under such circumstances, and to bring out his voice roundly and deeply, so that it boomed up along the echoing wall; but before I had a chance to grind my heel into his foot, and before he had got out the second word in his execrable imitation of Mexican as it is spoken, I heard a shout from one of the man hunters: "The gringos!"

They had made sure by the first word poor Denny sang

hat he was an outlander, and with ten thousand dollars a head laid on us, those hunters were not going to pick and choose and make sure of their men too fastidiously. They cut loose with a shotgun and two revolvers, point-blank!

Denny had thrust in the oars the instant the Mexican shouted. We had made a little distance in the meantime, and I suppose the excitement of the moment upset the aim of our enemies.

I yelled to Denny: "Down! Down into the bottom of the boat!" And I set him that example.

He remained where he was, sitting perfectly erect, laboring furiously at the oars. "I got you into this, and I'll get you out or die trying," says he.

And with that, we shot around a curve sufficiently great to cut off the shots of those jabbering, praying, cursing man hunters; the current, heading in toward the shore, caught us here like a helping hand, and we bowled off down the river in great shape. I was muttering at Denny:

"Are you hurt, kid? Did they snag you anywhere?"

"Of course they didn't," said Denny. "I'm a lucky man, tonight, and nothing bad can happen to me!"

He said it mighty bitterly, but I didn't press the point, because I knew that the heart of Denny was as cold as ice. He could not have helped hearing the voice of the Señor offering that price for his brother's head! Perhaps he sat up so erect in that boat because he really didn't care whether he lived or died.

He rowed well, with a good swing that shoved us along faster than I could have made the boat travel. He had learned something about oarsmanship in college. But I knew that we would have to take to the shore before long, for in some way or other the Señor soon would have the San Clemente alive with craft hunting for us.

I told Denny this, and he agreed at once.

"Besides," says he, "I've picked out the place for us to go."

"You have?"

"I have the very one," says Denny.

"Heaven bless you, then!" said I. "Head for it, lad. We need cover as badly as any two poor coyotes that ever were run with horses and dogs."

The current was taking us, and the oars as well, and

now Denny backed water hard, and then shipped his oar as we came to a landing.

"This is the place," said he.

"The place for what?" I asked him.

"The place we land."

"But they have these gardens guarded, Denny," I told him, and it was a fact I had learned long before.

"We'll be all right here," said Denny, "And there's nothing half so good for us to do as to land here."

I took his advice. I had not followed all his adventures since he left the house of poor Orthez, and I took it for granted that he had learned something which would be useful.

We let the boat go down the stream and we started up the stairs until the sound of a man clearing his throat just above us, made me stop. I turned to Denny, to know whether it was safe for us to go on, in spite of the fact that we soon might be seen; but he laid a frantic clutch on me, and by that I silently guessed that no matter what power he had in this place, it did not extend to the man above us in the dark.

I was uncomfortable at once, and a little more uncomfortable still when I saw a power boat come whirring down the current with a strong light whipping the shore. It came fast, traveling with the stream, and presently it struck its blinding white hand straight across our faces.

I waited, frozen, breathless.

Either the people in the boat, or the two men above us—for I had just heard another speak—were sure to see us, I argued, but I was wrong. I waited for the searchlight to sweep back at us like a saber stroke and fix us against the wall for a little further examination, at least. But they must have thought, on the boat, that we were guards at this house, and not fugitives so calmly standing there. At any rate, they went on, and left me softly thanking our luck.

The men above us? I suppose they were looking out to the water and the searching boat, not down toward us.

I heard one of them say presently: "I told you so!"

"You told me what?" says the other.

"That it was the Señor."

"Hush!"

"Ah, don't be such a coward. I can't be heard, here!"

180

"You can be. Anywhere! He has ears in the ground!"

"Then I stamp on his ear, curse him, and curse him again! The tyrant and monster! Bah! May he die in a slow fire!"

"I wish so, too," says the other. "But I wish you'd stop this sort of talk at once."

"Who have they been butchering at their slaughter-house up the river?" says the one who was so hot against the Señor·

"It must have come from his house, the firing."

"Of course it did, and some one has slipped through his fingers. I remember the time that the poor Greek got away from the house of the Señor and ran into the market place and begged protection from the police and the people. But the man in black came all alone and took him away, while he screamed and begged, and shrieked. That man was a coward, but I pitied him."

"We'd better take a turn around the side walls. Their hunted man may be coming this way!"

37 ... Romeo and a Cynic

"Now!" said the boy, and going past me, he led the way straight up the steps to where there was an iron gate closed, with spikes at the top. We helped one another over this, while I still wondered how Denny could know this place, and what would come of his knowledge of it.

But, of course, there was no time to ask.

We were in a big moonlit garden, much more formal and trim than that of the Señor, and we skulked through it slowly, from one shelter to the next. While we made that journey, I got out of the boy what had happened to him and what he had done. But only in phrases. He explained and dilated on nothing, but gave me back a few whispered words.

I remember that we had crouched at the side of some tall, flowering grass that looked like a species of bamboo, and we had a brief bit of dialogue which ran something like this:

"What house is it, Denny?"

"The Alvarado house."

"What? Where the Señor's lady lives?"

"Yes, that's why we're here."

"Are you crazy, Denny?"

"No, we're going to take her away to-night."

"Denny, tell me that you're serious, and not making a joke of me."

"She doesn't want to marry him. She has to if she stays here. So we're going to get her away."

He said that, and without waiting for an answer he led the way on through the garden.

Mind you, at that time I had not so much as laid eyes on the beauty, but for some reason I was not able to protest, for the quiet resolution of the boy broke down my resistance, amazed and controlled my mind. I went along with him, my wits stumbling, my head in a whirl, but unable to take a step against his wishes.

We crossed right through that hedge which surrounded the Pool of the Three Graces, where he had been caught. But the recollections of Denny made him pause here for a moment and look around with a sigh that was not all sorrow. I told him I hoped that he was enjoying the view, and reminded him that there were at least two guards at present in that garden who would ask nothing better than a chance to take pot shots at us, or run their knives into our hearts.

He gave me a glance, half smiling and half sad.

"Oh, Joe," says he, "I think we're going to win."

"We'll win a quick death," I told him, "and never a chance to enjoy that home in a crazy house which we certainly have earned."

I could not upset or depress him, however. He went on through the hedge on the other side of the pool—and was now in such a wild state of mind that he started walking openly down a path, with the gravel of it crunching loudly under his shoes. My own stockinged feet made noise enough on the small grinding stones, but I yanked Denny off the path and onto the lawns again, then knocked his knees from under him and got him down on the ground behind an open hedge of roses just as the two guards came promenading through.

They stopped not five steps from us and looked around.

I want to say that that moon was stronger, it seemed to me, than any sun; and when I call the hedge open, I'd have you understand a mere skeleton of young rose shoots, behind which we two lay flat, hardly breathing.

"I heard something," says one.

"Maybe you heard the two gringos," said the other, "the ones that the Señor will pay for." He chuckled a little.

"Curse him!" answered his companion. "I thought I heard steps—"

He turned from the path and made a stride or two in our direction. I looked him fair in the face, and in the face, too, of the riot gun he carried under the crook of his arm.

That fellow was keen as a whip. He had the look of a hunter in his lean face, and he turned his head slowly, like one whose eyes are noting down everything that falls under them.

My arm and leg muscles were beginning to tremble—I was that close to jumping up and running for it, in spite of the riot gun, when he turned away as abruptly as he had started, and went off down the path with his friend. A fine sight their backs were, in my estimation, and as good as any sunset, or other fancy picture, that you ever saw.

Denny and I crawled back into the brush, and there he headed on toward the house. I merely said: "You haven't had enough?"

"That was only a proof of the luck that's with us!"

I felt that I was hitched to a comet which was sure to ruin me, but I would not let go of it, though to this moment I cannot understand why. I had been so long accepted as absolute leader by Dennis MacMore that this sudden flash of decisiveness on his part left me helpless, it appeared.

We went on until we were close under a side of the house, and Dennis stopped beneath a big tree and stared up at an open window.

Before I could stop him, he cupped his hands at his lips and uttered a long droning note, vaguely like the hoot of an owl. It might have fooled the ear of a child of five who had only heard the bird once, but never a grown man.

183

I gripped him by the shoulders and shook him until his head bobbed.

"Dennis, are you mad?" I whispered. "Are you going to sing a serenade?"

But in a moment a white form glimmered in the dark square of the window.

Dennis stepped straight out into the blaze of the moonlight, and so suddenly that I could not stop him, only blundering after to the edge of the shade.

I heard a girl's voice, cautiously controlled, and trembling with excitement, call down to him and ask him what he had learned.

"I've seen him and done everything words can do," said Dennis. "He won't listen. He'll have you or die for it. He's put a price on me dead or alive because I interfered. Carmel, you are going away from San Clemente. I won't leave you here for such a marriage."

"You'll be heard, you'll be seen, Dennis!" says she and leans out from the window far enough for me to see her face.

All question about what we should try to do for her stopped in me at that moment. Somehow, when I looked up at her, I felt my broken nose and my ugly face as keenly as though I had glanced into a mirror. And staring from her to handsome young Dennis, I knew that some powerful pull was drawing them together. He had walked closer, his face raised to her, and he spoke with one hand lifted.

"I'll stay here till you come down to me," says Dennis. "I'll stay here and talk loudly enough to raise the house. Carmel, Carmel, you haven't the right to throw yourself away. Heaven made you for a beautiful life. With him you'll be in misery."

"We never could get out of San Clemente," says she. "Go away, Dennis. You're tearing my heart with fear for you!"

"I'll never go till you come down, or until they drag me away," says he. "Carmel, will you believe me?"

"What shall I do?" says she, leaning against the side of the window with a hand pressed against her throat and her head fallen back.

"Try for your freedom, if you have to die for it!" answers that young madman.

"Who is with you?"

"Warder. The best friend Heaven ever gave to a man. Carmel, why do you hesitate? Are you afraid to trust us?"

"No. But we'll fail. And the Señor will—"

"We've beaten him before. We will again. Is it love of servants and a big house and money that's keeping you here, Carmel?"

I heard her sob in an agony of indecision; then she made a gesture and disappeared.

Young MacMore came back to me with a stumbling step. He was like a man overcome with liquor.

"Now will you get out and give up this idea?" I asked him. "You can't persuade her—or are you going to sing a song to call her back?"

"She's coming down," said Denny to me.

"Coming down? You mean, she's actually coming down to try to leave San Clemente with us?"

"With us—yes, yes! Oh, Joe, I'm sick with happiness. I feel almost as though Heaven had brought me here, leading me by the hand, so that I could do this, and save her! She'll be here," he went on, mumbling and whispering to himself. "She'll be here in a moment—Carmel. You'll see her, Joe. You'll touch her hand."

"I won't," said I. "I'm off now to save myself, if ever I can get out of the man trap that you've led me into! Goodby."

I held out my hand, but Denny laughed silently in the shadow of the tree and would not take it.

"You won't go, Joe," said he. "You could no more turn me down and leave me in the lurch than you could take wings and fly. Why, man, d'you think I'm afraid that you'll desert me? It's for her, Joe!"

"Confound her," I answered. "She's flesh and blood like every other woman. And if they find us here with her—which they surely will—they won't merely kill us, they'll burn us inch by inch. I'd rather drink a glassful of poison than take a fool chance like this."

"Talk along—talk yourself out," says young MacMore. "I like to hear you. Good old Joe! You've carried the burden of me for so long, that you couldn't shrug me off your shoulders now!"

He still laughed, and dropped a hand on my shoulder, while I stood fascinated, frightened to death, resolute to

185

leave at once, but with a slight ache in my heart that kept me there.

And Denny did not try to persuade me. He merely stood there with his hand lightly on my shoulder and waved his other hand toward the house.

"Do you see that climbing vine?" says he.

"Dang the climbing vine!"

"Don't say that. Is it honeysuckle? Let me tell you, Joe, that when I look up that vine and breathe the fragrance of it, I know that the perfume will last the rest of my life."

"It's pretty apt to," I told him bitterly, "because we'll both be stiff before we're out of the garden, probably."

"Who cares about death?" says this young madman. "Who cares about death? It's the way we come to it that matters, and to go to it with Carmel at his side is the finest death that a man could find, if he went out hunting and asking the proper way!"

Then I saw it. I had been blind, of course, not to have guessed when I saw him talking to her beneath the window. I got him by the shoulders and jammed him back against the tree trunk.

"You dunderhead, you thick wit, you flabby calf!" said I to him. "You're in love!"

38 . . . All Aboard

WHAT A BLIND MAN I was not to have perceived it long before, by something new in his voice when he so much as mentioned her name! And now he merely laughed happily, drunkenly, at me as I accused him. As if we did not have enough trouble already on our hands without adding a sentimental mess like this!

Well, I had barely turned back from Denny in despair, when around the corner of the house comes hurrying, and pausing, and hurrying again, San Clemente's famous beauty; but she only looked to me like a small child that needed a good deal of fathering and mothering from the world and would have to get it, now, from a jailbird and cow-puncher and gunman like me on the one side, or on the other side from a moon-brained youngster such as Dennis MacMore.

She came up to the edge of the shadow of the tree and stopped there, while I waited for Dennis to go out and greet her, but he could not move. Even in the shadow of the tree, I could see how violently he was trembling there with his head thrown back a little, and his lips parted, and the look of a drowning man about him.

So I went to Carmelita myself.

She was the bright star, the proud beauty, and all that, but just at this moment, I can assure you that she was simply a terribly frightened and uneasy girl. If you'd had a picture of her, you would have said that she was standing in the rain, and not in the moonlight.

"I'm Joe Warder," I told her. "And if you really want to get away from your house, I'm bound to say that we'll give you all the chance that we can."

I knew beforehand that she did want to make the try, because she had jumped into riding clothes before she came downstairs. I wondered a good deal about her, too, as you can imagine, because there she was out of her room at midnight and talking alone with one man she had never seen before, and a second man whom she'd met for the first time earlier that evening.

She answered me with a worried, frightened murmur that meant nothing, and then her eyes went past me toward Denny, and I knew what had happened, and why she was there. I had to draw her in under the dark of the tree, or otherwise, I suppose she would have stood there minutes, just like Dennis, struck with ague.

To rescue myself from San Clemente would be hard enough, to help two others made it ten times harder, and burden myself down with two momentarily mad persons —how could I do that and call myself an intelligent human being? Yet as I looked from one of them to the other and heard their foolishly casual words as they met, and listened to the tremor in their voices, I knew that Denny, after all, had been divinely right in risking everything to get her. I knew why the Señor, after all, was willing to take her with or against her will. If I had been a tyrant, I think I might have wanted to try the same thing.

For, as the colonel said to Denny, she shone by her own light.

Then we were standing all together, whispering, trying to make our plans, but La Carmelita had the only good sense. While I was fumbling at ways of getting horses and dashing out of the town, or else of stealing along on foot, Carmel said quietly: "There's only one thing that will carry us away from San Clemente. That's the river, I think."

She was right. I could see that, after she had pointed the way, and I was willing to march along the path she selected. Certainly the stream would be guarded, up current or down, but so would all the other exits be. And the water might carry us smoothly off.

We started for the river at once, with the girl leading anl young MacMore beside her, while I kept a few steps back, feeling a good deal like the pilot of a ship. These two, mind you, had not said a word to one another about love, but now as they started out together on this high adventure, I saw them turn toward one another for one glance in the bright moonlight, both of them bare-headed, so that they seemed crowned with light, she smiling up to him, and he smiling down to her, so that it was as though she had stepped into his arms.

But still no word was said between them, and they went on as fearless as flame toward the water.

We had to wait several long, long minutes crouched in the brush near the river wall, for the two guards were back there, leaning over the water and muttering to one another; until we heard footsteps come up the stone stairway that ran down the bank, and a man appeared from the river to say that he came with a message from the Señor, begging all the people along the river to keep a good lookout, because probably two great criminals, gringos, were in hiding somewhere along the way. There was an offer of ten thousand pesos for the head of either man. And, furthermore, the affection and trust of the Señor would be specially lodged in all who helped him in this search. Particularly he hoped that the good house of Alvarado would be a fortress to him.

One of the guards said, naturally enough: "Wherever else they are, they haven't come here. We've had our eyes open, I tell you. And there's enough shot in this gun to blow both the scoundrels to pieces."

Says the other watchman: "Come in and have a glass of wine. It's as sour and bitter as green lemons, but still it makes a warmth inside you."

The messenger said he was worn out from pulling up against the current on this side of the water, and he went in gladly with them.

"That means there is a boat at the bottom of the stairs," said the girl.

Furthermore, the river gate had been left open at the head of the stairs when the messenger came through, so the three of us trooped and scampered down to the bottom of the stairs.

There was a long, narrow, little boat, built like a canoe very nearly. I took the oars; the girl and young MacMore crouched in the bottom of the craft; and we struck off up the current with such a strength of joy in my heart, for one, that I felt as though the air I breathed were new air, and the strength would never go out of my arms. There was a good wind behind us, which neutralized the run of the current to some extent, and there were two or three little blunt-bowed sloops standing up the river, bringing vegetables to the market of San Clemente. Their sails flashed under the moon, and before I had rowed fifty strokes, I began to wish that we had a rag of one of those sails to help us along.

Why not go downstream?

For the good reason that that would most surely be the direction in which the Señor would expect us to flee, whereas upstream he would be likely to maintain a far less strict guard.

After a few minutes, the boy relieved me at the oars. He did not swing himself as fiercely into the labor, but he was so much more crafty that he was able to push us rapidly along through the water. I crouched down in the bottom, because we felt it was well to show only one person in the boat, and I watched Denny swinging back and forth, with a brightening of his face as he lurched forward and looked at the girl, then the slower strain backwards, his face tilting a bit toward the sky.

Each of us, I think, felt the same wild joy as we put out our hands to take liberty; but none of us spoke a word while we pushed up the river. Every detail of that scene is burned into my mind, and particularly how we passed up under the end of the bridge, while voices laughed and pealed above us as though we had been seen and now were mocked at; and a heavy cart rumbled like thunder down over the wooden planking and sent squirts of dust down at us through the boards.

I was at the oars again when we pulled out on the farther side. The great *sabinas* threw enormous shadows, now, that stretched halfway across the stream, and keeping fairly close to the left-hand shore, I felt that we were reasonably safe for the time being.

So we watched the lights close on our left pulse past us with the strokes of the oars, and the roof lines of the houses on the farther side walk slowly past us. Nothing was going downstream, at this time, but the three cargo craft of which I was speaking continued upstream, two of them faintly winking in the distance and one of them drawing very near to us until we could hear the crunching and bumping of her bows against the ripples of the current; we could hear the strain of her cordage, too; and the groan of the mast in its stepping as the wind freshened and heeled the sloop over. There was a crew of two, one man at the tiller barking orders in a harsh voice, from time to time, and a boy working forward at the ropes, heaving and hauling and never speaking a word.

Well, as I saw that old creaking merchantman come laboring up the stream it looked to me the sweetest sight and the prettiest flight that I ever had seen. No buzzard on the wing ever seemed as graceful to me as that scow did by the light of my aching arms and shoulders.

I lost one stroke to lean and say to Denny: "We're going to board that craft!"

"We have no weapons, man!" exclaimed Denny.

"We have an oar apiece," said I. "You take the boy forward, and I'll tackle the man aft."

He agreed to that without much arguing, for he could see that even leaving the labor of rowing upstream out of the picture, we had an infinitely better chance of getting through the guards in this boat than we would have if we had to keep on by ourselves. As for the girl, she simply raised her head until the moon flashed once on her face, but then she abandoned the idea which she was about to speak and sank back again into the shadow.

Now I put the nose of the boat over into the deeper water, where the current laid hold of her like a hand.

"Sheer off!" roars the voice of the steersman in the sloop. "Sheer off, or I'll run you down, by San Clemente!"

I had picked out a Tartar, it seemed, and when I glanced astern at him, I saw that he had a pair of shoulders like a Hercules and a great bull-throat left open down to his hairy chest.

"I'll swing her nose right into him," I said in a low voice to Denny, who was now crouched at my feet. "You—Carmelita—"

I was brusque enough; but she answers as cheerfully as you please that she will do what she can.

"Catch onto a trailing rope, or the bulwark of the sloop, if that's not too high, and scramble on board after the two of us have cleared up the deck. But if we lose—then drift back down the current with this boat! You'll come to less harm in that way."

She nodded. Like a good soldier she raised no objections and she asked no questions at the moment of battle. So we turned straight in at that scow and in another instant we thumped against the side of it so hard that we almost capsized on the spot.

"You donkeys! You long-headed burros!" yelled the boatman at the stern. "I told you I'd run you down, and there you go!"

But we already had stepped over the low bulwark, and I had turned from him aft, on the run, while MacMore went forward after the boy.

39 ... The Señor Hails

THERE were about five steps from where I boarded the sloop amidships to where the steersman stood at the tiller, but in between was the most cluttered-up deck I ever saw, for there were great baskets of cabbages, and big-

191

ger ones of onions piled up, and a bed of cabbages never made a good running track. I sort of fell aft, while the skipper bellowed: "River pirates! We'll send them below, Tony! Never fear!"

Fight? That fellow loved a fight. There was real joy in his face as he let that tiller go and lurched forward to meet me, looking bigger and wilder the nearer he got to me. He did not yell to the shore for help, though his bull's voice might readily have carried that far, but he simply came driving to get into the fun.

I made a pass with the edge of the oar, intending to punch him in the face, but he put that stroke aside as if it had been nothing and got out, at the same time, the revolver he had been tugging at as he came in at me. I told myself I was gone, but jumping over a crate, I started for the head of the skipper the hardest punch I ever used on a human being. It had every ounce of strength in my body from heel to the wrist; it had all my affection for Denny, and my admiration for his beautiful lady; it had my fear of the Señor, and my horror of the shadowy thing, El Tigre. All of that poundage of flesh and emotion was hurled forward in that blow, though it was a quarter of a second late, I saw. For the skipper had his revolver out and almost jammed into my face as he pulled the trigger.

It did not need any great imagination for me to taste powder and lead and feel the bullet crash through my set teeth and out the back of my head. Instead, there was merely a hollow click as the hammer hit on the cartridge without exploding it. A hundredth part of a second later, the punch I had started with such hope landed on the skipper.

It hit him fairly. My power was my own good will and muscle; the accuracy was a matter of luck, but the luck panned out and that punch landed squarely alongside the jaw of the big Mexican on the spot which is called the button. The sound of it was like a clapping of hands together, or the fall of a plank; and the shock of it gave me a pain in the funny bone and turned my right arm numb and tingling to the shoulder.

I expected to see the big fellow fall—no matter what his size—but it was exactly as though he had been standing braced with a post at his back. The ship, unguided at the tiller, had payed off the wind and now was whirling in the current, while the boom passed with a groan and a swish just over our heads; and I felt that my own brain had given way, as I watched that greaser stand there. He simply grinned at me, and he kept his arms hanging at his side. It was the most horrible thing that ever happened to me to see him stand there, mocking me, inviting me to hit again and break my hand if I chose, but without anything for him to fear in the blow.

Well, cast-iron man or not, I determined to keep on attacking as long as I could. My right arm was about useless, but I poked feebly at him with my left and shoved the blow home against his huge barrel of a chest.

And the man of iron crumbled like a figure made of sand!

That first blow had stunned him, all right, and the last touch finished him, even though he could keep his feet for a second after the blow. I've seen it happen in the ring, for instance.

Now he lay spilled on his back on the deck, looking up at me with the same grin of mockery, though his eyes were a trifle empty.

I looked forward. There by the mast stood Carmel Alvarado with the half of a broken oar in her hands, while MacMore struggled up to his feet, and another figure lay twisted on the deck. Down the stream, already far behind us, slid the abandoned boat with the current.

I ran foward to see what had happened, and as I came up I saw that the head of the fallen boy was slashed across with crimson. Carmel looked sick and white, as though she were about to faint.

"Have I killed him? Have I killed him?" says she. "Oh, José, have I killed him?"

"José" meant me, of course.

She had not killed him. She had merely broken his head for him, and a mighty good thing that she had. Because almost as a matter of course Denny had gone down. He had attacked as bravely as any hero, as headlong and fierce as you please for life, liberty, and his lady love; but all of that desperation did not do him much good when his first punch missed and he found himself in a pair of arms that crushed him as though he had been a girl. A second later he was on his back and over him the moon slid a silver finger down the blade of a knife which the Mexican boy steadied for a mere instant before driving into the hollow of Denny's throat.

In that instant of balance and pause, as you might say, Carmelita arrived with the stub of the oar which Denny had broken as he boarded. She had intended to follow my directions, but when she saw Denny actually going over the side and into the battle, her heart was too much for her. It drew her after her lover and brought her up just in time to save her knight and whang the victor over the head with the oar handle.

In five seconds we were masters of that little craft, and Denny went to the tiller. He knew not only something about rowing, but he had sailed a bit, too, and under his directions, we righted the ship on her course, helped by a good stiff hand of wind that was shoving brisker and brisker up the stream.

I handled ropes and ducked the swinging boom, while Carmelita was busy saving her "dead man." A twist of rag around his head really was all that he needed, because he was a son of the skipper and as tough as his father, who now sat up and rubbed his jaw, blinking at us all.

I had his revolver working, by that time. A bit of cloth had wedged in beside the hammer, and that was why it had failed to go off. I shoved this gun under the nose of the poor skipper and told him exactly what was happening.

"We are running away from the Señor," said I. "We're going to tie your hands so that you can't bother us, and we're going to gag you if we have to, but we'll do no harm either to you or to your boy, yonder. And we won't touch your cargo, either. Lie still and take this quietly, and when we leave you, we'll give you enough money to make you wish to get hit on the jaw every night of your life."

When I ended that little speech, I saw that his small eyes were opening and opening, and growing brighter and brighter.

"You are Señor Warder!" he says suddenly.

I was sorry that he knew my name, because it was undoubted that he also knew he would get ten thousand for my head if he could betray me to the police, but he only answered himself, saying: "Then how is it that I am still alive? Señor, you chose to strike me with your hand instead of a bullet. Your hand is almost like a bullet, for I felt it pass through my brain and knock sparks out of my spinal column. However, I am still alive, and for that I thank you and Heaven!"

We tied the skipper and his son, as we had agreed; but they swore by everything holy that they would make no outcry to betray us, and, in fact, they were so entirely in our hands that I hardly feared anything from them. They sat on the deck and talked to us as cheerfully as you please until the boy began to notice La Carmelita and opened his mouth like a fish, with a fish's great eyes.

"Padre mio, padre mio!" says he. *"Es La Carmelita! La Señorita Alvarado!"*

I knew in an instant that the pair of them had seen her before—probably during that every-night performance of the promenade. But the moment that they knew she was with us, they fell as silent as stones, and looked at one another, or over the bulwark into the run of the water.

It showed that they were a decent pair, that they should have taken it so much to heart—the stealing of San Clemente's beauty by a pair of gringos, I mean.

Young MacMore called me to the tiller and advised me to gag them both at once, and I considered it. However, I decided not to. They had given me their solemn words of honor, and they looked like the stuff that honest men are made of.

In that I made a great mistake, and it was one more lesson to prove that mighty few men are worthy of being really trusted.

We were past the wall of San Clemente, now, on each side of the river, and we saw the last trouble that we probably would meet. Over at a landing on the right bank there was a little stern-wheeler tied up, with steam up, and a dozen or twenty men aboard her, all armed to the teeth—I could see the winking of the moon on the guns. In the meantime, a boat slid out from the shore and came rapidly across the current down toward us, with four men pulling at the oars and some one standing in the foresheets. I knew we were to be hailed. Perhaps we'd be searched, and in that case we'd have to fight. Bad odds against us, of course, but at least we had weapons now. That skipper was not the sort of a man to run the San Clemente River without guns, and from the little cabin La Carmelita had brought out a good rifle—Winchester—and another Colt revolver that hadn't had all the oil it needed, but that would probably shoot straight enough at close range.

I gave that gun to the boy, because he was not likely to hit any target with any weapon, even the best. I kept the rifle and the better revolver for myself.

Now I sat on my heels beside the captain and asked him if he would speak for us to the boatmen who were coming out, and he finally grunted out that he would, though he said that it would take ten years of praying and candles burned to the saints to wash the flavor of his lies out of his mouth. I gave him fifty dollars to raise his spirits and pay for a part of those candles, and he saw the point enough to wink at me.

There was a man, that fellow!

Carmelita and the boy I got out of sight. MacMore's glistening finery was doused under a ragged slicker as he stood at the helm, and so we stood on through the meager current of the shallows and watched the boat come on out to us.

The man in the sheets interested me the instant I laid eyes on him. And when the boat came closer I knew that it was the last man in the world we wanted to meet, but one. It was the Señor!

He was standing there with one hand on his hip, regardless of the way the boat bucked as it cut through the rough water of the central current, and much as I feared him, I think I admired him almost more.

He had sent the bulk of his men to watch other outlets, but with a true general's instinct he had come to the right point to handle the affair for himself.

Then his great voice sent a hail ringing across the water to us, and my heart stopped beating.

40 ... Hope in Our Hearts

I said that skipper was a man, and he proved it now. Of course, he knew that as I sat out of sight now behind the bulwark I had a gun trained on him, but he stood up free and easy near the mast and talked to the Señor.

"Who are you?" says the Señor.

"I'm Juan Niño."

"I know that man," says one of the boatmen. "Ask him why he is up here, because usually he carries his vegetables straight to the central market."

"Do you hear that question?" sings out the Señor.

"I am beating up to Los Gatos," says the skipper, Juan Niño. Then he added, proving that he was a good, fluent, and natural liar: "I am sick of the San Clemente prices. This is a town only meant to make the rich richer and the poor poorer!"

"Who is at your helm?"

"My son."

"Do you know this man?" says the Señor again to his boatmen.

"Yes. Very well. He's honest. There's no better man on the river than Juan Niño."

"For saying that," said the skipper, with a laugh, "I'll forgive you ten pesos of that money you owe me, friend."

The whole boat crew chuckled at this, but I, peering out through a crack, saw that face of the Señor was as fixed as stone.

"At any rate, we'll board this honest man," says he. "Give way, and fall in there on his quarter. Niño, you have no one else aboard you?"

"No one," says Niño. "But come aboard, Señor. I have here a good bottle of red wine. It is more than a year old and it tastes of its age."

The boat of the Señor was almost beside us, and I was rising to my knees to open fire with the Winchester when

Niño said this, and I heard the Señor utter a brief exclamation of disgust and impatience.

"Sheer off," said he. "They are not there among those cabbages, I take it. Put back to shore!"

This he said, and had the boat turned off, when hardly ten feet from him stood his own brother at the helm of this boat. It was the greatest piece of luck that ever I saw—and the greatest slip made by that keen man.

Off they went, with a powerful beat of oars and grunting of oarlocks, while the wind freshened behind us and drove us strongly up the stream.

Relief flowed like cool water over my heart; the knotted muscles of my forehead relaxed; we had stepped across the line to freedom.

Up the stream we went; the oars of the skiff were flashing nearer to the shore well behind us, and we were above the little stern-wheeler, when a shrieking voice broke out forward. It was young Niño.

"Help, in the name of Heaven!" he yelled. "La Carmelita is here and the two gringos. Oh, Señor! Help, help!"

I could not speak. I could not move.

And I heard the skipper say with a really wonderful calmness: "I shall die for this, and he will live. And at last there will be a rich Niño to walk in the outer promenade in the Plaza Municipal!"

This he said when the hangman's rope, you might say, had just fallen around his neck!

Well, I got to my feet with a lurch, by this time, and I saw the boat landing, and the men from it rushing toward the steamer. They would not trust to oars to overtake us, but they would soon be at us with that sharp-prowed boat.

However, we trimmed the sail, and heading a little closer to the shore, we made as much of a reach up the stream as we could.

We did not have long. For the steam was up in the stern-wheeler, and in another instant we heard a deep-throated shout of many men as she turned out into the current. She hit it so strongly that I could see the bow wave spring out like a sheet of thin ice curving back to the river.

When I saw her speed I knew we would have to get to the shore at once, and we turned the bows of the old boat straight in. I cut the rope which tied the hands of the skipper, and shook hands with him.

"Come with us if you will," said I.

"I would rather die in San Clemente," he replied, "than live beyond the Rio Grande. Adios, and good fortune to you and your hard fist, Señor Warder!"

That was the last I saw of him, and in some ways he was the most remarkable man that I ever saw. I mean, that I never have seen another who could face death with such cool blood. Yet he had not worked the flavor out of life. The red of his cheeks showed that he flourished day and night.

The boy we let alone. We could get no change from him by knocking him over the head, though he sat cross-legged on the deck with his back against the mast, fully expecting to be done for any minute. However, now the prow cut deeply into the sand and mud of the bank, and the three of us scampered ashore, swinging down over the point of the prow.

Willows grew thickly before us, and as we plunged into them, I looked back and saw the steamer rushing across the stream after us at a prodigious rate.

We hurried on. I remember looking at my watch as we crossed a patch of open moonlight, and seeing that it was a quarter of an hour after one o'clock. Yet how much already had been crowded into that night of nights!

Our bad luck had made us land in semi-marsh. Every moment we were splashing into thick, malodorous water and slime, and then struggling out onto half-dry ground again. The light was baffling. It made water look like land, and land like translucent silver water. But through a world of patched black-and-white we struggled on across the marsh and came out on open fields beyond.

I was a bit in the lead, trying to find out the easiest way, and as we left the woods and had crossed a fence, I looked back to see the pair of them climbing the fence side by side; and I remember that a sort of sad compassion for them came over me, as if they were children.

We went on at a run, and it was a pleasure to see La Carmelita keep up. She ran well, with a good swing to her and her head straight up. Fear takes your wind quicker than work, and fear was not sapping her strength. Now and then young MacMore would look across at her, and every time she had a smile ready to flash back at him, that jewel of a girl!

However, we could not last long across country—a country bound to be peppered with the men and the horses of the Señor. Horses, horses, were what I wanted. My feet—which you must remember had been without boots for a long time—were pretty badly bruised and cut, by this time, and made every step a miserable business, particularly when we struck a thorny hedge. La Carmelita faced it bravely enough, but she simply could not get through. I was already stepping on tacks, as you might say; and then I heard the noise of the hunt break out of the willows behind us, and the rapid, fierce voices of the many men as they ran forward.

I looked back, and the moonlight was sufficiently bright to show the long dark line springing out at full speed.

So I picked up Carmel and went through that hedge in spite of torn body and stabbed feet, and so came out on the other side and found myself standing in the more than velvet softness of deep dust on a little road. And that road ran north, around a bend, and north lay our safety, and our country, and the law which assures the happiness of honest men.

Now that thing rushed over my mind with a wonderful force, and it was like the blowing of a good keen wind, whipping away a mist and letting me see the face of the truth. Law I had first hated, and then been enslaved to; but suddenly I saw it as a good and beautiful thing, because it kept beautiful women like Carmel Alvarado, and weak-handed, great-hearted men like MacMore, from being sacrificed.

In the first half second I felt the joy of that soft dust, and had this thought; and then I heard the jingling of harness, the beat of trotting hoofs, and finally a voice that broke out singing, close at hand.

In the distance, behind us and toward the marsh, the pursuers must have seen the team, for they set up a wild roar; but words were indistinguishable in the confusion of many voices, all warning him not to give us aid, I suppose. But all they succeeded in doing was making him draw up as he came to our corner, so that all I had to do was to step up and show the revolver six inches from his nose. He was a big, ugly, broadfaced fellow, with a huge fat paunch;

but he got out of that seat like a scared cat and went through the thorn hedge as though it were a puff of smoke.

We piled into that little buckboard and I let the pair of mustangs go at a sharp trot.

There was no great need of speed just now, because we certainly were leaving the Señor and his man hunters behind us, and so I kept the ponies down to a moderate pace, and told MacMore, who sat with the girl on the rear seat of the wagon, to hold the rifle ready and keep a good lookout.

A good lookout indeed!

When I glanced back at him, I saw her in his arms, and their first kiss.

Well, they had worked hard enough to deserve a moment off, I suppose; but I roared at them, and told them not to be fools, or El Tigre would chew their bones before the morning came.

I was almost glad that I had that name to throw at them, because it scared them back to common sense and opened their eyes again; but having named the Indian, I grew mighty depressed.

Perhaps it was because I so long had been on the trail of him; it must have been more because I knew that he was a friend of the Señor; but in some way a mysterious surety grew in me that I was bound to meet El Tigre, and perhaps before this very night was ended. Call it dream, call it foolish instinct; but, at any rate, it was correct!

We were not out of the danger zone. We would not be until the far Rio was crossed. But in the meantime, the country opened before us, we climbed into the hills so that San Clemente lay white and beautiful behind us, and for this moment we breathed easily, and hope flowered in each heart of ours, I suppose.

41 . . . El Tigre Shows His Claws

A HORSE willl trot and pull you farther and faster than he will pack you on his back—that is, if the road is at all decent. The road through the San Clemente hills was not decent at all but we managed to keep on going. Why the wheels didn't break, I don't know, because we were continually crashing through brush and whacking over projecting rocks. That trail was the kind that's more traveled by wind and water than it is by wheels. It looks like a road from a distance and like a ditch close at hand.

We slugged steadily along, however, squeaking on at a walk where the surface was too rough or the grade too steep; and then trotting once more as the opportunity offered, while I realized more and more completely that we were gone geese!

At our rate of travel, we certainly were not distancing the wild riders that must have poured out from San Clemente to pursue us. And now as we topped the first ridge, we turned and looked back for the last time upon San Clemente. The moon was far down, but it gleamed on the white walls; the lights were mostly out, but a few still marked the Plaza Municipal; and I saw the silver of the river, widely looping through the place. It was wonderfully beautiful, more beautiful, even, than it had seemed to me when young MacMore and I first sat out on the mountain shoulder and looked down at it, as at a fort. But while we looked down there, I saw a red fire bloom on one of the lower hills, and then, by Heaven, leap on top of a summit of the second ridge, straight before us!

Think what one might, I knew that that was probably the beginning of the end for us, and they were marking out with fire the straightest road for new riders and old to take if they wanted to be in at the death of this hunt. I could see them coming on their mustangs, like so many Indians. And somewhere in the distance, probably yonder where that second hand of fire had gone up into the sky, was El Tigre himself!

If so much was known about our course—though we had not seen a human soul for a long time—there was no use plunging straight ahead. Instead, I turned off to the left on a wretched excuse for a road that once had been, I suppose, a timber drag. Up this we went from the bottom of the valley, cursing at our squeaking wheels, and at the snorting of the tired horses, and the creaking of the harness. We ourselves talked very little, and in soft voices.

When the girl told me that she thought we had very little chance in the rig and should take to our feet now, I assured her that she was wrong, and that everything was going as well as possible. She did not entirely agree with me, but she would not argue the point, and so I managed to keep up the spirits of the pair for a little while.

We got up to the top of the second ridge without trouble of any kind, and from that ridge, I looked down on a wider and better road dipping into the next ravine. The pines which had stood in close ranks up to this point, now spread out, growing much bigger, but farther apart; so that all down the hillside there were streaks of moonlight and great splotches of black—the very worst conditions in the world for seeing anything unless it will move fast across the field of your eye.

Something about that utterly peaceful scene troubled me, I didn't know why, and I reached from the driver's seat to a pile of rock which rose like cord-wood at the side of the way. I dislodged a fifty-pound boulder that went off down the hillside first at a trot, then at a gallop, then racing wildly along, crashing through brush, and thumping against trees.

Before it was halfway to the bottom of the grade I was glad that I had taken the precaution, because that whole hillside sprang into life. Out from behind the trees sprang men on horses and men afoot. A tumult of shouting began, and guns started in shooting at imaginary targets.

As for me, there was nothing left except to veer off to the left through the open woods. We went lickety split, of course. No matter what happened, if we wanted to salvage a few more seconds of life, we had to move, and we paid quickly for our speed. We struck the ridge of a half-rotted log, then bounced onto hard rock, and the buckboard broke down.

It was the strangest wreck I ever saw. The wheels seemed to give way all together by a mutual agreement. Denny, of course, fell out head over heels in the crash, but equally of course he got up unhurt.

There we stood in a great natural clearing, with boulders and a few old logs around us, and up through the woods to the north and the south and the east came the pursuers. They came in a host, shouting to one another, then yelling like fiends, while their horses rushed forward.

If anything was clear, it was that we had our backs to the wall and could not run farther.

"We camp here," I said to the girl and MacMore, and pointed to a natural nest of rocks close by. We got the horses into that round of stones which stood up five and six feet high, so that we had only to fill in a few interstices in order to have a good breastwork.

MacMore had sense enough to realize that and frantically set to work piling stones, and the girl with him. I let them work, while I kept my rifle ready. I intended to have a little satisfaction by peppering one or two of these fellows before they got our scalps, and so I had the rifle at my shoulder the instant I saw a rider come flickering through the last of the forest moonlight and shadows and into the open.

I covered him right over the heart, but I could not shoot! My dreams had come true, and a pretty nightmare they made. With his long black hair blowing over his shoulders, naked except for a loinstrap, his dark body and thick shoulders looking enormously strong, and, even in the moonshine, his face deformed by a huge puckering scar that ran all along one cheek, there at last was El Tigre before my eyes and under my gun, while I, like an incredible fool, gaped at him, and trembled more than ever a novice did because of buck fever. I trembled and shook so that that big target swayed back and forth across the sights, and at last fled away among the trees with a wild screeching cry that trailed over his shoulder.

He disappeared. Other riders boiled at the edge of the woods, before the warning cries told them that there was danger in the clearing, and I would have bagged three or four of the hottest riders who dashed out into the open and then hastily swerved back again, had it not been that at this time Denny came and caught my arm.

"She's dead!" cried he, and he pointed to where La Carmelita lay.

"She's seen El Tigre, I guess," said I. "She'll wake up presently, and you be sure to tell her that this is no time or place to cry."

"You'll find her braver than a man," says Denny to me.

Well, I believed that, but I also believed that I really would find her dead, before long.

Then I fell silent, listening to the fiends as they screeched in the woods around us.

Well, it was not very pleasant to look out through the cracks in our fortress walls and see the hugeness of the trees and notice the nakedness of the rock-strewn clearing. In one foretaste I knew the agony of long thirst and hunger that lay before us. Already my throat was dry.

I had another thing that surprised me a good deal. The horse on which El Tigre had ridden when he rushed out of the woods was very familiar to me. If that were not Larry, my own mount, then my eyes were no good at all! And yet it should not have been so very surprising. Once in the hands of the Señor, of course the gelding might very well be passed on to the chief of the bandits.

About this time I had something to do besides speculate vaguely on the future. Bullets began to comb the rocks, some of them fired from high up in the trees about the clearing. But these shots stopped as suddenly as they began, and I could understand why. The Señor wanted to have back La Carmelita, and, therefore, he would not allow an indiscriminate bombardment. I wondered if there had not been a savage argument between him and the wild man, El Tigre. However, the trees were again quiet, and we crouched in the pale of the moonlight, speaking very little, and then only in whispers, and now and then rising a bit to peer out at one of the crevices among the stones in order to keep watch against surprise.

"Señor Warder! Señor Warder!" called a voice from the nearest trees.

I answered, and the voice named itself as Pedro Oñate, and asked a truce to come to make a parley with us. I gave him my word, and the rascal jogged straight out to us on the back of a pinto. He sat there in the moonlight and waved a gloved hand at us. His proposal was what I expected. If we would allow La Carmelita to go back to her people, El Tigre was willing to permit the pair of us to escape.

"Accept the offer, señor," says Pedro to me. "As surely as there is a Heaven who hears us both, I speak to you as though to my own father, because I know what I owe to you. But El Tigre is more furious than I ever have seen him. If you delay long, every one of you will be killed, man and woman!"

Carmel Alvarado started to answer that she would go, but young MacMore stopped her.

"Go back to El Tigre," says he, "and tell him that we all are happy and prepared to die!"

As I look back on it, it seems to me as though Denny were taking a good deal on his shoulders, at such a moment; but at the time, it seemed the most natural thing in the world to have him speak as he did. Which shows how close we were to one another in that pinch of our lives. I looked back at the two, as they stood close together, with Denny talking and the girl staring up at him as though he were talking heavenly wisdom. Perhaps he was, for that matter.

So Oñate turned his horse and went away, though I must say for him that he acted as though he would have given a hand to change our decision; and the three of us settled down quietly and comfortably to wait for death.

The moon was behind a mountain, now, cutting us off from the direct light; but still it was not below the level horizon and, therefore, the air was softly filled with its illumination.

"This is the end," I heard MacMore saying to the girl. "And one hour like this with you, Carmel, is worth more than a long life to me. I shall die happily!"

"I shall die with you," she replied to him, "unless something happens."

"Nothing possibly can happen," he said. "You can see that?"

"There are miracles," says the girl. "El Tigre himself may still be placed in our hands, my dear!"

"Miracles!" says I to myself, thumbing the stock of the rifle. "El Tigre may be placed in our hands!"

But all at once I stopped sneering, because a wild thought had jumped into my mind and made me sit on my heels, agape like a child.

42 ... With His Face to the Ground

How SHOULD she, I often wonder, have thought of speaking those words—"El Tigre might come into our hands!" Well, of course, it was fairly obvious that he was the only key that would unlock the door of our prison.

I pondered on him, probably riding around through the trees at the present moment, ordering his men, preparing some fiendish and crafty surprise; for his mind always was filled with expedients. And then it jarred home in my mind that, if Larry it were that he was riding, I did actually have a hand on his actions that might prove stronger than he thought.

Then I looked to the rifle. The magazine was full, the mechanism worked smoothly. I looked to the revolver, and I remember barely hearing the girl whisper on the far side of the clearing: "José is about to do something."

"Dear old Joe!" says Denny.

They couldn't very well guess that I was actually about to whistle the lightning out of the sky and bring it here to singe us! But that was my idea, and a moment later I sent a loud, quick whistle into the air—the call which Larry had grown used to on a hundred campaigns with me, and which he was in the habit of answering at the gallop as far away as he could hear the sound.

I gave that call, and instantly heard a crashing among brush on the southern rim of the trees.

To that point I turned, and by thunder, there came Larry streaking it for me like a little racer, with El Tigre out of balance on the saddle, and clawing to get back in place. He was halfway to the rocks when he managed that job, and at the same time I fairly drew a bead on him, when he leaned forward, and the tossing head of Larry came in between me and my target.

Why didn't I shoot Larry then? His fall would have stunned El Tigre and I could have finished the copper-skinned brute while he lay helpless on the ground. It wasn't the universal shriek of dismay and excitement that was now breaking out from the trees all around us that disturbed me; it was simply that I couldn't kill the poor fellow as he came running to my call. No, not even though my life and that of two other humans depended on the act.

If those wild men among the trees were excited, it was nothing to what I felt. El Tigre was coming in on me a mile a minute when, getting erect, he grabbed the reins.

But he did not pull them in! No, sir, the run of the horse had made the desperate courage of the charge leap up in the heart of El Tigre, I suppose; for now he gave out a war whoop that made the clamor of his followers seem like nothing at all, and digging his heels into the ribs of Larry, he urged him still faster for our little fort.

He carried a revolver in his left hand, and now dropping the reins, and managing Larry with the grip of his knees and the sway of his naked body, he pulled out a short-hafted hand-ax from behind the saddle and sent Larry on at the rock wall with another whoop of frantic joy.

I got a good bead on him now, standing a little to the side, and I chose the hideous face, all twisted out of shape by the pull of the scar; so that when he yelled, his cry was all on one side of his face.

I took a good, careful bead, and fired.

Well, I made a clean miss. I had shot at plenty of men before, but when that monster came rushing up on me, getting bigger and bigger, somehow it started me shaking all over, as it had done in the first case. At any rate, I missed him clean, at six yards!

And as I missed him, Larry went into the air like a bird off the ground. It was mighty good jumping. And even in that last flashing instant, it seemed to me that I saw joy in the bright eyes of Larry as he cleared the wall.

That was all that I did see for the moment, for the revolver of El Tigre flashed in my face and I went down with a feeling as if somebody had laid a heavy club along the right side of my head.

I was not unconscious entirely—more like the pugilist who sprawls in the ring, trying desperately to get back to his feet but without any chance of making his muscles obey him.

In the meantime, I saw and heard everything with a perfect clearness—only my body was made of lead, without muscle.

Larry flashed overhead, landed, and turned sideways to avoid running head on into the farther wall. It was his flank that thumped against it so heavily that he grunted and a shower of the stones rattled down.

But Larry was not my main concern now. I remember distinctly how El Tigre threw up his moccasined foot over the neck of the horse and leaped for the ground.

Young MacMore—there never was a gamer lad on this earth!—ran straight at the monster, firing his crazy old revolver as he came. Of course he did not hit the mark, but then I saw El Tigre do a strange thing. He didn't send a bullet through Denny's head, and he didn't split his head open with the ax. Instead, he closed in, grasped the gun out of Denny's hand as easily as though from a child, and cast Denny away from him with a back stroke of his arm.

I never had seen such an exhibition of power; and all this with the needle of Carmel's dreadful screaming stabbing at my brain.

El Tigre whirled on me with such a shout that it blotted out my senses like the explosion of heavy ordnance. It was I whom he wanted, of course, though that hardly explained his deliberate waste of time in sparing Denny. The ugly brute came at me with a leap, for he could see that I had recovered a little, and though the blood had streamed down and made me blind in one eye, yet with the other I could see well enough to kill him—and my hand already was on the rifle!

He saw that, and he came fast. He had dropped the revolver in his skirmish with Denny, and not stopping to pick it up, he came in with the hand-ax to split open my skull.

Then Denny saved me. Rough-handled by that monster already, and now with Carmel clinging to him, without a weapon in his hands, that boy tore himself away from the girl he loved and came plunging back at El Tigre, and threw his weak arms around the great torso of the bandit.

"Joe, Joe!" he was yelling at me. "Shoot!"

I heard the snarl of El Tigre like the snarl of a dog. Even then he did not pole-ax Denny, but with the force with which he cast him off flung him half senseless against the wall of rocks, while El Tigre swayed up the ax to finish me.

Too late, El Tigre!

If I had been twice as far gone, the sight of little Denny's heroism would have cleared my brain, I think; and that cry of his sent a white flame through my mind and body and made me well. I had rifle ready in an instant, and just as El Tigre threw the boy from him the second time, I shot the wild man through his thick body. He came on one more step at me, but then toppled slowly to the side, and the ax clanged uselessly upon the stones.

That, then, was the end of my trail!

Now, when these things were happening, still half of my mind was bent upon the danger that lay outside the little ring of rocks, and I jumped up without a stagger.

It was time to look out, for from three or four sides of the clearing mobs of men had started across at us, yelling with excitement and rage and fear for their leader.

"Shoot, Denny!" says I.

And at the same time opening my throat wider than a wild cat, I yelled my joy and victory, while I pumped bullets blindly at the nearest mob. And Denny, on the other side, was equally whooping it up, and blazing away with a revolver he had picked up.

It wasn't our shooting that did the work, for I really don't think that I landed on any of the scoundrels; but by the fact that we could give them our attention they knew that El Tigre was finished; and just as some ancient army used to turn and run when it heard of the death of its king, so that mob turned and poured back for the shelter of the trees as though a thousand demons were after them. Long after we could hear the crashing of the underbrush, as they still swept onwards!

I dropped the rifle then and went back to El Tigre.

Carmel was crying in the arms of Denny, and Denny himself was weeping and laughing like a woman. Well, he

210

had shown himself enough man to save us all, a moment before!

El Tigre was about done for when I kneeled beside him. His breathing had a horrible faint bubbling sound to it, by which I knew that his lung was nicked; but there was enough light to show me something mightily interesting about that scar on his face. I mean to say that there was a bit of it loose and turning up, and when I touched it, I knew it was mere tape, and no scar at all. One jerk pulled it off, and the twisted face turned suddenly into that of the Señor, of Patrick MacMore!

I looked down at him dizzily, and saw one hand go up and cover the place where the scar had been. His eyes cleared, too, and his lips stirred.

I leaned over him and heard him whisper.

"Cover my face from Denny! Here's the price to buy your tongue. Promise me, Warder, and here is wealth for you!"

And he passed into my hands a little soft bag of chamois. I've already told you what the contents were!

"Promise?" says he, his dead eyes yearning up to me with the last agony.

"Before Heaven!" says I.

And El Tigre shuddered from head to foot, and died.

I looked one half second into the big eyes, fixed upward, and an odd thought came over me that you would not have expected to find a place in my mind, just then: I suddenly decided that it had meant something in the world to be The MacMore.

I dropped the sack of jewels into my pocket and turned El Tigre face down on the ground.

Denny came to me, then, and in a shaken voice said that he wanted to see the famous man face to face. That gave me a touch of the horrors, I can tell you.

I merely said: "Denny, he's dead. Don't insult him now. He was brave enough to deserve something better than that from you!"

It was pretty sharp talk, but it did work. And presently Denny says: "He could have brained me, Joe. No matter what a monster he was, he did his fighting with warriors. I mean, with the hard hitters, like you! Aye, Joe, I'll let him be!"

That was how we left the great El Tigre, with his face

turned to the ground, and went off through those woods with never the sound of a human being about us.

The birds of the air buried him, I suppose, and the wolves.

43 ... By Moonlight

THAT MARCH north was as hard a thing as I ever undertook, but we got through it—chiefly because of one mighty good turn that Pedro Oñate did for us. However, I'm tired of telling about small things. After the death of El Tigre, all other matters seemed pretty trivial.

So at last we got across the Rio Grande and breathed again what always seemed to me a different air.

The wound in my head had healed pretty well, though I still had a bandage tied about it; Denny and Carmel were already man and wife at the hands of a parish priest on the way north; and the same evening that we crossed the river, I said good-by to them.

Well, it was a hard thing to do, but I did it. And what made it easier was that ever since the death of El Tigre, in spite of myself I couldn't quite feel the same about Denny.

He was as fine as ever, or finer. But on account of him I knew that the strongest man, the greatest fighting machine, the keenest brain I had ever known had laid down his life. For that, surely, was what El Tigre did in sparing the boy.

Now I had a little talk with them both in a hotel room in a dusty little border town, while five reporters waited outside raising a ruction to get at us. They didn't know much, but at least the rumor had come north long ago that El Tigre had been killed by a "gringo," and people had kindly put down the job at my door.

I said to Denny: "Old son, I've got some bad news for you"— he had just been saying that some day he'd take the chance again and would surely get his brother out of the wild country—"and the bad news is that your brother is dead."

212

He sat up as stiff as starch, his eyes big, but his mouth steady and straight.

"And you're The MacMore now," said I, "and a dang good one you'll make, you and your missis. And this is how I happen to know."

I took out the chamois sack and handed it to him.

"From what you've told me," I said, "this was the Señor's. He never would have given it up, alive. And therefore, when I took it from El Tigre, I knew that he was dead. But I kept the news back until we had the river behind us. However, you're The MacMore!"

"El Tigre!" says Denny. "The monster murdered—"

"Of course he did," said I. "You could tell by the look of him that he could never keep friends long with any white man. Eight years were a miracle of constancy, with him, I suppose."

"The MacMore?" says Denny to himself, fighting back his grief. "I don't think I'll ever wear that title, Joe. Patrick was the last of the old fighting clan."

"Aye," says I, "maybe you're right, because your brother was out by himself as a man!"

Denny begins to walk up and down the room, working his hands into fists and out again, and while he fights with the first pinch of his sorrow, Carmel comes to me and puts her hands into mine.

"I know!" says she.

I stared down at her. By Heaven, her eyes were filled with tears!

"I always knew," she says to me. "And still, in a way, I think I loved him almost as much as I dreaded him."

And she lifts up her face to me.

"Padre José!" says she. "Kiss me, José," says Carmel.

Which I did.

There's one thing you can count on the newspapers for, and that's a quick finish of every bit of true excitement.

Now, when I turned the nose of Larry down the main street of the old town, I expected that people would get stirred up a bit when they saw me, but they didn't.

I went by Bud Larkin's house. It was late afternoon, and Bud was sitting out on the porch in his shirt sleeves. I noticed that the shirt was silk, with red elastics to hold up the cuffs from falling down over his hands. He wasn't in-

213

haling a cigarette, either, but a long-lined cigar was in his teeth, which he puffed as though he knew how.

Bud didn't say anything to me. He merely waved his hand, and somehow, by that, I knew that he and Guthrie had blown their bank and were sitting pretty on the profits.

Well, that made me sigh again!

And now I came down past the blacksmith shop, where the MacLean boy and young Si Hammer were standing around, and they gave me a wave and a call, but nothing worth stopping for. You see, the newspapers had played it up for a week, and everybody had read the story out to the end, and now they were pretty tired of the whole affair.

Most of the oxygen and ozone was out of me when I came to the marshal's office. Horton was in. He had a couple of big politicians in his office. One was the ex-governor, and another was a rich cattleman from up on the Staked Plains. That's what the kid in the outside office says to me.

"And who are you?" says he.

"I'm a poor gent," said I, "that's turned up looking for a hand-out."

"Well, set down and rest your feet," says he, "but the marshal keeps a padlock on his purse."

"You go in and open that door," says I, "and tell the marshal that Warder is here and only has a minute to stay. I guess that he won't be able to see me, though."

"He'll bust me on the nose, I suppose," says the boy, "but I'll take a chance for you, old-timer. Are you one of his old men?"

He opened the door far enough for a whiff of stale tobacco smoke to come rolling out. He says something and there's a yell from inside.

Horton came out in two jumps, tucked me under his arm, you might say, and marched me back in.

"Get out of here," says he to the governor and the cattle king. "I'm through with you boys, because I've got a real man to talk to, now. This is Warder."

"Yes?" says the governor, politely interested.

"Dang your hide," said the marshal. "This is the last man on the border! Look at him! He's easy to remember by his nose!"

214

They shook hands with me and laughed a little, and went out without being embarrassed.

And I then spent the evening with Horton.

He did everything fine. He arranged for a fine dinner, and everything from soup to cigars, almost like the old days when I stepped through the long green in New Orleans, and sipped absinthe frappés, and cursed the waiter for having the claret too cold. It was almost like that. It was near enough, anyway, for the whole of the old days to come rolling back over me.

And while we were finishing up this long program of eats, the marshal talked about one thing and another, and how the boys were getting on, and a new fellow by name of Gloster who had a lot of promise, but needed to be worked up by an old hand, like me.

"I'm not working up any new hands," said I.

"And why, son," says the marshal, "after the long lone hand that you've been playing? I should think that you'd like a little company, from now on, for a while."

I considered this.

"The way of it is," said I, "that company is like clothes. I like it cut to order, or else not at all. Even you, Horton, would only do for me about once a month."

He grinned at that.

"You won't see me that often," said he. "I'm going to keep you busy burning up this border, Joe. I need you pretty bad."

Then he went on:

"And as soon as I get the whole detailed story from you, I'm going to write out a report on this that'll make all Washington open its eyes and tell itself that the West is still producing men."

He waited a while longer.

"You can start anywhere you please, Joe," says he. "But to suit me, you might begin with that El Tigre in person. I'd like a lot to know what he looked like, for instance!"

I chewed the butt of my cigar for a long while.

"I only seen him by moonlight, Horton," I told him, "and so I don't suppose that I ever saw him right."

For the Sunday cyclist... for the cross-country tourist... whether you ride for better health, for sport, or for the sheer fun of it,

GET THE COMPLETE BOOK OF BICYCLING

The First Comprehensive Guide To All Aspects of Bicycles and Bicycling

JUST A FEW OF THE HUNDREDS OF EXCITING TIPS YOU'LL FIND:
- A simple way to increase your cycling efficiency by 30 to 40%—breeze over hilltops while others are struggling behind.
- 13 special safety tips for youngsters.
- How to read a bicycle's specifications to know if you're getting a superior one or a dud.
- How to know whether to buy a 3-speed to start with, or a 10-speed.
- How to select the right kind of equipment for touring or camping.
- How to minimize danger when cycling in the city.

▼ **AT YOUR BOOKSTORE OR MAIL THIS COUPON NOW FOR FREE 30-DAY TRIAL** ▼